Taylor Blake
IS A LEGEND

Taylor Blake IS A LEGEND

LAURA JANE WILLIAMS

BLOOMSBURY

LONDON OXFORD NEW YORK NEW DELHI SYDNEY

BLOOMSBURY YA
Bloomsbury Publishing Plc
50 Bedford Square, London WC1B 3DP, UK
29 Earlsfort Terrace, Dublin 2, Ireland

BLOOMSBURY, BLOOMSBURY YA and the Diana logo
are trademarks of Bloomsbury Publishing Plc

First published in Great Britain in 2024 by Bloomsbury Publishing Plc

A catalogue record for this book is available from the British Library

ISBN: PB: 978-1-5266-6805-9; eBook 978-1-5266-6819-6;
ePDF: 978-1-5266-6804-2

2 4 6 8 10 9 7 5 3 1

Typeset by Westchester Publishing Services
Printed and bound in Great Britain by CPI Group (UK) Ltd, Croydon CR0 4YY

To find out more about our authors and books visit www.bloomsbury.com
and sign up for our newsletters

For the Year 9 in everyone and everyone in Year 9,
and Ella, for the inspo

1

*I*f my life was a TV show, the cast of characters would be very, very small. In my life there's literally only:

- Mum, who thinks she's 'cool' and 'with it' and has a TikTok account that she updates *four* (!!!!) times a day. Cringe.
- Grandma and Grandad, who Mum is always shouting at for saying things that are a bad influence on me, when they're actually funnier than she is (I haven't told *her* that).
- Star and Lucy, my best friends who are also a couple and always together, so even though they are INDI-VIDUALS WHO HAPPEN TO BE PARTNERED, they really only count as one person because they're joined

at the hip. It's cute and everything, but I'm a bit jealous because I've never even kissed anyone, let alone had a boyfriend or a girlfriend or A PARTNER.

However! All that is about to change! Because now I'm in Year 9 I get to be a host for the French exchange program and I know – I can feel it in my BONES! – that good things are coming my way. Not to be dramatic but it's totally written in the stars. I have waited *years* for this. Years! But you're not allowed to take part until Year 9. WELL! Here I am, a Year 9 student all signed up for her very first French partner!!!!

Although Mum reckons I'm putting too much pressure on it.

'Darling,' she says, which is her new term of endearment for me. She called me *bunny* or *tater tot* or *bug-a-boo* for ages, but once I got into Year 9 I had to sit her down and explain that I am growing up now – if not already fully grown. As such, I found it infanticiding to be called anything that could be deemed a 'baby name'. ('Bunny,' she'd replied, '*infanticide* is when you kill a baby. I think you mean *infantilising*.' I didn't appreciate being corrected when I was trying to make a point; it felt a bit like whatever the mother version of mansplaining is. *Mum-splaining*. I said, 'Whatever way you slice it, Erica, please don't,' because calling her by her first name instead of Mum makes her purse her lips and try not to get cross, which is a way of me almost always winning the argument, tried and tested, because she often just sighs and gives up! Credit where credit is due though – she did pack the baby names in. I'm *darling* or *cutie* now. I can live with that.)

Anyway.

Star and Lucy say I have a habit of going off topic.

Where was I?

Oh yes, the French exchange. Mum says I'm putting too much pressure on it.

'Darling, this will be the first experience of many. It might be brilliant, or it might not be, but however it goes, your first French exchange won't be your last. And more than that, I hope you'll backpack through Bali, and go to India – god, the backwaters of Kerala? That's where I knew I wanted to become a writer, you know. Travelling the world, making mistakes, having grand adventures … I know I talk about France like it's the best thing since sliced bread, but you don't have to be a Francophile just because I am …'

Mum is always doing this. She starts her stories about me but we always end up talking about her somehow!

'Yes, yes,' I say impatiently. 'Living in Paris was the best three years of your life even though it's nothing compared to living in Crickleton now, and being my mum. I love you for that! But Mum – *Erica* – I need you to promise me that you'll be super cool and we can get loads of nice food in and, you know, let's just not be super weird when my French exchange partner is here. Don't try and relive your Parisian youth, OK? And don't be too English, either. Let's be *chic* and *sophisticated* and if you could just … let us get on with it?' I see her face fall a bit. I don't mean to be unkind. She loves using her French any chance she gets, and she's the one who bought me *How to Be Parisian When You're Not from Paris*. She read it when she was my age, so even though it's a bit old-fashioned it's still THE BIBLE!! I could quote that book off by heart if I wanted to. For example, the introduction:

How to Be Parisian When You're Not from Paris
Darling, you do not have to be of Paris to be Parisian, for being Parisian is an attitude. It is a state of mind. It is a way of being. The Parisian woman is nonchalant, has low-key style but high-maintenance skincare, and is proud but self-deprecating. She falls in love deeply and madly, and spins every event of her life into a story. She is wild and untameable, loyal but direct; she values herself and how she spends her time. The Parisian woman is the main character of her own world …

Isn't that just so wildly chic?! Mum always has stories about her time in Paris, and I've seen her photos. We finally went

4

for my eleventh birthday and ever since then I've been OBSESSED. The food was amazing, all the buildings and the cobbled streets were amazing, the Eiffel Tower was amazing. It was a dream! We came home and Crickleton seemed so boring in comparison; it's just so small and full of old people. So, I watch endless movies and read every book there is on France and the French and dream about the day I will return! When I got *How to Be Parisian When You're Not from Paris* for my last birthday, it cemented my love of the place even more. I've waited years to make my first proper French friend, and on the exchange it is finally happening! Ooh la la!

… And it's cool Mum is excited for me, but also, this isn't her exchange, it's mine. I just want her to understand! 'No offence or anything,' I add quickly, seeing the look on her face now I've tried to set some boundaries.

'None taken,' says Mum, very much obviously taking offence. But do you know what? I take offence first, because she's always telling me to own my voice, to not let anyone tell me what to think or do, to be a strong independent woman like she hopes she is. And yet she does an awful lot of telling me what to think and do and feel herself! She can't get cross when I disagree with her. That's a dictatorship.

'Any word on who we're getting, anyway?' she asks, opening and closing cupboards to check what she needs to add to the grocery order on her app.

'Not yet,' I reply. 'We all need to get our printouts from Madame Jones next week. Can I get the top of my ear pierced before then? Jessica Sanders got hers done at the cheap jewellery place at the shopping centre but they used a gun and it got infected and then she had to take it out to let it heal again, so I think I should go to the tattoo studio in town and have it done with a needle? But it's a hundred pounds. I really think I should have a top ear piercing before the exchange. All the French girls have them and I can just put a plaster over it for PE.'

'Taylor,' my mother says, not even taking her head out of the fridge, which I would get accused of being *rude* for if I did. My mother says eye contact is the first and most important bastion of respect, to which I said, well, not in China. Direct eye contact with someone of an older generation is a sign of disrespect there! To which *Mum* said, being deliberately obtuse is unbecoming. 'I am not paying a hundred pounds for you to have your ear pierced, even if I do think you'd suit it.'

All I heard was that Mum thinks my ear would look good pierced at the top, which, if you think about it, leaves room in her *no* for something closer to a *yes*. Time to be a bit more polite then – I reckon I can wedge the door open on her 'maybe' by tomorrow morning, latest.

'Oh,' Mum says, squinting at her phone. 'Grandma and

Grandad are FaceTiming. I'll bet they want to congratulate you on your first byline in the school paper!' She prods at her screen. 'Hi, Mum! Hi, Dad!'

'Hello, darling!' comes Grandad's voice. 'Is the world-famous journalist Taylor Blake there with you?'

'She is,' Mum says, pulling me into frame.

'Hi, Grandad,' I smile. 'Hi, Grandma.' They're holding a copy of the school paper, the *Register*, smiling like Cheshire cats.

'Your review is fantastic,' says Grandma proudly. '*Keeping Your Ion on the Prize with Science Week* by Taylor Blake. What a clever headline!'

Grandad chuckles. 'I'd say we don't know where you get it from, but we're pretty punny ourselves, so ...'

I roll my eyes good-naturedly. 'Must be in my DNA then,' I say, and they laugh.

Grandad clears his throat and keeps reading. '*Crickleton High has been celebrating Science Week. This year's theme was all about connections ...*'

Oh my gosh, this is so embarrassing.

'I wrote it, Grandad, I know what it says! Shush!' I laugh. 'You don't have to read it to me! It's only a hundred and fifty words, anyway. And about Science Week. I want to write about stuff that's important to me, not just reviews of school events. It's hardly a feminist manifesto, is it?'

Mum kisses the side of my head and says, 'We're just pleased for you, is all. And we all have to start somewhere.'

'Your first byline is no small feat,' Grandad says. 'Plenty of people *want* to have a dream, but not a lot of people actually *work* to make their dream happen. You're a doer, Tay. You go after what you want.'

I screw up my nose, still embarrassed. Who knew people being kind could be so uncomfortable? I sort of want them to keep going, because it's nice to be told you've done a cool thing, but at the same time my cheeks are burning and for some reason I want to cover my face with my hands.

'We're going to frame it,' says Grandma. 'Once you've signed it.'

'Ooooh,' Mum coos. 'I'll send a photo of it to Auntie Kate, too! She'll be so excited for you!'

Auntie Kate is Mum's best friend, and runs a yoga studio out in Bali. When I was seven, she went to a psychic, and the psychic told her I'd achieve 'big things'. She likes to be kept up to date with any of my wins, because she takes it as proof the psychic was right. I mean – if she is right, I'm not mad about it!

I shake my head at my family. 'You're all crazy,' I say, but everyone can tell what I mean is *thank you*.

'Oh, love, the time!' Mum says then, glancing at the kitchen clock. It's three o'clock. 'Aren't you late to meet the girls?'

'Argh!' I say. 'You're right. Sorry, guys, I've got to go!'

'Bye, darling, well done again!' Grandma says before we ring off.

Nooo! I hate being late for stuff! I feel like I miss out if I'm not on time. I put my hands on Mum's shoulders and flash what I hope is a winning grin, even though I'm not entirely sure what a 'winning grin' is. An enthusiastic one?

'Errrr,' I start, because I have to ask, but I am aware I'm doing a lot of favour-asking today. 'Have you put any money on my Starbucks card? They said I'm not allowed to just have a tap water and take up a table any more.'

Mum's face softens. She has a way of looking at me sometimes, all soft crinkled eyes and Smirky McSmirk smile, and it makes me feel funny. Like she might laugh at me but is trying not to, when I don't even know what I've done. Must be love, or something like it, I suppose. Either that, or she thinks I'm a fool.

'A fiver,' she says, her voice serious even though I can tell she's not really mad. 'And that's all! I had a job in Year 9! I think it's time to think about gainful employment for you.'

'Yup,' I say, going in for a kiss on the cheek. She likes it when I do that, and gets all huffy if I try to leave without it, like she's being ignored. But I never ignore her! Not on purpose! Sometimes I'm just BUSY. 'You worked for two pounds an hour in Great-Auntie Barbara's pine furniture shop when you were fourteen, cash in hand, which after the bus and your lunch left you with about fifty pence profit. I hear you! But think of how much less time I'd have for homework if I worked every Saturday! And at fifty p, you'd still have to give me money for Starbucks …'

'Hmmmmmm,' is all she muses, screwing up her nose like she doesn't want to unpack all that. 'Just go, you. Love you, Bug-a … I mean, love you, darling. Tell Lucy and Star I say hi.'

'If we come back here after can they stay for tea?'

That Look again. Earnest. Crinkle-eyed. A bit like she might cry, or burst into hysterics, if only she could decide.

'You know I love a house full of girls. Of course,' she says, and as I pull on my coat and walk down the hill I think: she's all right, Mum. It could be worse. Lucy's mum is a biology teacher at our school. Imagine THAT.

2

'What time do you call this?' Lucy yells playfully across Starbucks, from our favourite spot at the back. Her blonde hair is pulled back into a slick, low bun, so you can see the full roundness of her pretty face, her every expression heightened. An old man looks like he could be startled into an early grave by her booming voice, and a woman tuts loudly and shakes her head. I do an over-the-top *shhhhhh* face to her and then burst out laughing, which elicits more scowling from people but who cares, it's not a crime to have a laugh. We're not dead yet!!

'Grandma and Grandad called me about my review,' I explain. 'It held me up.' I slip into the chair opposite them. 'And then I had to go and take my copy of *Anna and the French Kiss* back to the library, and pick up the next one in the series.' I hold up *Lola and the Boy Next Door* triumphantly. 'I'll probably read it in about two days. I could read for hours! Especially about first kisses … *ahhhhh!*'

The girls have both got their drinks already – strawberry cream Frappuccino for Star, and a decaf iced latte for Lucy, because in the summer holidays last year she drank five espressos in a row and got so dizzy she went temporarily blind, so can't do proper coffee any more. We were all trying to develop A Taste For It on account of how grown-up it is. Drinking coffee, and eating just a square of dark chocolate for a sugar craving, and also drinking room-temperature mineral water with a slice of lemon: these were all things we'd decided to try in time for Year 9. But coffee makes your tongue fuzzy and a square of dark chocolate isn't as nice as a big bar of Dairy Milk and water is better with apple and blackberry cordial in it, orange at a push. *How to Be Parisian When You're Not from Paris* says every woman is allowed a little off-kilter quirk, though, so we've gone back to doing what we like, rebranded as eccentric.

'Yeah, your first byline!' says Star excitedly. 'How does it feel?'

I shrug. 'Cool,' I say. 'I mean, I'd like to write about my opinions and thoughts and stuff, but Mum says it's a good first step.'

'What?' asks Lucy, her blue eyes alight with curiosity. 'Thoughts and feelings like ... a *diary*?'

I shake my head. 'Noooooo,' I say. 'Opinion pieces. Stuff about the world and changing how we think. Feminism, the climate emergency, that sort of thing.'

'Bit deep for the *Register* ...' says Star dubiously. 'Don't you think?'

'Yeah,' agrees Lucy, which: *of course* she agrees. Lucy is obsessed with gossip, and gossip only: local gossip, school gossip, celebrity gossip – even gossip about people she doesn't know! 'You could do something about, like, which teachers are secretly dating, or, or ... Oh! The school play apparently has *tons* of drama happening backstage ...'

'No pun intended?' I joke. She pulls a funny face. I knew she'd suggest something like this!

'If you wrote about that, you could make it really funny by writing about them like they're actual actors, like film stars. But it's really just Millicent Monroe in Year 10 being a diva ...'

'Maybe,' I say, but I can't help feeling like they don't get what I mean. What I'm trying to *achieve*. Not that it matters. I don't really 'get' Lucy's gossip obsession, or Star's love of fencing (it's ... people poking each other with sticks? Whilst wearing white?), but I still love them like sisters.

I go and get a mango and passionfruit Frappuccino and

am surprised to be told I've got enough loyalty points for a free drink next time. Huzzah! Take THAT, Mum.

'We've been making a list for the exchange,' Lucy says when I go and sit back down, ever the organised one of the three of us. She's a natural leader, and makes it easy to follow her commands. 'All the things we have to make sure to do when they're here.' She looks over the paper they've been scribbling on. 'I've said wear a beret, a neck scarf and a mac, and sit at a cafe outside on the pavement. I think they'll be expecting that, don't you? I know we like being back here out of the way at Starbucks, but that's because they normally let us stay as long as we want. When the Frenchies are here should we go to the independent cafe around the corner on Blunder Road?'

'Offft,' I say. 'Their chairs are those iron ones that dig into your back and make your bum cold.'

'I said that!' exclaims Star. Her voice is so soft and sweet. Me and Lucy are definitely the lounder ones, and Star is gentler, less likely to overreact or get silly. She's the calm one. 'Dad thinks going there gave him piles.'

'Now there's a thought,' I quip. It's one thing thinking about my own bum, but quite another to imagine Star's dad's bum too. Although I'm not actually that sure what piles are. I'll google it later. I suspect I'll immediately regret it, but knowledge is power. It's astonishing how often grown-ups mention piles, to be honest. Makes me a bit afraid of getting any older.

'Still,' Lucy insists, using her special 'in charge' tone of voice that if we lived fifty years ago would have been called *bossy*. But I actually called her bossy once and let's just say, her reaction means I never will again!! 'It's nicer there, isn't it?'

Well, that settles that, I think. *If Lucy has decided.*

'What do you want to add, Tay?'

'She's going to say boys,' Star interrupts cheekily, right as I say …

'Boys, of course!'

We look at each other, blinking.

'What's wrong with that?' I ask. Star and Lucy have officially been a couple since the middle of Year 7, but ever since they met on the first day of secondary school, have been in each other's orbit, like planets with the same centre of gravity or something. We've been a tight threesome since we all got put in the same form together and me and Lucy got all protective over Star when our form teacher was backward about her being trans. That teacher has left now, praise be. He was so old he's probably in a nursing home, where he can be a bigot in peace. Star and Lucy became girlfriend and girlfriend not long after (partner and partner, ACTUALLY, as Star gets a bit annoyed if you gender her relationship) but it didn't really change much, except now they always sit side by side at Starbucks and hold hands and I always go opposite. But it's still the three of us, as much as it ever was. The three musketeers, Tay and two queers! (I'm allowed to say that because Lucy was the one who invented it.)

'I'm sick of being the only kiss virgin in our year,' I complain, frowning. 'Honestly, there are probably Year 7s who've had more action than me. We can't all meet the love of our lives on the first day of school and run off into the sunset together. SOME OF US have to wait for a coach of French boys to pull into town before our real lives can begin.'

'Charming,' scoffs Star, and I can't read how much she's joking and how much she's serious. 'So we're just filling your time before you get a boyfriend?'

'No!' I counter, outraged. 'If you wanna be my lover, you gotta get with my friends,' I say, quoting the Spice Girls, Mum's favourite band when she was my age. She plays them on long car trips. 'But come on, I am *fourteen years old* and never been kissed.' I see Lucy go to open her mouth, but I hold up a hand dramatically. 'I know you're going to say your piece about how *no self-respecting girl waits to be kissed, you could go off and do the kissing yourself, Taylor.* And I know fourteen isn't really *that* old to have not been kissed. But still! I want it! And I don't dream about making the first

16

move. I dream of a boy looking so gaga at me that he can't even remember his own name. He just wants to make me happy. I dream about how tight he'll hug me and how he'll pull away and look at me so seriously, all intent and *brooding*, and then he'll lean in and do fantastic things with his lips. I dream about feeling all … *weak-kneed* from his touch …'

'Is that how I make you feel?' Lucy asks Star.

Star laughs, loving the joke. 'I can barely walk you make me so weak at the knees!'

Lucy giggles, satisfied. I tap a finger on the piece of paper where they've been doing their list.

'Write it down!' I insist, copying Lucy's *leadership voice*. 'Write *Taylor to get her first kiss*.'

'You've waited too long, that's your problem,' Star says with a serious nod. Her dark eyes cloud with concern. 'You've made it too much of a big deal in your head. I'm worried you're going to be—'

'No!' I interject. 'Don't say I'll be disappointed! People don't go mad from desire, fighting wars, penning poetry and going to number one on Spotify's most played songs about the way their heart beats because kissing *isn't* brilliant. Kissing is excellent and everyone knows it.'

Star looks at Lucy, and Lucy grins.

'See?' I cry. 'You both know it! Plus, for the record—'

'Oh! For the record! Hold on, let me get out my phone to

record this,' Star teases. She knows how much I like things duly noted. 'If it's for the record!'

'For the record!' I say again. 'If I wanted to just go and snog some random, I could. It's not about having a first kiss so much as having a *special* first kiss. And I can't think of anything more special than an actual French boy. It's called French kissing for a reason, after all!' I sigh deeply. 'It will be like *Amélie* meets *Moulin Rouge* meets *Emily in Paris*. I'm going to fall in love next week!'

'Yes, I've heard that's how it works, that you can pencil it in your homework diary in any slot you chose.' Star again. She's being uncharacteristically spiky today! What's got into her?! She's starting to bug me now. Lucy can tell, because she hits her arm as a way to tell her to put a sock in it.

I know that really they're only trying to make me laugh, but honestly, I am embarrassed that I'm a kiss virgin. But since I am, it's going to have to be epic when it finally happens. I can hardly snog Bilious Billy from the bus, so called because if he's not farting from one end he's belching from the other. Although … there was a moment before the summer holidays when I *did* consider it. You know, with Billy. When he's not belching, he does have a bit of a twinkle in his eye …

But no. A girl must have some standards. And because of those movies I love, and the books I read, and Mum's Paris stories and *How to Be Parisian When You're Not from*

Paris ... well, who could blame my standards for being high? *How to Be Parisian When You're Not from Paris* says:

On Kissing

It is all-consuming, passionate, the secret the Parisian woman carries with her: a love affair can be fuel for the Parisian woman, a kiss the flame that sets alight her world. The Parisian woman kisses the way she lives her life: dramatically and whole-heartedly. She treats every kiss like a once-in-a-lifetime performance!

I mean!!!!!!

'Girls,' says the person in charge of cleaning the tables. 'I'm sorry but we've got a rush on. If you're done with your drinks I'm going to have to ask for your table back.'

The three of us automatically look towards the counter, where there's a queue backing up to the door.

'OK,' Lucy tells her. 'We won't be long.'

The woman nods with a smile at Lucy, a courtesy that wouldn't have been extended to me or Star. But people always like Lucy. She's all blue eyes and blonde hair and she has a fringe. Girls with fringes always get treated nicely. I think it's because they can't see properly and so always look just a tiny bit like they need extra help navigating daily life, when in fact they're just in need of a trim.

'Mum says she'll cook tea for us,' I tell them. 'Did you bring the story? We could do some of that in my room and drink the Shloer she saves for parties out of wine glasses? I saw some under the stairs.'

The 'story' is our project we do together. It's Harry Styles and Tom Holland fanfiction, and we take turns adding to it to make the others laugh. It's quite good, though, if you ask me. There's something about writing to impress your mates. It really makes you try hard. The teachers at school are missing a trick with that one. If our geography homework was based on lols, we'd all be getting As.

Star pats her bag. 'Got it right here,' she says, with a mischievous grin.

'Come on then,' I say. 'Let's go. Maybe my next chapter will be all about what Harry thinks of the Frenchies. I'll bet his first kiss was when he was about ten. I bet he came out of the womb kissing, even.'

'He was eleven, actually,' says Star matter-of-factly. 'A friend of a friend when they were watching a film.'

I shake my head at her. Imagine what else we could all remember if we weren't so absolutely gaga?

After we've all had tea at mine and Star and Lucy have gone home, I sit with my notebook on my bed and make list of articles I'd like to pitch for the *Register*. Ms K says writing is collaborative, and editors like to shape pieces as much as writers like to write them, so it's about striking the interest of your editor (aka the Year 13s who run it) and letting them shape the idea. I tap my pen against my lip and have a think, then I write down:

- *Why You Should Make Friends with the New Kid*
- *More Drama Offstage Than On: Meet the Dramatic Stars of Crickleton High's Theatre Club*
- *Feminism for Beginners*
- *Why You Should Care About Feminism*
- *The Case for Abolishing GCSEs*
- *Something about volunteering?*
- *Maybe a quiz? Climate emergency?? Different people's obsessions and hobbies??*

I'm not really convinced by any of what I'm coming up with, but maybe inspiration will come once I start writing the pitches. I'll ask Ms K what she thinks. Anyway. Tomorrow is a new day and one step closer to the French exchange, aka *Vive la kiss!*! The French exchange starts in Year 9 and happens here every other year when we're the hosts, and in France every other year when they're the hosts, so that by the end of Year 10 you've been both host and hosted. Imagine if it was the year to go to France! That would be even more special for a first kiss. Le sigh. Hmmm. Must go to bed. *How to Be Parisian When You're Not from Paris* says sleep is vital for a fresh and dewy glow:

Sleeping Beauty

Every Parisian woman knows the rules: drink your water, spritz your face mist generously, and the trick to wearing as little make-up as possible (for heavy lips and eyes are the opposite of chic), sleep like a child, for hours and hours, and make no apologies for it. You'll be bright-eyed and fresh-faced effortlessly.

Just as I'm about to turn out my light, Mum taps on the door to say goodnight.

'Darling,' she says, as she pushes down on the handle. 'I just want to get your thoughts on this TikTok I've done …'

Urgh! Mum and her 'Writer's TikTok'! When she's not teaching creative writing at the nearby university, she writes these bizarre time-travel novels that nobody buys (her words, I'm not being mean!), so is always trying to find new ways to reach readers. But … TikTok, Mum, seriously?! She needs to get a life!

'Mum …' I start, but I am silenced by a massive shriek.

'Ohmygod!' she trills when she sees me. 'Taylor!'

'What?!' I shriek back. She's scared me! 'WHAT?!'

'Your face!' she says. I rush to the mirror. I am covered in blue ink. Ah. My pen. It must have leaked on me when I was doing my 'thinking'.

'Oh my god,' she says, starting to laugh. 'That was terrifying! You fool!' Mum says, kissing the top of my head. 'Don't worry about the TikTok. I think it's going to take you a while to wash that off and get clean.'

'*Scrub* it off, more like,' I say, trundling off to the bathroom and grabbing a flannel from under the sink. This had better not stain!

'Don't use my best cleanser!' Mum shouts through to me. 'It's expensive!'

Oh *sure*, I think. I'll just stay blue forever!

3

*H*mmmm. Mum's still standing strong on the upper-ear piercing. Says she won't part with a hundred quid at the drop of the hat, which is fair play on one hand, because it's not like I have a spare hundred pounds either – but on the other hand it does rather ruin my life, and I'm sure she could stretch to it if she really wanted to, maybe as an early Christmas present. I should definitely have nice cute jewellery for when the Frenchies come. I don't want them to think I'm *provincial*. (Or do I mean proverbial? Must google.) Maybe I'll experiment with being one of those girls who wear a lot of rings, you know the ones, they don't go all the way down your finger but sit in the middle bit below your first knuckle, and some below the second knuckle, all bohemian and fashionable. The last rings I had weren't proper gold though, and turned my fingers green when I washed my hands. That wouldn't be bohemian *or* fashionable, but rather scrubby and unkempt-seeming. Much to consider. I'll see what Star and Lucy say.

Anyway, I should concentrate. We're all in a meeting in the hall, to talk about the French exchange and code of conduct with Madame Jones and Monsieur Brown (have you ever heard of such boring names for French teachers?), the ones in charge of it all. They have a million PowerPoint slides to go through. Incredible how some teachers can make even the most amazing thing to ever happen to you in your life seem boring. Maybe there's a column in that? Or … oh! I could write a column about the French exchange! That would be cool!

I *try* to look interested, so that the teachers know I'm up for it and give me one of the better exchange partners. I imagine that's how it works. You can't go pairing a dud with somebody ready to live life to the fullest. That would be cruel for both sides. But I keep feeling eyes on me from across the room. You know when you just *know* somebody is looking at you, sort of like how you can just *know* you've not got a very good mark on a test right before they give out the results? That gut feeling? Two minutes ago I was minding my own business, doing my interested face, when I looked to the left where the boys in the year above are sitting. Tommy

Tsao, renowned class clown, was vaguely looking in my direction, but didn't make eye contact. But just now I've looked over again because he's ... staring at me?? Having a Year 10 boy look directly at me is a bit like looking right at the sun and then seeing spots afterwards: I feel all stunned and a bit scared, like I've made a mistake and should know better. And yet, OK, I can definitely feel that it *is* his eyes on me now, I'm deffo not wrong. Ewww, this is so uncomfortable! Is he trying to psych me out? Why? I've never even spoken to him before. Mum says once you get into Year 9 the older kids start talking to you. Is she right?? I try looking away from the presentation to pick at the skin around my nails so that my eyes are firmly down, but last about three seconds before I can't resist looking up again and—

GAH! WE HAVE JUST LOOKED RIGHT AT EACH OTHER!!!

It's like I've touched a live wire and got an electric shock.

I wonder if he's doing some sort of a dare.

I think I've gone red. Urgh! Stop, stop, stop! That's the thing about getting embarrassed. We have all these PSHE lessons about talking about your feelings and acknowledging your emotions because a problem shared etc. etc., but with embarrassment, it's like the more you know you're feeling it the worse it gets, as if it likes the attention. I go all blotchy when I colour up, patchy down my neck and up to my eyeballs and it takes ages to calm down. And now Star is looking at me, like I'm a beacon of shiny red, Rudolph the Red-Nosed Reindeer of the French block, begging for everyone's eyes on me when I'd actually rather just disappear.

Goddammit! Year 10s! They're horrible!

Although. That said …

He's pretty fit, Tommy Tsao. Quite tall and plays on the boys' hockey team and has this dark shaggy hair that he has to flick out of his eyes. I wonder if he has to wear an Alice band for sports, like premiership football players have to do. It makes him a bit less intimidating to imagine that. He used to go out with Natalie Redcock (unfortunate name), but they broke up after the summer when she cheated on him on her holidays. Whoever she met when she was away must have been a proper ten-out-of-ten, because I don't think I'd ever cheat on somebody with eyes like Tommy Tsao. But what am I saying? I'm getting ahead of myself. I can't cheat on *anybody* because OH YES! SINGLE FOREVER TAYLOR BLAKE HERE AND REPORTING FOR DUTY! Cheating means being committed to kissing one person and then snogging another, and as everyone in the world knows, I'm a kiss virgin.

I look up again.

This time, something in me finds the absolute bravery to hold his eye. I don't know what comes over me but it's like I'm Katniss Everdeen, standing my ground and refusing to be bullied into submission. I might be the colour of a ripe tomato but I've got nothing to lose: I don't know who this Tommy Tsao thinks he is, but he can't just be all goggly-eyed and distracting because he feels like it. I am my mother's daughter! I will not be made to feel intimidated by a boy! Even a Year 10 one!!

One second goes by, and then one more. It feels like ages. In a bonkers way, I almost want to laugh? Look at me go, staring down Tommy Tsao. And then the most bananas thing happens: Tommy Tsao does a sort of cross-eyed face and sticks his tongue out a bit, really fast, so nobody else sees, and the shock of it makes me hiccup into a little laugh.

'I assume that laughter is your way of volunteering for clean-up duty after the welcome breakfast, Ms Blake?'

Madame Jones. She's fairly young and actually quite pretty too, for a teacher, but somehow talks like she's sixty, like she read a book on how people in authority should sound and so is practising on us. *Ms Blake?* I hate it when teachers use your last name – they never do it to the boys, only us girls.

'*Je suis désolée,*' I squeak, definitely less tomato and more positively purple now. Everyone is looking at me because the noise I made was so stupid. Bloody Tommy Tsao! I could kill him! This is his fault!

Madame Jones carries on with whatever she was saying

and I try to focus on forcing a hole to open in the ground so it can swallow me up and I no longer have to weather this horrid mortal coil. I have no idea if Tommy Tsao is looking at me, but I know Star is, right beside me, because best friends know what other best friends are thinking, and I don't have to hear her voice to know she's asking me: *Tay, what the hell is wrong with you?*

'Tay, what the hell is wrong with you?' Star says once we've been dismissed.

Told you.

I wave a hand and shrug like I have no idea what she's saying.

'Hmmmmm?' I muse, in a way that I hope is *insouciant*. I can't say that word out loud – I don't know how to pronounce it – but when I see it written down it seems like a sophisticated way to say *not bothered*.

'You were acting really … abnormal in there,' she says.

I look around to see if anyone we should be concerned about can hear us, i.e. Tommy Tsao himself. And there he is again! Looking over here as he files out of the hall with his mates all joshing around him. Star follows my gaze right as he lifts a hand and issues a little wave. At me!

'Is Tommy Tsao … waving at you?' she says, sounding exactly amazed as I feel.

'You saw that too?' I ask.

'Do you know him?'

'No!' I say. 'But he was staring at me, I think. Not to brag or anything. He was pulling faces.'

'Boys are such rubbish flirts,' she notes. I point out that I'm not much better.

We move through the throngs of people all leaving school at the same time, both of us looking out for Lucy, who had an intervention meeting for her maths because she's not been doing her homework, as she says she can't. I've offered to help her – not that I'm a brainiac with numbers, but … well, you just follow the formulas they tell you to do. It's not actually that hard. But when I said that to her she called me a swot in a mean way, not a banter way, so I left it alone. Lucy looks like a little angel, but she's got an attitude made of fire, and fire burns! It's great when she's on your side, but if you annoy her, boy oh boy will she tell you.

'What did I miss?' she asks when we find her.

'Tay has been flirting with Tommy Tsao,' Star says, kissing her on the cheek. 'Or trying to,' she adds wickedly. Honestly, I don't know how she's still considered the kind one in our Members Only group when she's starting to really get an edge to her lately. It's kind of fun, though …

'A Year 10?' Lucy asks, her blue eyes wide with shock.

31

I shrug. I don't want to make this a bigger deal than it needs to be.

'He was probably just bored,' I say. 'He was pulling faces at me. Whatever.'

'*Whatever*,' Lucy mimics, pushing her fringe out of her eyes with a flick, and I push her arm and she pretends to stumble from the force of it so that I roll my eyes like *what are you like, idiot*, and then we all laugh and make a group of petrified Year 7s stare like they might pee their pants.

We amble up to the Co-op, the posh one with the toilets, to go and look at what our Frenchies might like. Part of the briefing I *did* actually pay attention to was Monsieur Brown explaining that it might be nice to encourage our guests to make themselves at home – show them where the drinks and food are so they can help themselves and not die of dehydration or starvation whilst waiting to be offered, which is a good point really because I was once at Star's house for a whole afternoon during a heatwave before she offered me a cordial. I've never been so thirsty in my life. I kept hinting, but she didn't pick up on it. That was last year though. I'm braver now – as demonstrated by this afternoon, staring at Tommy Tsao right back. Thinking about it, it *was* pretty badass. Mature of me, refusing to be intimidated. Yay me!

'You know,' offers Lucy as we meander around the aisles, 'when I went to France when I was little, we saw a whole family eat bars of Milka between chunks of baguette. Literally chocolate sandwiches.'

'Gross,' I say. 'Sounds like a perfect way to ruin chocolate if you ask me.'

'I could eat a chocolate sandwich,' reflects Star. In her phone she's keeping a list of things we think our parents should get in – croissants (fresh daily, but frozen will do if CBA), Nutella (none of us are allowed it normally, but surely for guests it is a must), the aforementioned baguette ...

'What else do French people eat?' I say. 'Snails and frogs? I don't know where we'd buy those.'

Star says, 'Dad reckons they'll just want to have Starbucks and fish and chips.'

I sigh. 'Is that all England is known for? See, this is why I'm going to live abroad when I'm older.'

'Same,' says Star. 'I don't know why anyone would want to live anywhere other than New York.' Star wants to be a restaurateur, opening up loads of fancy places for famous people to eat in. I think that's *so* original. Who else thinks like that?!

'Or LA,' notes Lucy, who is planning on being an agent for actors out there, something that I can totally see for her. She'd be all barking orders down the phone about contracts and deals, but from some fancy cafe drinking green juice and busy being gorgeous.

'Or Paris. Do you know my mum lived in Paris right before she decided to have me, and chose *having a baby* over FRANCE?'

'Couldn't she have had a baby *in* France?' asks Star, a wicked glint in her elfin features. 'I've heard they do that there.'

'Ha, ha,' I say. 'Apparently she wanted to make sure she had help, so came back to Crickleton because Grandma and Grandad are here and they could babysit.'

'So she chose Crickleton over Paris? Whoa. That explains why she sometimes uses French words in her TikToks though.'

'Oh yeah!' agrees Lucy. 'She says a lot of *oui!* and *oh la la!*'

'Guys,' I say, pulling a face. 'You know the rule.'

'Don't talk about your mum's TikTok,' the girls drone in unison.

'Exactly,' I say. 'Thank you!'

Mum's one and only rule for my social media that I must obey is that Mum has to follow my account and I have to follow hers, but I try not to watch anything she posts. It's just so embarrassing! All these videos about creating characters and pacing plot where she uses a pointer to her whiteboard and tries to talk 'young'. NO THANK YOU.

'Moving on,' I say. 'I definitely think French Taylor already has her upper ear pierced.'

'Just go to the jewellery place in the shopping centre,' Lucy says, lingering by the crisps and picking up a packet of Quavers. Then she puts it back and picks up some Monster Munch. Then she puts the Monster Munch down and moves on. 'It's cheap there. Surely you've got birthday money saved up?'

'Only fifteen pounds,' I say, picking up some Monster Munch for myself. Lucy sees and nods, circling back to get herself the bag she obviously wanted all along. I check the time on my phone. 'Oh,' I say. 'I have to go soon – I still need to put the finishing touches on the spare room.'

For my Frenchie's arrival I'm going to put rolled-up towels on the end of the bed and a chocolate on the pillow like a hotel. Isn't that so classy?!

As we stand to pay, I look around in case anything else sparks inspiration. Garlic – the French love garlic with everything, don't they? Oh, and eggs! In *How to Be Parisian When You're Not from Paris,* it says that every woman should be able to snaffle off to the kitchen to make her love a quick omelette. That sounds simple enough. I might not be cooking snacks for my partner – she can help herself, as per Monsieur Brown's advice – but hopefully she'll be bringing her sexy male friends over, and within hours the best-looking one will see how cool and funny I am, and talk about how he's always preferred English girls over French girls, and he just *had a feeling* he'd meet somebody special, but he had no idea that in meeting me it could be somebody *so* special. He'll be talking about how maybe he could stay for the term, or the rest of the school year, his parents won't mind if he explains … and I'll say 'Are you hungry? I could do us a quick omelette,' and after he's eaten he'll push his knife and fork together, wipe his mouth with one of those linen napkins (I'll have to ask Mum to get some) and then lean in, tipping my chin up with a finger and whispering *mon dieu*, and whatever the French is for *you've got no idea how beautiful you really are, do you?* and then it will happen, the kiss, like tasting the future and everything that might well be possible in this life that suddenly has so much more promise … Heaven on earth …

'Hello? Love? I said that's 65p,' comes a voice. The checkout woman. I shake myself from my daydream and tap my card. God, the exchange needs to just hurry up and get here!!

'I hope all our partners are friends,' Lucy says excitedly as we tear open our crisps and head up towards the hill where we normally say goodbye and walk in three different directions for the night. I can see her 'organising' light come on, and sure enough she says: 'We could do a sleepover all together. Star, will your dad say it's OK to do it at yours? You've got the biggest room.'

'I'll ask,' Star says, going in to nick a Monster Munch.

And then there he is again! Tommy Tsao. How mad is that? Some boy I've never noticed before in my life suddenly everywhere, all day, every place I go? And get this: LOOKING RIGHT AT ME AGAIN, SMILING!!!

So it wasn't an accident before, in the French meeting. Hmmmm!

He's in a group, a bunch of Year 10s draped over two benches at the edge of the park, laughing and joking and generally being unapproachable.

'Smile back!' hisses Lucy, not so much a leader as genuinely bossy in her surprise, face agog at this turn of events.

I feel a bit stuck to the spot, and it takes a lot of effort to smile back. Then I remember I'm cross at him for getting me into trouble and relax my face again. And in the time all this happens, one of the girls – I think her name is Anna – has looked over to where we are and back to Tommy again, her face thunderous like we're pathetic for even existing.

'You know they're in Year 9, don't you?' I hear her say, and so we take it as our cue to scurry away like sad little mice. As we trot off though, I do see Tommy say something back to her. I watch his lips move. They're so nice. I'll bet he's a really good kisser …

Not that I'm thinking about kissing Tommy.

Obviously.

I mean.

OK, fine. Maybe a bit.

'I think … he *fancies* you,' Lucy says slowly, delightedly, and it's weird that she seems so a) shocked by this and b) utterly thrilled, as if she herself has just discovered somebody fancies *her*.

'I don't even know him,' I say.

But on the inside I think: *Omg, what if he does!!!!*

4

I'm late leaving school tonight, because I can't stop thinking about what that horrid Year 10 said yesterday, when she made out like Tommy was stupid for smiling at me because I'm a Year 9. Year 9 is very cool! It's my favourite year so far! So this morning in geography I started to make notes on an idea about why Year 9 will be the best year of your life and I'm trying to flesh it out on one of the computers before I go home. The inspiration is burning bright! So far, I've got:

> ***Which school supply is king of the classroom? A ruler. But which year is the best in the land? I have to say, it's got to be Year 9.***

Years 7 and 8 are all about being little fish in a big pond, finding your feet and figuring out what's what. And Years 10 and 11 are all about the exam treadmill: you've picked your GCSEs and that's it now, you've got to study and study hard! Which leaves lovely Year 9, like an island of calm in the middle of the school storm …

In Year 9, you get to join in the hosting for the French exchange (if it's a hosting year at Crickleton High. If it's the French school's hosting year then you get to go TO FRANCE! How amazing is that!) and finally get to hold positions of responsibility in school clubs, like being able to write in this very paper. My mum got her first job in Year 9, making her own money. A lot of us get more relaxed rules from our parents in Year 9: being able to go into town on a Saturday, or staying out later or having friends over. What's not to love about all that!

Basically, Year 9 is when our maturity kicks in but we haven't got loads of responsibilities yet. It's the best of both worlds! And to anyone who disagrees, I say: nonsense! But maybe that's a column somebody else can write … as for me, I've got to dash … I'm busy having FUN!

It's over 150 words and needs some more jokes in it, but it's a good start. See, this is where writing for the *Register* has its limits. If I had 500 words, I'd be able to be so much better. It's very frustrating! But still, I'll take what I can get. Maybe I should start googling other places to write, too, like the local Crickleton paper maybe, or something online. I print off my piece and put it in my bag to show Grandma and Grandad – I'm going there for tea, and they always have good ideas …

'Hey, Taylor.'

I look up from where I'm studying the bus map. I know every bus and every route, because it isn't hard – this is Crickleton, not outer Kathmandu. But I like to look at it all the same, all the names of the streets I've known my whole life, all the connecting stops that could, in theory, take me from my own front door to the whole rest of the county, or even the country – the world! – if I had the fare. I find it comforting, looking at where I am and what I know, with just the hint of possibility about what lies beyond it all, if I'm brave.

It's funny, but as I drag my gaze away from the map to whoever said my name, I hallucinate that it's Tommy Tsao. Tommy Tsao stood there all tall and floppy-haired and half-smiling with his lovely nice lips, in his hockey gear, waiting for me to say something back. I've got him on the brain! The way he waved at me after the French meeting yesterday has been playing on my mind so much that I'm imagining he's actually here.

I blink once, then twice and three times, until the apparition in front of me says: 'Are you OK?'

It really IS Tommy Tsao! *Zut alors!*

In the split second before I open my mouth to speak, I imagine saying something cool and calm and collected, something devastatingly chic that leaves him wanting more: something like *hey* or *oh, it's you* or just a simple *Tommy*, with maybe a shrug or half-smile that he'll spend the rest of the day wondering about, like he's made me wonder about him. But before I can regulate myself I sort of splutter out crossly, like it's an accusation: 'How do you know my name?'

I sound rude and abrupt. I didn't mean to!

'Urm,' he says, looking from left to right like the answer might be either side of him. 'I asked around. When I knew you were doing the exchange. Because I hadn't noticed you before.'

I must pull a face because he adds, a bit panicked, 'Not in a creepy way. I just didn't know. I'm Tommy, by the way.'

Now, there are several ways to take all this. On one hand, Tommy Tsao is not only talking to me, but went to the trouble of finding out who I am once he knew I was doing the exchange program!! On the other hand, I am so plain and boring that he'd never even noticed me before, and telling me so is a bit mean. On the third hand (??), he's also just introduced himself because his ego isn't so big that he thinks I already know, which is very sweet, really. Of course I know who he is! The whole school does! He's the star hockey player, the most popular boy there! He's sporty and handsome and cheeky – the holy trifecta of popularity!

'Oh,' I say, because I am *soooooo* smart and cool and funny and used to talking to boys in Year 10.

Not.

He nods, like I've said something worth agreeing with (it's like we're both having conversations with people who aren't each other and we can't quite line up what we're saying) and then the bus pulls up and I think, *Well, that's that, well played, Taylor, you've really left an impression there. Excellent job. Lucy will be organising you a World's Best Flirt party in no time. Jeez.*

But then once we're both on and have tapped our passes, Tommy *doesn't* walk away and pretend not to know me because I'm such a dud. Instead he gestures for me to slip into the seat opposite him in the four-section, which I do, wondering what the heck is going on. Am I suddenly friends with him?

'So why are you leaving school so late?' he says. 'Were you at a club or something?'

Oooh, I'm glad he's asked. This is going to sound *so* impressive!

43

'Actually,' I say, in my most confident voice, 'I was working on a piece.'

'A piece of what?' Tommy asks, looking at me but then quickly looking away out of the window, like he's scared to.

'I'm a writer,' I say. 'I write for the school paper?' I pause, waiting for him to make a noise of impressed awe. But he doesn't. It's like he hasn't even heard me.

'Don't read it,' he says, and it makes me mad, because that's a bit rude! Can't he at least say, like, *Oh! Wicked?!* But then he catches my eye and smiles really wide and it makes my insides feel all gloopy, like they've melted, and I'm not mad any more.

And then I remember.

'Hey,' I say, with a cheeky point of the finger. 'You got me in trouble at school yesterday. I'm supposed to be cross at you!'

The bus pulls away from the kerb, where it will wind through suburban streets for the fifteen minutes it takes to get to Grandma and Grandad's. I always go to Grandma and Grandad's on a Tuesday. I usually walk. How peculiar that the one day I get the bus is the one day Tommy Tsao does too.

'Yeah,' Tommy says, running a hand through his hair. 'Sorry about that. That noise you made was really funny.'

'Really *embarrassing*, more like,' I say, and then I pout, but it's a funny pout, and I think we're both relieved to

44

realise that I'm … flirting? Like, quite well now? Or at least better.

'You just looked so serious when they were talking. I thought, How is this girl able to be so interested in such a long and boring meeting? So when you looked my way, I had to try and make you laugh.'

'Mission accomplished,' I say.

'My bad that you got in trouble though.'

'You're forgiven,' I say, pursing my lips but in a funny way.

'Phew!' he says, pretending to wipe his brow.

It's interesting being this close to him. He grins at me, and I find myself grinning back. His dark eyes are even dreamier than I thought, and he has a dimple on one side of his mouth but not the other, which is even cuter than being symmetrical somehow. After a beat it feels weird to still be looking at him, so I look away … But when I dare to sneak a glance back up, he is totally still staring at me, only he looks away really quickly like he isn't, and then I get another beat to study his face again. Then he looks back and our eyes lock once more, and we laugh – about what I don't know, but we're definitely in on the same joke together, even if I'm not sure what the joke is. It's a nice feeling, being part of a little club with him.

'So you excited about the exchange?' he says finally.

'Yeah,' I say. 'My first time hosting. I can't believe there'll be a French person in my house!'

'I went there last year,' he said, 'and my partner was a bit of a loser. Didn't want to do anything, didn't like to leave his mum for too long, that sort of stuff. Obvs I've got the same partner this year so I can return the hosting favour or whatever, but I'm bummed about it. He was so lame.'

'Yeah,' I say uncertainly. 'That sounds crappy.'

In my head I think, *Awwww, that poor person getting all nervous about Tommy Tsao in their house!* It makes me wonder if Tommy just wasn't a very good guest. But then who wouldn't love hanging out with him?

'Let's see how it goes!' he adds. 'Although I'm only doing it because my mum makes me. I could take it or leave it myself.'

Hmmm. He's a bit of a Debbie Downer. Or is he just doing what loads of boys in my year do and playing it down because he thinks enthusiasm is 'not cool'? Ironically, I find fake boredom more boring than actual boredom.

'Well, I'm really excited,' I say. 'I'd like to live in France one day. I'm a bit of a Francophile ...'

'Yeah?' he says. 'How come?'

'We went a few summers ago,' I say. 'And I just love it. The buildings were just so incredible and dramatic, and I like *pain au chocolat* and *moules frites*. And I watch loads of movies set there, and read books set there too. The French just have this way of living that I think is so sophisticated, like they know what is important in life. They're creative and cool. And Mum's always on at me to make plans to travel, to see the world. Crickleton can be a bit boring. I want a *big* life, if that makes sense. To do everything it has to offer!'

'Nah,' he says, and it's a bit dismissive. 'Crickleton's got everything you need! Cinema, shops, places to eat …'

'Yeah,' I say, 'but don't you want to, like, do those things in other places? Other cultures?'

'We go back to China once a year,' he says with a shrug. 'But I don't really like it.'

I feel a bit deflated. He doesn't like much, Tommy Tsao. But he's getting more confident the longer we talk, and I have to admit I quite like the attention. He keeps staring at my mouth when I'm talking, which at first makes me self-conscious, like I've got carrot in my teeth from the coleslaw at lunch, or lip gloss smeared everywhere. But today I didn't have coleslaw in my sandwich and I didn't wear lip gloss to school … so it's as if he's letting me know he likes my mouth. Like … well, OK, I don't want to sound full of myself or big-headed or anything, but … I just get a really strong feeling that he's wondering what it would be like to kiss me. And now that I'm wondering if he's wondering that, I'm wondering what it would be like to kiss *him*. Imagine if I kissed a Year 10! Imagine if I kissed THE Tommy Tsao!

The bus slows down and Bilious Billy from my year gets on. He gives a nod of acknowledgement and I feel bitchy for looking away but I don't want Tommy to know I know him. I can't explain why.

Billy sits down in front of us and it's not long before the smell of rotten eggs permeates the air. And I mean proper rotting eggs, like ten-day-old rotting eggs, totally foul. What are Billy's family feeding him?! It is *not* normal to do farts that smell that bad, honestly. I surreptitiously pull my sleeve over my hand and put it to my nose and mouth so I don't have to breathe in the air, watching as Tommy gets a lungful and nodding in Billy's direction because I can't have him thinking it's me, farting like that and almost killing everyone on board, silent-but-violent style. Tommy bulges out his eyes and coughs a bit too loudly. I don't like Billy's farts but it would be cruel to call him out on it and I don't want that. I pull a face at Tommy, who puts his hand over his mouth and nose too, and then he's laughing, and I'm laughing, and he moves to open the bus window a bit and the smell passes but we're still laughing – we can't stop! Every time I think I might be able to pull myself together I look at Tommy and burst out into giggles again, and every time he gets a bit more serious I make him laugh, and on and on and on it goes, right up until:

'This is my stop!' I say, seeing Grandad on the other side of the glass. The bus is already pulling away, thinking nobody is getting off, so I have to leap up like my bum is on fire and shout, 'Hold the bus, please!' and I peg it down the aisle and almost fall over as we brake to a stop. I'm so flustered I almost forget to look back at Tommy, but he shouts, like he doesn't care who hears: 'See ya, Taylor!'

I get off and turn around in time to see the bus drive away, Tommy looking at me through the window. I raise a hand to say bye. I'm going to have to report back about all this ASAP in the group chat!

'He's a handsome lad,' Grandad says.

Ohmygod, that's the last thing I need, Grandad sticking his nose into my love life. Ewww.

'Hi, Grandad,' I say, giving him a hug. He didn't have to meet me off the bus, but when I rang to say I wouldn't be walking he said he'd stretch his legs by going to the top of the drive to wait. I'd forgotten he'd said that until now. I wish he hadn't seen me wave to Tommy. That's my personal business.

'Are you courting, then?' he says, as we head the twenty or so steps to the bungalow.

'Courting?' I repeat. 'Grandad, this isn't 1930.'

'Going out, then! Friends with benefits!'

'Grandad!' I shriek. 'Don't say friends with benefits to me!'

'What?' he asks. 'Why not? That's what you call it when girls and boys are pals, isn't it?'

49

I die from grossness on the inside. 'No,' I say. 'It means ...'

I can't bring myself to say it. He's in his sixties – I could kill him!

He pushes open the door to the bungalow and I take off my coat and shoes as he says, 'Go on, explain it to me.' Then he shouts through to Grandma, 'Rachel! She's here!'

'It's when,' I say, steadying myself with a deep breath, 'you're friends with somebody mostly, but *sometimes* you ...'

I wiggle my eyebrows suggestively, to fill in the blanks. He just looks at me.

'Have s-e-x,' I whisper, totally mortified, right as Grandma appears at the doorway from the lounge.

'Oh Christ!' Grandad splutters. 'Well, I'm pleased for you if you've got a new boyfriend, but I certainly don't think you should be up to that just yet. Nobody buys the cow if they can get the milk for free. Remember that, won't you.'

And with that he slips on his slippers and fumbles on through to his armchair, leaving Grandma looking at me, amused. I can't believe me and Grandad just talked about sex!

'Taylor, love,' Grandma says, and I brace myself for some big talk on how I shouldn't be dating boys or kissing boys or even really thinking about boys. I feel guilty for something I haven't even done, like I've been caught being 'loose', even though Mum says there's no such thing as 'loose', that that's a term from the patriarchy to oppress *women who can't be*

50

tamed. 'I just want to say,' Grandma continues, and I hold my breath. 'I don't think you should be doing the nookie *quite* yet, but whatever you do …'

Oh god, oh god, oh god. This is *mortifying.*

She presses: 'Don't wait until you're married to do it. You'll only be disappointed.'

My grandparents, folks.

I really love hanging out at Grandma and Grandad's house. I don't technically have a dad, because Mum got pregnant from a sperm donor, so my family is really small. It's just me and her, and Grandma and Grandad, and we're all really close. I tease Mum for choosing Crickleton over Paris, but every Tuesday after school, and some Fridays or Saturday afternoons, I get to be fussed over and cooed at in a way that if Mum did it I'd be annoyed, but for some reason when Grandma and Grandad do it, I don't mind.

I do some maths homework at their little dining room table as Grandad does the crossword and Grandma walks about from room to room. I ask her what she's doing in case she needs any help, but all she says is that she's 'doing her jobs'. The nature of these jobs is unclear, but I'd be fascinated to get a pedometer on her to see how many steps she gets in a day. She must cover about ten miles, just in this tiny little bungalow. It only takes four steps to get from the living room to the bathroom, maybe six to get from the bathroom back to the kitchen. So you can imagine how many laps she's doing.

'What do you want for your tea, love?' she asks, in between moving some clean laundry through from the kitchen where the washer is and reappearing with dirty laundry from the basket in their bedroom.

'Have you got any eggs?' I ask.

'I have,' she says. 'What you thinking? Egg and soldiers?'

'Omelette, actually,' I tell her. '*How to Be Parisian When You're Not from Paris* says every girl should master making one.'

Grandma chuckles. 'You and that book,' she says. 'You're just like your mum was at your age: passionate and intense about *everything* she got into.'

'Thanks? I think?' I say, not quite understanding her point. Then I let out a snort of laughter. 'Is that why she's so into her TikTok now?' I say. 'Obsessive tendencies?'

Grandma shakes her head good-naturedly. 'I wish I even knew what this TikTok is,' she says. 'When people talk about their kids getting into social media, I thought they meant teenage kids! Not a forty-five-year-old!'

'She says it helps find new readers for her novels,' I say.

'Seems to me to be a lot of pointing at words on a screen, or ... what do you call it when you mouth the words to things?'

'Lip-syncing?' I say.

'Lip-syncing!' Grandma hoots. 'But whatever pays the bills, I suppose. Although I'm surprised between the writing and the university teaching that she's got the time. You don't go on it much, do you?'

I shrug. 'I've got an account, but only to really watch videos of Harry Styles at his gigs.'

'Well,' Grandma says, 'you stick with your books. I've got some excellent steamy romances for when you're a bit older. Mills & Boon, they're called. Ooooh, they've kept me company many an afternoon!'

I've seen the books of which Grandma speaks. They normally have pictures of muscley men in half-undone shirts, and women with their dresses falling off their shoulders. I'd prefer to reread *The Fault in Our Stars* again – I've got an old battered paperback that Auntie Kate got me one Christmas. It might make me cry, but gosh it's so romantic and beautiful. And all the bits in Amsterdam are nearly as good as reading about Paris.

'I will have to read this *How to Be Parisian When You're Not from Paris*, though,' she adds. 'See if I can pick up any tips for when your exchange partner is here.'

I sigh, half amused and half mortified at the thought.

'No,' Grandma continues, her eyes alight with mischief. 'You're right. I can tell by the look on your face what you're thinking. You're thinking: Grandma doesn't need to *read* a book about being *très chic*, she could *write* a book about being *très chic*! And you know what? You're absolutely right.'

'You read my mind,' I say, laughing. 'Now. This omelette. What do I do? I'll cook for all of us.'

'Ooooh, get you,' Grandad says from his chair, but I can tell he's secretly a bit impressed. 'I'll take mine with cheese and a side order of baked beans, please. And some buttered bread. You can't beat beans and an omelette with a slice of buttered white bread.'

I pretend I'm a waiter and 'write down' his order in the palm of my hand, a joke we've done since forever.

'Anything else for you today?' I ask him with a flourish, and he shakes his head with a smile.

'Just a cordial, please.'

Grandma shows me where everything is and asks if she should *sous chef* or leave me to it. I say leave me to it. How hard can it be? *How to Be Parisian When You're Not from Paris* specifically uses the word *snaffle* when they talk about disappearing off to make a quick omelette. *Snaffle off to make a quick but delicious snack*, or something like that.

I put two eggs in a bowl and barely get any shell in with it, heat the pan and spray in some oil and put in a knob of butter. I salt and pepper the eggs, sprinkle in some cheese, and then pour the whole mixture into the hot pan, watching it bubble as it cooks.

I remember what Grandad said about wanting bread and butter, and his beans, so whilst it cooks I busy myself wading through the tins and finding bread plates and going through to the dining table to clear my maths homework and put out the table mats. I decide to make the effort and go the extra mile with some floral napkins (paper, not cloth) from the side cupboard, and the nice water glasses. As I work, I think about Tommy Tsao and how he was watching my mouth back on the bus, and the look on his face after I waved goodbye. I suppose if he's doing the exchange I'll be seeing a lot more of him over this next week, but even if he does fancy me (still a big if!! I don't know how to get confirmation!) there's two things to consider: 1) I'm not actually sure if I fancy him back? I might just enjoy that he's a Year 10, and the attention in general. I mean, who doesn't like to think somebody could be crushing on them?! And 2) If I do decide I fancy him back, I think my first kiss should still be with one of the French boys, to set the tone for the rest of my love life. In fact, it will set the tone for my life in general! I want to be a chic and cool adult, one who walks around outdoor markets with a string bag full of fresh fruit and a baguette poking out like on Pinterest. I'll have a wardrobe full of white T-shirts and well-fitting jeans, like they tell you about in *How to Be Parisian When You're Not from Paris*, with an oversized navy blazer for the spring and an artfully battered leather jacket for autumn.

How to Dress Like a Parisian

Don't try too hard, but always make the effort. Jeans, always. Ballet flats, or loafers. A blazer, to smarten up any outfit. A small silk scarf, either around your neck, or tied to the handle of your handbag. Oversized sunglasses, for the mystery. A man's shirt, and an oversized jumper that slips off the shoulder. Always a trench, sometimes a leather jacket …

Imagine having a wardrobe like all that!

I'll have a really cool group of French friends (plus Star and Lucy when they visit) who I'll sit outside cafes with, drinking tiny cups of espresso and saying intelligent things about art and philosophy before going to parties where everyone works in theatre or newspapers or fashion. I won't ever settle. Not like in Crickleton, where 'culture' is the annual Christmas market and that's about it. Everything I've ever wanted, I will make happen, and so that starts now, on my first ever French exchange! When I was in Year 7, I remember when it was the French exchange but obviously I wasn't old enough to host. It was so amazing seeing all the

Frenchies walking the corridors at school – they were all slouchy and European and COOL. You could spot them a mile off! It just seemed so exciting to be hosting actual real French people in their houses, like soooo grown-up because of this super special and fun responsibility. And then last year, after everyone went to France, they all came back seeming so much more *mature*.

I want that version of myself – French Taylor – to be more and more real. A French boy as my first kiss feels vital for the story of how the rest of my life will unfold, like if I get this wrong it will pull me off track. A French kiss with a French boy to start Crickleton Taylor's morphing into French Taylor. It's a must! I was even on the French exchange planning committee for some of the events. They're the stuff of legend, and our year *has* to live up to it.

Suddenly, the big fire alarm goes off and I realise that the whole tiny bungalow has thick black smoke billowing through it.

The omelette!

I race through to the kitchen and start coughing manically from the smoke, but quickly turn off the hob, right as Grandma comes through and grabs a tea towel so that she can take the pan without burning herself, dumping it in the sink and turning on the cold tap. Grandad launches himself into the tiny kitchen too, opening the window and waving his paper under the smoke alarm to try and get it to shut up.

There's the wailing of the alarm, the wailing of Grandma, and cries of Grandad screaming, 'What the heck, Tay! That was our best pan!'

Needless to say, my omelette skills are going to need some work.

5

English class, right before lunch, and out of everyone it's *me* who has to stay behind For a Chat. It's pizza day in the cafeteria, and I'll bet it's just the end bits with no cheese left by the time I get down there, especially because I need to stop by the French department for my exchange partner info too. Classic. It doesn't rain but it pours!

'My two shining stars of the class,' Ms K says, as Jason Clementine slams the classroom door shut and it's just me, her and the other kid she's asked to speak with, Duncan Higginbottom. Duncan Higginbottom, also known as: The Boy Who Never Speaks! Seriously, I know literally nothing about Duncan, aside from the fact that he always seems to have a book in his hand. He's one of the quiet ones who sit at the front and never volunteer for anything but always get top marks. I wonder what it's like to have so little to say. If I ever do get told off, it's for contributing *too* much.

'You buttering us up for a favour, miss?' I ask, because you can say things like that to Ms K and she gets the joke.

'In a fashion,' she replies, with a playful grin. I sort of frown, a bit confused, and look at Duncan to see what he thinks, but his face gives even less away than his non-existent voice.

I wait for her to say more, grinning as she is, and when she doesn't I prompt: 'Well, go on then, those that don't ask don't get and all that.'

She nods, and goes to get some papers off her desk. I really like Ms K. With some teachers you don't care if they get rage-y because you know they're just a miserable person who didn't read the part of the job description that said teaching involves working with kids and now, twenty years into their career, they're livid with themselves. Ms K isn't like that. She asks us questions and actually listens when we reply, and she doesn't have those stupid one-liners that e.g. Mrs Bates in maths thinks are funny: 'The bell doesn't dismiss you, I do!' etc. etc. etc.

'I'd like you both to consider entering this.' She hands us both a flyer, the words REGIONAL LOWER SCHOOL PROSE AND POETRY COMPETITION emblazoned at the top. 'You write so well – both of you – that I'd be confident in your chances of success. It's for the county, so you'd be judged beyond the talent within the school, and I think you're ready for that. You both really impressed me last year, and I'd like to be the teacher who keeps an eye on your talent. Nurtures you, you know. A mentor, if you like.'

I get top marks in English as well, and it was last year with a school competition that got me thinking properly about being a journalist one day. Duncan came second, I think – I don't really remember, I was just so excited to have come first. It makes me feel quite proud that Ms K just said she wants to 'nurture' us, like we could be little wordsmiths in the making. See, that's what I mean about her. She makes you feel good. She cares. I eye up the leaflet. It's got the crests for a bunch of local schools: St Ann's, Lower Lane, and even Lady Manners – I know about them because their school newspaper is *six pages*! It wins awards! I read about it online, when Mum sent me an article about it.

Lol. An article about a school paper's articles. That's funny.

'OK …' I say, remembering I'm supposed to be concentrating. I'm not really sure how you're supposed to respond when you get told to enter a competition, even when you're super flattered. Thanks? I'll think about it? OK, whatever you say?

'The deadline is tight,' she continues. 'I've had a mountain of paperwork – I'm a teacher, I always have a mountain of paperwork, lol –' Ms K actually says things like *lol* out loud – 'and I only just got around to getting the details. But if you could rustle something up I'm sure it would be brilliant, and you'd make me so proud if you gave it a go. The theme is BECOMING, which you can take to mean however you want.'

I look at the poster again and then for some reason at Duncan, who obviously isn't saying anything, because he's essentially mute, so he's just standing.

'Miss,' I say, and she looks at me all big eyes and full of hope.

'Yes, Taylor?' she replies, and I feel bad I'm not going to say anything more profound.

'Is that all? It's just, we're missing pizza day.'

She laughs, nodding. 'Yes,' she says. 'Go! Go get your pizza!' She does a shooing motion towards the door, and we shuffle out. 'Send me something ASAP if you're going to do it though,' she insists as we go. 'By which I mean: I look forward to seeing what you come up with!'

I laugh at her – she's funny, for a teacher – and am surprised to hear a noise beside me THAT IS ONLY DULL DUNCAN, HE WHO NEVER SPEAKS! I must look shell-shocked, because he looks at me like he regrets existing and says quickly, 'Sorry. I just … she's funny, Ms K.'

It's like I'm watching a giraffe in a dress suddenly give a physics lesson.

'I don't think I've ever heard you speak before,' I blurt out, before I can stop myself.

Why am I like this? Other people have filters, or can run what they're about to say through their brain so their brain can give a thumbs up or a thumbs down. Me? I let everything slip out, like … diarrhoea. That's it. I have the verbal equivalent of an upset stomach.

'It's the first time it's happened, actually,' Duncan bats back. 'I'm glad you were here to bear witness.'

I narrow my eyes at him, and it takes half a second too long for the penny to drop that he's kidding.

'Oh my god,' he says, breaking out into a massive grin. 'I'm joking, Taylor. I've been saying full sentences since I was at least ten and half. Not to brag.'

He's about half an inch taller than me, sandy blond hair and blue eyes. Stocky. Not cute, but not *not* cute. He's waiting for me to respond, to see if his joke has landed. I give him a good old-fashioned eye roll (if in doubt, act unimpressed!) and a deadpan, 'Ha, ha.'

We walk. I certainly don't mean to, on account of not knowing him, but we fall in step down the quiet corridors, vacated by everyone for lunch. God. Dull Duncan speaks? And is sarcastic and witty? Who knew!

'Are you following me?' I say, once I realise we're both going in the same direction.

'I was about to ask you the same thing,' he replies. 'I'm going to the French department.'

'Oh,' I say. 'Same.'

'For the exchange partner info packs?'

'Yeah,' I say. 'You're doing the exchange too?'

He shakes his head, smiling. 'Wow,' he comments. 'Nice to know I've made such an impression in the *bazillion* meetings we've all had about it, when I've literally sat across from you. Cool. That makes me feel *amazing*.' He's so banter-y that I suddenly have this thought, this moment of, like, *Who the heck is this boy?!* The Duncan I'm walking with is *nothing* like the Duncan who I sit behind during English class, and apparently French class too? He's … a bit of a laugh? Honestly, this is really shocking. The girls probably won't even believe me; they'll accuse me of hallucinating, like I did at a sleepover we all had in Year 7, right before I got the flu.

'I'll bet you don't even know what the other thing we have in common is, do you?'

I crinkle my brow. 'English class, obviously,' I say defensively. Like, excuse me if I do not know the ins and outs of everything Duncan Higginbottom does!

'No,' Duncan says. 'The paper?'

'Oh!' I say. 'I just had my first byline for the paper!'

'I know,' he tells me. 'I was your copy editor.'

I stop walking and look at him. 'You were?' I say, actually quite shocked. I didn't even know Year 9s could be on the editorial staff. I thought you had to be in upper school for that, or sixth form.

'I was.' He nods.

I take this in as I start walking again.

'Do you write for the paper as well?' I say. 'Or just edit?'

'Just edit.' Duncan shrugs. 'I know it's weird, probably, but I like being behind the scenes and helping everyone else be better. Shaping the overall paper rather than writing bits for it. If that makes sense?'

'Kind of,' I say, because it doesn't, really. Why wouldn't you want your name there as a byline? Editorial get tiny fine-print credits that you can barely read, they're so small. 'If you have any kind of sway with the paper, can you get them to make it two pages instead of one? So we get higher word counts? I have more to say than the measly hundred and fifty words we're allocated!'

Duncan laughs, a sort of hoot that makes me feel really proud for being funny, even if it wasn't on purpose.

'I'm serious!' I say. 'Or can't you start your own paper, online, and then hire me to write whatever I want, however long I want?'

'Sure.' Duncan says. 'We can call it *The Instruction Manual*, since you're so good at telling people what to do.'

'Hey!' I pout. 'Not other people. Just myself. You only get one life. Gotta go for it, et cetera.'

Duncan nods, considering this. I don't know what his nod means. I was only joking, anyway, about the online paper.

'I do write a few things,' he offers quietly. 'But only sometimes … I don't like to show people. Ms K is good at twisting my arm with the competitions and stuff.'

As we round the corner, there's a knock on the window from the outside, and it's Tommy with all of his mates. Tommy looks totally embarrassed and it's easy to gather that it wasn't him who knocked to get my attention, but rather the friend of his who is now doing that stupid joke of wrapping his arms around himself and turning around so that from behind it looks like he's snogging someone. Everyone roars with laughter and somebody ruffles Tommy's hair and, when Tommy doesn't really respond, gets him in a headlock until Tommy pushes him off. All I can surmise from the whole thing is that Year 10 boys are about as mature as Year 7 boys sometimes, which feels … depressing.

Duncan doesn't comment on the scene we've just witnessed, he just says with a point, as if none of the last fifteen seconds even happened, 'I was told Madame Jones's office …'

'Same,' I say, happy to ignore the idiots outside. What were they expecting me to do, a fan dance? As we reach Madame Jones's office, Duncan pulls at the handle, heaving back the door to let me go in first … only I don't move, because Monsieur Brown is pressed against Madame Jones, near her desk, and they are SNOGGING!

Madame Jones screams, 'Joel!' in a really high-pitched voice, and Monsieur Brown looks at us standing in the door, appears to consider throwing up on himself, and then grabs at Madame Jones's face and holds up a finger as he leaps back, eyes wild and face flushed like a lion interrupted mid-kill.

'Got it!' he cries. 'I got the eyelash!'

Everyone stays where they are. Madame Jones eyes him up like he's totally lost the plot, until she seems to realise something and suddenly launches into action.

'Yes!' she yelps, and then the rest of her words fall out of her mouth all jammed together, with not a breath between them. 'The-eyelash-gosh-that-was-really-causing-me-some-bother-yes-ouch-thank-goodness-you-were-here-Monsieur-Jones-I thought-it-was-going-to-be-a-trip-to-A-and-E-that!'

Before she's even finished speaking Monsieur Brown is following her lead, saying: 'I-WAS-JUST-GETTING-AN-EYELASH-OUT-OF-MADAME-JONES'S-EYE-DON'T-YOU-EVER-KNOCK-I-COULD-HAVE-BLINDED-HER!!!'

I'm all for taking the mick out of my teachers when the situation arises, but I get the sense that now is *not* the time for jokes, no matter how ridiculous this all is. Monsieur Brown is actually *spluttering*, a word I'd only ever read about in books, but I know exactly what it means now he's doing it. He's gone all posh and indignant, too, which is weird because normally his accent is broad Yorkshire.

'We'll come back, sir!' Duncan announces, barely concealing how hilarious this whole thing is. Hilarious and *gross*. Teachers DOING IT??? Yuck, yuck, yuck. How can Madame Jones even fancy Monsieur Brown? His coffee breath is *notorious* around school, it would be like licking the bottom of an espresso cup over and over, until your tongue was all furry and you'd either have to scrub it with a toothbrush or chop it off. How depressing for me, though, that even *they* are getting kissed?!

I don't realise I'm *still* staring at them until Duncan pulls on my arm, and I slam the door shut again and we peg it down the corridor until Mrs Bates from maths sees us and bellows, 'SLOW DOWN RIGHT THIS MINUTE! THIS ISN'T THE SUNDAY RACES!'

The combination of what's just happened, Mrs Bates being ... well, Mrs Bates, and the sudden high from running so fast and for quite a long way, too, is enough to mean we push through the double doors to the outdoor courtyard and collapse into absolute hysterics.

'Oh. My. God!' I squeal. 'Madame Jones and Monsieur Brown! In her OFFICE! Gross!'

'I was just getting out a very dangerous eyelash,' Duncan mimics, quite spot on actually. 'Oh no,' he says in his normal voice. 'Hold on, he has a moustache, doesn't he?' Duncan holds up a finger under his nose to act as said moustache, and then carries on. 'Don't you ever knock? That could have been dangerous!'

'Yeah,' I say, 'dangerous for his …' I finish the sentence by making kissing sounds. It makes Duncan laugh.

'Dangerous for his reputation, too,' points out Duncan. 'That man had better give me straight As for the rest of the term.'

'Oh,' I say. 'So you're not in my class for French? I have Madame Jones.'

Duncan raises his eyebrows and then rolls his eyes in the exact same way I did earlier, when I didn't know what else to say.

'I swear I'm a ghost in this school,' he says.

'If I can see you does that mean I'm actually dead too, and haven't realised yet?'

Duncan rolls his eyes again. 'As if. Everyone knows who you are, Taylor.'

And then he walks away! Just like that! Before I can say anything back to him!

I scowl, trying to figure out why what he just said – which is obviously untrue, everybody does *not* know who I am – sounded like an accusation, like there'd be something wrong with that.

'Good luck with your competition entry!' I find myself yelling at his back, and under my breath I add, suddenly mad at him, 'Too bad I'm going to beat you. *Again*.'

I spend the walk home re-enacting the whole fake-eyelash-in-Madame-Jones's-office scene for Star and Lucy, who can't decide if the most shocking thing is teachers SNOGGING or that Duncan Higginbottom not only speaks, but has banter, too.

'Maybe he's just one of those speak-when-spoken-to types,' suggests Lucy thoughtfully. She's a powerhouse, Lucy, but she *is* good at giving people the benefit of the doubt. 'You know, what's that saying? Something like it's better for everyone to *think* you're a fool by staying silent, rather than talking too much and everyone *knows for sure* you're a fool.'

'Oh yeah, I've heard that saying before.' I nod. 'Well. He's definitely not a fool. And now I am absolutely going to enter Ms K's competition, *and* I'm going to beat him.'

'Get it, girl,' says Star, snapping her fingers all silly and dramatic. I snap my fingers right back and we laugh, and then I head on up the hill by myself, ready to go home and do loads of beautifying in the bathroom, since the exchange finally starts tomorrow!! Time to bring my A game: face mask, pluck my eyebrows, do a deep-conditioning mask for my hair made from old mashed-up bananas ... I'm going to shave my legs, too, but only up to the knee because Lucy says the biggest mistake her mum has ever made was shaving her thighs as well. She says it's such a big job, and the hair grows back so fast, that it's like trying to paint that bridge in San Francisco that as soon as you're done you have to start all over again because it takes so long.

I don't see the girl who lives opposite at first, standing out on her doorstep. It's not until I'm closer that I spot her in her fancy private school uniform. Her name is Morgan, and when we were really little we played together a bit. I thought as we got older we might always be friends – something to do with our names. Both our parents wanted something gender neutral so I don't know, I figured maybe that bonded us a bit. However. I don't know how to explain it, but there's something that gets in the way of us being proper friends. The older we get, the more going to different schools feels like we're just in different worlds. I know it isn't a kind thing to say, but as Star has pointed out before: not everything that is the truth is nice to hear. Anyway. When we *have* hung out, it's been like deciphering a code, talking to each other, sort of how it must be for the Spanish and Italians: languages so close they almost understand each other, but not really. Her world is fancier school uniforms and Saturday-morning classes and school trips to Costa Rica for three weeks in the summer. Crickleton High just isn't like that. And so, we've drifted.

I go to lift my hand to wave – you know, no need to be rude, et cetera – but realise she's got a boy with her! Now, I happen to know full well that at Morgan's house there's a no-boys-in-the-house rule, because her mum told my mum, and my mum told *me* she thought it was a bit distrusting and old-fashioned. Fair play to her though: She's not breaking the rule if you go by technicalities. *Technically* the boy isn't in her house so *technically* she isn't doing anything wrong …

Anyway, even if I *did* wave she wouldn't see me because Morgan and her visitor are SNOGGING. With eyes closed! And he's holding on to her waist!!!

I feel like a pervert, looking over, but I can't look away. I open the front door and even as I turn around to close it, I've got such a good view that I linger a bit. They are *really* going for it.

I find myself going upstairs to look out of Mum's bedroom window, standing just far enough behind the curtain that hopefully I won't be seen. Even if you only time the kissing from when I got home (and trust me, they'd obviously being going at it ages before I got here) we're looking at a solid, what? Eight minutes? Probably more like nine or ten. I try moving my mouth as if it's me who is doing the kissing, and it hurts after about ten seconds. Haven't they got sore jaws by this point, like when it takes too long to chew a toffee Quality Street?

Something must be in the water today, what with the French teachers at school and now this. I hope it rubs off on me. It's like everyone in the world is getting their snogging on. Surely I will be next!! Praise be, please, Lord!

OH MY GOD.

He's kissing her neck now!! This is basically pornographic! Children could see!

I move to get a better look right as, luck would have it, Morgan looks up at the bedroom window, and I swear to god it's dead in the eye. I hurl myself to the floor in a panic like an army sergeant sacrificing themselves on a bomb, crawling on my hands and knees to the bedroom door and then going down the stairs on my bum so as not to be seen. I don't want Morgan to still be looking at the house and see a shadow pass by the front door if I stand up, so I keep crawling through the hallway into the lounge, which is obviously the moment Mum decides to come out of her 'writing studio' (aka *office*).

'What on earth are you doing?' she says, seeing me on all fours.

I swallow, desperately trying to think of an excuse.

Mum settles on, 'Get up, darling,' then goes through to the kitchen to flick on the kettle. 'You're not a cat.'

Oh my god, this day!! It can't get any worse!

6

I've spent too much time lolling in bed this morning – I should be getting ready! But instead I've fallen down a hole of googling things like *first kiss technique* and *how to kiss* and *what does a first kiss feel like?*

I want to be prepared for this week. Now that the exchange is here, in T-minus six hours (!!), it's dawning on me that not only do I want my first kiss to be special, but I want it to be *good*. *Teen Vogue* says there's no such thing as a bad kisser, but that bad kissing *can* happen. That's terrifying! I could have a bad kiss and the boy could get the wrong impression because he hasn't read the same article and he could think it's my fault, that I really am a bad kisser!

At least my first kiss being with a French boy will mean if he does pie me off afterwards, I probably won't be able to understand. My French isn't that good. And also, he'll be leaving soon anyway, which … well, will be awful if I really do fall in love, but if everything goes wrong I can, luckily, pretend none of it ever happened.

I think this is called hoping for the best and preparing for the worst.

Apparently you're supposed to keep the first kiss you have with somebody under twenty seconds, which must mean Morgan and her boyfriend have been doing it for a long time, because their snogging was for about twenty *years*. Google says you have to breathe in and out through your nose, and try not to breathe into his mouth. Google also says you get a massive adrenalin rush that makes your heart beat fast and gets the blood flowing. I hope that doesn't mean my awful blushing thing happens. Imagine thinking you were kissing Normal Taylor and then pulling away and finding out you've actually been snogging a tomato.

Urgh! The agony and the ecstasy! Honestly, waiting to be kissed is HORRIBLE! It is occupying more and more of my thoughts.

I had better take my mind off it all. Time to get up.

HOLY MOLY! I've just gone for my morning wee and was halfway through brushing my teeth when I looked up into the bathroom mirror and … I've got an almighty mountain of a spot, right on my jaw! It's big enough that it is obvious from any and all angles: no matter which way I turn my head, it's painfully visible, like a mutation or deformity. This is *not* fair. Not at all! My face mask last night was supposed to give me a subtle and sexy glow, not make my face into an assault course! I get the odd spot with the best of them, but I just so wanted to feel my best self today of all days!!

I turn on the spotlight at the side of the mirror to get more light on it, and then rummage around for Mum's magnifying mirror too. It's a humongous red bump, but it doesn't have a head. This is good and bad. Good because if I leave it, I think with a bit of make-up it can be disguised enough so that it isn't the first thing you look at when you see me, more like the third or fourth thing. Bad because potentially it could develop a yellow head throughout the day, and then it will *undoubtedly* be the first thing you see. I don't want all the French boys to think of me as a pus-filled spot for the whole week. First impressions today are going to be *vital*.

Dammit! Star says spots are OK to squeeze if they have a head, but if a spot bleeds when you squeeze it it's because it isn't ready and That Is Bad News. But running my finger over it, I reckon I could squeeze this one, if I push hard enough …

… OK, I shouldn't have tried squeezing the spot.

It's bleeding like gangbusters and I've held a tissue over it for ages and ages but it's still not really letting up. I've had breakfast and quickly finished some geography homework and there's a crust around the edge of it now but still oozing in the middle. Crap-pants. I've made it eleventy million times worse. AND my hair is so greasy from my leave-in conditioner that I could charge nits to use it as a slip-and-slide adventure park. I need to talk to Star and Lucy right now.

I snatch my phone from the dining table and open our Members Only group chat and fire off messages as fast as my fingers can type.

Members Only

Me: *EMERGENCY! EMERGENCY!*

Star: *OMG, what?*

Lucy: *Are you OK*

Me: *NO!!!!!! Meet me in the usual toilets before form! SOMETHING TERRIBLE HAS HAPPENED!*

Star: *WHAT?!*

Star: *Taylor????*

Star: *TAYLOR, WHAT HAS HAPPENED?*

Star: *Oh my god, you can't just be all dramatic this way and then disappear!*

Star: *OK. Fine.*

Star: *ANNOYING!*

'WHAT HAVE I TOLD YOU!?' screams a horrified Star when she sees me. Both girls are in the toilet, as requested. 'This didn't have a head, did it?' she clarifies, and I shake my head, ashamed.

'What am I going to *do*?' I moan, looking again in the mirror. At least it's stopped leaking fluid now. But if I even so much as nudge it, not only is it really painful but it starts bleeding all over again.

Lucy uses a finger to tip my face towards her and gives me a sympathetic once-over.

'Oh, Taylor,' she says. 'You idiot.'

'Solutions!' I tell her. 'I know I'm an idiot but I need help! Not reminders of my lack of intelligence!'

'I think you need to draw the eye away from it,' she says. 'So when we look at your face we focus on something else. Didn't you say *How to Be Parisian When You're Not from Paris* talks about that?'

'Yes,' I say. 'On page 145. They say pick out a feature and make the most of it. But ... I don't know, Luce. You sound dangerously close to suggesting a forehead tattoo ...' I tell her.

She rolls her eyes. 'I was thinking, like, eyeliner?'

'Oh,' I say. 'OK, yeah. I do quite like my eyes. Have you got anything with you?'

'No,' Lucy admits. 'But let me see what I can do …'

She disappears for less than a minute and reappears holding a black eyeliner pencil triumphantly.

'Whoa,' Star says appreciatively. 'What else could you source if we asked you?'

'I don't suppose you can find me a do-over for getting to school this morning?' I ask.

'What do you mean?' says Star, as she grabs the eyeliner off Lucy and waves her hand in a way which I take to mean: *lean against the sinks and let me focus.*

'Tommy Tsao was at the school gates when I got here,' I say, careful not to move my face too much as I talk so I don't get stabbed in the eye. 'I don't think he was waiting for me, obviously, but he was loitering, waiting for *someone*. And I think he was going to talk to me, but I didn't want him to see my face so I ignored him and just kept walking.'

'What makes you think he was going to talk to you?' Lucy asks, watching Star do her work.

'He said, "Hey, Taylor! Can I talk to you?"'

'Oh,' says Lucy, and I can tell she's disappointed in me. 'Sounds quite likely you've dented his ego, then.'

'Don't straight boys do the whole "treat 'em mean, keep 'em keen" thing though?' asks Star, using a finger to smudge something away from one of my eyelids before going back in. She must be putting quite a lot of eyeliner on. 'It could have worked in your favour ...'

Lucy scowls, unimpressed. 'I don't think we should be encouraging mean behaviour as a seduction technique,' she says. 'That's like when we'd get pushed over in the playground or get our hair pulled when we were at primary school, and some stupid adult would say, *Oh, they've done that because they like you!* We shouldn't be horrible if we like somebody! We should be extra nice!'

'I wasn't horrible on purpose!' I yelp, outraged she'd think I'm awful.

'Well, you were,' points out Star, standing back to admire her make-up skills and pointing a finger to signal that I should turn around to the mirrors again. 'But only because you didn't have another choice. I hope.'

'Exactly,' I say, right as I get an eyeful of my reflection.

Whoa.

I don't look smoky-eyed and chic, I look ... absolutely wild.

Star has drawn big thick circles around my eyes in black eyeliner, like I'm in a sketch show and have picked up some booby-trapped binoculars that somebody has put shoe polish on.

'I know it's a bit thick,' she starts to say, as I lean in closer to make sure this really is as bad as I'm fearing. I poke at it in horror. 'But when you talked I got a bit too thick on one side, so then I had to even it up by going thicker on the other side, and then I went back to try and make it neat …'

I can tell by Lucy's horrified expression that she's thinking what I'm thinking.

'I can't go out there,' I say, gesturing to the toilet door, 'looking like this. They'll detain me under the crimes-against-style act!'

'But, to be fair,' Lucy says, like now is the time to see all sides, 'nobody will be looking at your spot now …'

'Lucy! No!' I squeal. 'No, no, no! Oh god, this is terrible. Thank you, Star, for trying …'

'I did my best,' she says, in a small voice.

'I know you did,' I say, reaching out to her shoulder. 'Thank you. I just think maybe this hasn't had the desired effect? I think I should try to take it off and …'

I don't know how to finish that sentence. And what?

'I've got an idea,' says Lucy. 'BRB.'

God bless her resourcefulness. She disappears once again and I set to using a paper towel and some cold water to rub off some of these black marks. It doesn't work *brilliantly* – I end up looking like I've just woken up after smearing my face across a pillow because of bad dreams. But maybe the Frenchies will think I've been up all night snogging one of my many lovers? Maybe??

'I'm back,' says Lucy triumphantly, as she pushes back through into the loo, followed by a Year 8 who seems more than a bit alarmed by us – whether because we're in the year above her or because I look like I do, I'm not sure.

'Here,' Lucy says, handing me something.

'A plaster?' I say.

'Just put it over the spot and if anybody asks say you cut yourself.' She shrugs.

'But this is … blue!' I say.

Star giggles lightly, and I give her a dirty look.

Lucy looks between us and explains: 'That's all they had in the school kitchen. Plasters have to be blue in kitchens so that you can see them if they fall off into the food …'

'Now there's a thought,' gags Star.

So anyway, long story long, that's how I go meet the French exchange students off their coach with greasy hair, charcoal-rimmed eyes, and a bright blue plaster across the bottom of my face.

An excellent first impression.

Not.

I find my welcome beret all screwed up in my coat pocket, so furiously try to straighten it out right as a big brown coach heads up the school drive and circles the roundabout at the top. I shove it on my head at what I hope is a jaunty and casual angle. Me, Star and Lucy are the last ones out there, and I swear down as we approach, Monsieur Brown has got his hand on the small of Madame Jones's back, but then he sees us and whips it away quickly, looking guilty, as well he should. Teachers getting it on is *horrid*.

Alas, there's no time to be dwelling on that (luckily for Madame Jones and Monsieur Brown!!) because Here! They! Are! God, the first day of the rest of my life. Here's where it all begins! When I'm interviewed on TV for winning a big journalism prize or writing a book and they ask me about the most important parts of my life story, I'll start here, on the first day of the French exchange. Nothing that has come before matters really. A different Taylor is born today: grown-up, mature, and *friends with French people*. Ooh la la!

There's an excited murmur across the group, which gives way to a bored murmur as nobody gets off the coach, but rather stares out the window with unblinking eyes, looking at us, a bit unimpressed. They don't look French. There's a teacher, a skinny guy with a beard, standing at the front droning on and on at them, and even Madame Jones whispers to Monsieur Brown: 'Gosh, he's going on a bit, isn't he?'

I suddenly realise that everyone has got bits of paper with them that they've unfolded, with a photo of their exchange partner and some details about them. But I never got mine – I was supposed to pick it up when Duncan and I walked in on … well. What we walked in on wink-wink-nudge-nudge.

'Miss, I never got my exchange partner's information,' I say, and as Madame Jones turns around she visibly startles at the sight of me.

'Taylor!' she says. 'You're looking … different.'

I know better than to ask whether that's good different or bad different.

'I cut my face on an open cupboard door in the bathroom,' I say, a line that took ten minutes of workshopping with Star and Lucy. A lie should be simple but believable, Star had said.

'Oh, I'm sorry to hear that. I thought they only had plasters like that in industrial kitchens.'

I try to think fast, come up with a reason why I've got access to blue plasters from industrial kitchens.

'Mum's been doing a course, miss. A … pastry course, at one of the restaurants in town.'

I don't know where that came from.

'Oh!' says Madame Jones. 'Oh, that's very interesting! I'd love to do something like that! Do you happen to know the name of the restaurant at all?'

I can feel Lucy and Star shaking with laughter beside me, the losers. So much for supportive pals!

'Urm …' I say, saved by Tommy Tsao yelling out: 'Miss! They're getting off!'

I lock eyes with him and shoot over a grateful smile. He looks a bit taken aback – sort of opens his mouth and closes it, like a fish, and creases up his brow like he's confused. I make my smile even bigger, remembering what the girls said about being extra nice.

'Nice hat,' he says to me, and loads of people turn to stare – to look at who TOMMY TSAO is talking to!! – and from his tone I know he means the opposite of what he's actually said. Ouch. I must have upset him when I ignored him this morning.

Madame Jones claps her hands and starts babbling in French to the bearded guy off the bus, and tired-looking Frenchies file off behind him. Everyone starts holding out their bits of paper and locating their partners, until it's just me and Duncan at the edge of everything, watching on sadly, like dogs at a butcher's window begging for a sausage.

'We never got our partner info, did we?' I say.

'We did not.' He nods. 'I suppose we'll get the only ones left at the end …'

'The Bounty bars of the French exchange,' I say. He laughs.

'You're funny,' he says. 'I didn't know you were funny.'

I know exactly how to reply to this.

'That's the first time it's happened, actually. I'm glad you were here to bear witness.'

He grins, and I feel a jolt of pride at being so quick-witted.

'Duncan!' Madame Jones barks across the crowds. 'This is Pierre! Your partner!'

Duncan waves at a gangly dark-haired boy in skinny jeans.

'And then there was one ...' he says over his shoulder, walking away.

It's not officially home time, but everyone on the French exchange is allowed to leave school now to take their partner home and let them get settled after the journey. I try looking for a solitary French girl who is obviously waiting for a partner to scoop her up and take her home, but everyone seems coupled. Lucy has her partner, Star too, and they wave goodbye and say they'll text later and eventually there's just a handful of people and Madame Jones says, 'Everything all right, Taylor?'

'I still don't know who my partner is,' I remind her.

She frowns, as if to say, *Ahhhh, shoot. You're right.* She saunters off to the bearded guy and does some talking with big hand gestures, looks over at where bearded guy points, and then they look at his clipboard together, Madame Jones's face getting darker and darker, like a cloud is moving across her features to reveal that she is displeased.

She comes back over.

'Well,' Madame Jones says, clapping her hands together, and her voice is like it's forced happy, not really happy. 'There's been a little miscommunication. You're paired up with Axel, who I thought was an *Axelle*, as in the feminine. Not the masculine. Monsieur Toussaint thought Taylor was a boy's name, not a girl's name. And so …'

I blink several times, trying to digest what she's saying.

And then the bearded guy comes over with a boy who looks about seventeen, all brooding eyes and wavy hair and *an actual nose piercing*, and says, 'C'est Axel. Axel, Taylor.'

'THIS is my French exchange partner?' I squeak.

'If your mother doesn't mind …' says Madame Jones. 'Monsieur Brown could potentially take him, but he'd be on the sofa bed and if you've already got everything set up for him, it seems a shame to deprive you of the exchange experience because of *gender*.'

I know for a fact that Mum will say the same thing. God bless my liberal, open-hearted, forward-thinking mother!

'OK,' I say to Madame Jones, trying to contain my excitement. And then to Axel – tall, handsome, dreamy, *FRENCH* Axel – I reach out a hand and say, in my best accent: 'Enchantée.'

He takes my hand.

His hands are big and soft, like I've aways thought Harry Styles's would be.

I dare to look him right in the eye (so big! So deep!) as he shakes my hand and says in a gruff, SEXY voice, 'Enchanté.'

Oh my god.

My partner is a boy!

A CUTE, BEAUTIFUL BOY!

This is the best day of my life!!!!!!!!!!

7

'Oh, darling, that's fine! It'll be fun! Gender is a social construct anyway,' Mum says, when I call her to tell her about Axel being a bit different than either of us were expecting, i.e. he's a boy.

I *didn't* tell her he's got deep chocolate-brown eyes that look like you could dive into them and get lost. Or that he's handsome but not *too* handsome. Is that a thing? I also didn't say that he's taller than most boys in my year, like he's not really fourteen but, like, a Year 11 or something, nor that he's got what looks like STUBBLE. He's like a movie star! If Madame Jones tells me he's actually quite famous in France for starring in a Netflix original, I'd believe her. God, *that* would be legendary. I could be his equally famous journalist girlfriend and we'd be known as France's most dashing couple, getting photographed with pop stars and politicians and hosting dinner parties where everyone laughs at my witty observations about culture and life, and Axel looks on adoringly and everyone says how they wish they could have a love like ours.

Wait. What was I saying?

Oh. Right. I didn't tell Mum any of that. I skipped over all the delicious details of Axel's dishy and brooding hotness, as I didn't want her to think I fancy him. Which I do, obviously, because I have eyes. My skin is on fire and my brain feels like it has swollen in my head from … well, I don't know. Firing too many thoughts? About him? I've never felt so aware of my own body, my own skin. I can feel every breath I take in a different way, and all the hairs on the back of my neck are prickling, standing to attention. A real live French boy in my house! *Sacré bleu!* Talk about the universe doing me a solid.

My phone pings, so I pull it away from my ear to see Star has replied in the group chat. I've told the girls my partner is a boy and Star's reaction is: *OMG, SERIOUSLY?! Is that even allowed?!*

My phone pings again. Lucy. She says: *Oh my god! I mean, trust you to get a boy, Erica is the only mum cool enough to agree to it!* She follows that up with: *Wait. Does your mum even know yet?!*

'Taylor? Are you still there?' Mum. I put the phone back

to my ear. 'If you don't need anything else I need to get back to work. I'm not going to hit my word count today otherwise.'

'I'm here, Mum,' I say, trying to focus.

I watch Axel swaggering – actually *swaggering* – over to catch up to Duncan's partner. I think his name is Pierre. Axel is standing with one hip jutted out and nodding a lot as Pierre talks, and then he leans in to air kiss each cheek. It's *so* cool. Imagine Bilious Billy kissing another boy on the cheek to say goodbye? Boys here just don't do that sort of thing – sometimes they can barely even hug. The Europeans are *sooooo chic*.

I scratch my head under my beret – it itches like crazy. It suddenly occurs to me that none of the actual French people had on berets themselves. Did I misjudge wearing one? Axel catches my eye as he does some more swaggering, and I tug it off my head, my cheeks illuminating bright red. I can't help it. It's like he sees right through me, to, like, *my soul*. Although it's going to be very inconvenient if I don't figure out a way to control that. I can't be blushing crimson every time he looks at me. He'll think I'm shy, or aloof, and that could get in the way of whatever is obviously blossoming. Because he must be feeling this too, right? I will myself to keep looking at him, to not blink or look away. I even try a smile, but it feels complicated trying to do it all at once, like patting your head and rubbing your tummy. I'm almost staring at him, and my eyes feel a bit dry, actually, but I can't afford to project anything other than supreme confidence. Axel looks away first, knitting together his eyebrows like he's confused.

Hmmm.

No smile back.

Maybe *he's* the shy one?

If that's the case I'll have to be extra confident, to make up the shortfall. I can do that – open the door for him to let me in, that sort of thing.

'Taylor!'

'Sorry, Mum,' I say, coming back to the task at hand whilst also stuffing the beret into my pocket, then smoothing down my hair in a way that I hope is nonchalant and casual. It's so slick my hand practically skids off it. 'Thanks for understanding,' I continue. 'We'll see you at home. We won't be long.'

'Right-o, bug,' she says, ringing off before I can remind her not to call me that.

'We'll see you tomorrow, Taylor,' Madame Jones says when she notices that I'm off the phone, all big smile and a clap of the hands. 'Sorry for the confusion, but it's all worked out in the end, hasn't it? *Au revoir*, Axel!'

Axel looks shocked at being directly addressed. Definitely on the shyer end of the spectrum, then.

'*Au revoir*,' he says back, then he looks at me. I try to think of the French for *this way, then!* but all my French has left my head. I open my mouth to speak, close it again, open it and then settle on the English.

'Let's go,' I say, with a point for emphasis, and Axel nods, his face set in what looks like, confusingly for me, a slightly concerned expression. What could he possibly have to worry about? This is going to be GREAT!

In my head, the walk home was going to be a sophisticated saunter through Crickleton with idle chit-chat and lots of pointing out wonderful local sights. In reality, Axel has two bags that are really *really* heavy, and it slows us down and also means we're both a bit out of breath at schlepping them through town, which suddenly feels devoid of cute things to point out now the sun is behind the clouds and all the shops are starting to shut. I thought I'd be with a French girl and we'd be best friends by the time we got home – *How to Be Parisian When You're Not from Paris* says going for a city walk with somebody is an elegant way to spend time, because it's low pressure – but Axel and I can barely string full sentences together in one another's language, so there's lots of me gesturing at things (the newsagent's … the Co-op … the park …) and giving them a thumbs up or a wavy hand motion that I hope translates to mean 'so-so'. I'm basically giving mime reviews of where I live, like a sickly pop singer who daren't risk their vocal cords before a big concert.

This is the opposite of great.

When we pass the baker's I say, 'Do you like ...?' in English, because truly it's like I've never spoken a French word in my life. I can't remember a single thing! I scramble for a way to finish the question. I have no idea why I started speaking before I knew what I wanted to say. '... *bread* ...?' I settle on. BREAD!

Do you like bread?! Ohmygod. My chat is officially a zero out of ten.

'*Oui*,' replies Axel, like he's not actually that sure. '*Et toi?*'

'Yes,' I say, and I use my free hand to pat my belly. 'Very much!'

If I made a fool out of myself like this with Lucy and Star, they'd take the mick out of me until we all ended up laughing, and it would become an in-joke we'd refer back to for ages in Members Only. Not so with Axel. He watches me pat my stomach and squints his eyes like he's concluded I'm an idiot and filed away the information in permanent ink. It makes my palms sweat.

'Are you excited for the exchange?' I say, not ready to give up so soon.

'Of course,' Axel replies. '*Oui*.'

I nod and try to hold eye contact again, but Axel seems to

be avoiding it. He's probably just taking in his new home for the week. Fair enough, it's a lot to process. He's basically been taken across the Channel, handed to a stranger, and told to enjoy himself. That's a lot! When it's my turn to go to France next year I'll bet I feel a bit uncertain at first too!

Thank god we're home, then. Maybe Mum can talk some French to him to reassure him I'm awesome.

'This is us!' I announce, trying to sound cheery and welcoming, and Mum flings open the door, where she stands with Grandma and Grandad, everyone waving and smiling and WEARING BERETS AND STRIPED T-SHIRTS! They look absolutely bonkers, all shouting out, 'Hello! Welcome! Hello! *Bonjour!*' in a big mash of enthusiastic loud voices and insane facial expressions. I look at Axel. It's like he's considering making a run for it.

Before he can, though, everyone ushers Axel into the house – whether he wants to stay or not – and through to the sofa, where Grandad sits on one side and Grandma on the other, patting his knee and grinning. Did I look that bonkers in my beret?! I dread to think. Oh god, this whole French-person-in-my-house thing is more overwhelming than I thought it would be. I should have phoned home and told them NO BERETS! This is mortifying.

I drag Axel's bags up to the guest room and by the time I get back down, Mum is standing in the middle of the living room giving a monologue in French – which, OK, I sort of wish I could speak as fluently as she does, but Axel can't get a word in edgeways. I loiter at the door, not knowing how to rescue him, but then he suddenly bursts out laughing at whatever Mum has said, and it's like the best music you've ever heard, his big laugh. And then Mum is laughing too and Axel is babbling away so fast I only catch the odd word. *Oui … c'est magnifique …* something about *unfortunately it is true*.

'Where's your beret?' Grandad asks me suddenly, when there's a break in the laughter. 'You got that especially! Show Axel, love! We all match!'

Axel looks at me, framed by the doorway, and I blush *again*. Those eyes, I swear down. They're *heaven*.

'It was itchy,' I say. 'I had to take it off.'

Grandad looks at Axel. 'We wanted to look the part,' he explains.

Axel smiles, and Grandma says: 'Have you got a beret too?'

Axel shakes his head.

'The beret …' he says. 'It is … not so common.'

I could die. I knew it! I knew I shouldn't have worn it! Dammit! What a terribly un-chic first impression!

'Would you like an omelette for tea?' I blurt out, desperate to redeem myself and my family. 'I can make you one? With cheese?'

Everyone looks at him expectantly in their berets.

'It is possible?' Axel says, in his adorable accent. 'To try fish and chips?'

'I knew it!' cries Grandad, slapping his thigh. 'I said, didn't I, Rachel, he'll want fish and chips!'

Grandma nods, conceding that yes, he did say that.

Mum babbles a French version of, *Yes! Of course! Whatever you want!* and we organise Grandad to drive Mum up the road to the good chippy, but Axel barely touches what is on his plate, even though he says he likes it. I think he's disappointed, and just trying to be polite. Grandma has his extra mushy peas, and Grandad takes his half-eaten haddock. I eye up the last of his chips, but decide against eating them. I've embarrassed myself enough.

As I clear the dishes, Axel says he will go to bed. It's only 7.30 p.m. Mum and Grandma and Grandad have been as cool as I could have hoped, hats and T-shirts aside, but I'm letting myself down. I haven't impressed him as much as I'd like. I can't help but feel like all this is getting away from me, and it hasn't even properly begun …

'*Bonne nuit*,' I say half-heartedly, and once he's gone I think: *Or is it* bonne soirée?

Why can't I remember a single French word?!

8

Members Only

Star: *My partner is so quiet! It's super awkward. How are you two?*

> **Me:** *OMG same! Do you think it might get better as time goes on?*

Lucy: *Mine is OK, her English is really good! Her grandma is English*

> **Me:** *That's good for you then! Mine went to bed really early*
>
> **Me:** *I felt like he was disappointed or something*

Star: *Nooooo, he was just tired I bet!*

Lucy: *Mine went to bed at like 7.30!*

Me: *Axel too!*

Me: *OK, that makes me feel a bit better.*

Me: *I thought I'd done something wrong*

Star: *Let's see how the icebreaker day helps ... I need it to work because it will be a horrible week if it goes on like this!*

Lucy: *I think our girls are friends, Star, so maybe when we're all together that will help!*

Lucy: *And don't forget Taylor has been on the planning committee for events too – Taylor, it's good stuff we're doing, right?*

Me: *Right! Yes! Especially the English picnic day!*

Me: *I hope Axel knows your girls as well, and we can all hang out together!*

Everyone on the exchange program meets for a buffet breakfast in the school canteen, which basically means all the English lot on one side of the room, and all the French kids huddled at the other, with Monsieur Brown glaring furiously at Madame Jones as she flirts with the French teachers in the middle. I watch as Axel leans in to his friend Pierre, talking animatedly so that Pierre laughs. It's interesting to see him so relaxed with his friend, compared to the rabbit in the headlights we had in the living room last night. Although he's been friendly enough this morning, eager to get to school and see what the day has in store. He practically bounded down the road and through the gates, asking me questions about what we'd be doing. (In English, as it happens. Now he's warming up, his English is very obviously better than my French! But that wouldn't be hard, considering everything I've ever learned has conveniently left my head forever. I'll bet it all comes flooding back once this is over! Urgh!!)

Monsieur Brown gives a big welcome and explains that, as an icebreaker activity, we'll be doing a scavenger hunt. Each set of partners has to pair up with another, to make a group of four, and half the clues will be in English and half in French. Everyone has to work together to solve them, and the winners get a prize.

'I'll bet the prize is a signed copy of the textbook he co-wrote,' quips Lucy, and I snigger because it's true. She can be so quick and funny! Monsieur Brown is notorious for making everyone in his classes buy his textbook at the start of every school year, directly from him so he gets a bigger profit. Mum says it's fair play, since teachers aren't paid well enough, but there *are* some mistakes in it, which puts a bit of dent in her defence of him.

Star nudges me hard in the ribs, and right as I'm about to nudge her hard right back, I see that she's trying to warn me that Tommy Tsao is heading over. OMG!!

'Y'alright, Tay?' he says with a flick of his hair. I can *feel*

Star and Lucy raise their eyebrows at each other and suppress a squeal, even if I can't actually *see* it.

'Hello,' I say, trying to stay calm. I can't believe he just called me *Tay*. That's not my name! It's TAYLOR. TWO syllables. But I guess when you're a Year 10 you can do that, give people nicknames. 'How's it going?'

'We gonna be in the same team?' Tommy asks. 'I feel like you're proper clever, and I like winning.'

Star and Lucy are holding on to each other, shaking with laughter. I'm going to kill them later. Tommy looks at me with big puppy dog eyes, and it gives me a funny feeling in my lower pelvis. My heart beats quicker. If this is what it's like to have a simple conversation, who knows what it will be like before a KISS. It doesn't bear thinking about!

'Urm …' I start to say, a bit starstruck at being singled out this way, but then Axel comes over and I'm reminded who my true crush *really* is. I have to remember, no matter how many butterflies Tommy gives me: Tommy might be a Year 10, but Axel is *French*!

Tommy looks between us as Axel says, 'We are with Pierre and Duncan, yes?'

I shrug at Tommy, who seems really angry at this turn of events, and look across at Pierre and Duncan, who gives me a small wave like he's sorry to interrupt.

'Sorry,' I tell Tommy, and he mutters something about *it's all right*, but it doesn't sound all right from his tone. Welp! *C'est la vie*, Tommy! *Je suis désolée!*

Anyway, that's how I end up traipsing all around the school fields with Duncan Higginbottom, following Axel and Pierre, who, it turns out, are actually very competitive and do all the work. Duncan and I are just along for the ride. We try to help at first, but in the end simply follow wherever the boys go in silence, eventually exchanging the odd eyebrow raise to communicate: *What are they like, hmmmm?!* until eventually Duncan speaks, as I've learned he can do.

'Pierre was so excited to come to school today,' he tells me as we wait for the Frenchies to solve the next riddle. This one is in French, so I don't even pretend I can be of assistance. 'I think he's best friends with Axel, and wanted to see him.'

'Yeah,' I say. 'Axel was the same. Must be weird, being in some strange English person's house on your own.'

'That's what my stepdad said,' Duncan comments.

'Yeah.' I nod, repeating myself. I don't really have much more to say than that. Not to Duncan. I wonder how the girls are getting on. They're working together, because just like they hoped, their partners are friends.

The boys shout out an answer and shoot off past the sixth form block. How they even know where to go is beyond me – it took me until halfway through Year 8 to properly understand the layout of the school and they only got here yesterday.

'So,' Duncan presses, and I get the feeling he Wants to Chat. There's nothing better to do, I suppose. 'You working on anything good for the paper? Or for Ms K's competition?'

I pull a face. 'Still thinking about the comp,' I say. 'But I was brainstorming some ideas for the paper the other day, and I'm just polishing an article about why Year 9 is the best year of your life.'

'Oh yeah?' Duncan says. 'I'd love to read that. You should send it to me.'

I can't tell if he's being sarcastic, so sneak a look at him. He nods again, for emphasis. I think he might mean it. 'Seriously,' he adds. 'I live for words. I know that's really geeky, but …'

'No,' I say, thinking of how neither Lucy nor Star has ever asked to read a draft of my work. Not that they should or anything, it's just a weird new feeling to feel like somebody is interested in the process. 'I get it. Same.' We turn the corner right as the Frenchies turn the next one, just catching sight of the back of them. Duncan points, and we head that way. After a while I add, 'I suppose all I want to do is have thoughts and put them down on paper in a way that makes other people able to understand them, and hopefully agree with them. Thanks for being interested.'

'We're a pair of geeks,' Duncan offers, and I'm about to protest when I see his cheeky grin, so I pull a face instead.

'Cool geeks,' I say.

'Cooks?' Duncan suggests. 'Ceeks?'

'Ceeks,' I laugh. 'Yes. We're a pair of ceeks!'

Duncan laughs too, and starts to say he'll write down his email address for me, but I'm suddenly distracted by Axel and Pierre off in the distance, sitting in the middle of the school field. They've got a cigarette! On school grounds! Where anyone could see!!!

'Are they ... *smoking*?' Duncan asks, seeing what I'm seeing. 'Gross!'

'I know,' I say, because smoking is, like, very 1950s and obviously kills you. Even *How to Be Parisian When You're Not from Paris* says don't do it:

Smoking Kills

It might surprise you to learn that smoking, so quintessential in old French movies and photographs, is not at all fashionable in the modern day. Standing outside in the rain like a drowned rat, to end up smelling like an ashtray? Horrible! Wrinkles around the mouth? Non. Smoking is the reserve of old men and silly schoolboys. The Parisian woman leaves it well alone.

But as we walk over (am I going to tell them to put it out? Is Duncan??) I find myself mesmerised by how they take a puff and pass it back and forth between them. The smoking is disgusting but Axel's attitude is … well, *sexy*! I don't think I really understood that word before now. The way he shrugs when he sees us, like he knows he shouldn't and he doesn't care, and the way he holds it. He seems so grown-up. I notice his hands and his fingers, how long and elegant they are. I've never noticed a boy's hands and fingers before, not ever. I'm consumed with a weird urgency to flop down next to him on the grass, as close as I dare – which is exactly what I do. The smoke smells terrible, but they're nearly done, fortunately. This is the closest I've been to him, actually. I can feel the warmth of his skin radiating close to mine.

'We are the champions!' Axel says, holding the scavenger hunt clues aloft. The way he turns his head, sitting so close to me, it could be so easy to kiss him, you know. My tummy does a flip at the thought. Mmmmm.

'Well, *you* are,' points out Duncan. 'We didn't really help. Well done.'

'We are a good team,' says Pierre, grinning at Axel.

And then Pierre and Axel go back to murmuring in low, hushed French, with Axel practically turning his back on me. Huh. I like how he relaxes with Pierre, but I don't like Pierre getting *all* of his attention. It's all very well being in

108

school together, and I know there's some group trips and stuff organised – I even helped to plan a traditional English picnic, later in the week! – but I can't help feeling like we all need a big party, outside of a school event, to hang out together and find excuses to slink off arm in arm. I hadn't thought of that before, but now it seems obvious: We need to be out of school uniforms and away from the glare of teachers. That's how first kisses happen in almost every single book I read – the main girl has to find a moment alone with her guy. I'm sitting so close to Axel, but what do I expect, that he'll kiss me right here in broad daylight? No. That's not how it will happen, is it? I need to get him somewhere quiet, where he's relaxed but it's not weird to pull him away from his friend. And a party is the perfect place! Among the hustle and bustle of fun that everyone will *no doubt* be having, Axel and I will disappear together, realise our unquestionable affection, look into each other's eyes and fall into the most passionate first kiss ever.

'You two are good friends, yes?' I hear Pierre say to Duncan. I realise he's gesturing at me. I don't mean to pull a face, but I do, apparently, because I see something like disappointment flicker in Duncan's eyes.

'Not *close* friends,' he says slowly. 'But …'

'Yeah,' I say, feeling awful if I've made him feel bad. But we're not friends, are we? I've only spoken to him twice!

'New friends,' I offer, and Duncan looks happy with that. I am too, to be fair. I like that he understands the writing stuff. It would be nice to know somebody who 'gets it', even if that somebody is the quiet boy from the front of the class.

'Us too,' says Pierre, and Axel adds, 'Friendship is so powerful, isn't it? It's the most important thing.'

I don't really know what to say to that, so I lie back and look at the clouds and think of how we should definitely have a party. I can ask Mum if she minds – I'm 99 per cent sure she'll say yes, we can have one. She's totally the 'coolest' mum out of all my friends' parents, TikTok habits aside! We could have Shloer in wine glasses and put out little bowls of crisps, push the furniture in the living room back to make a dance floor. It's already been almost twenty-four hours of the exchange, and they're only here six more days. It's no good wasting any more time if I'm going to secure this kiss from Axel. I like what he said about friendship being powerful, though. That's very mature. Sasha Broadwell and Barry Singh are boyfriend-girlfriend, but I've never even seen them talk to each other. They just walk around holding hands and then when their mates come over he talks to the boys and she talks to the girls. That's *got* to be boring. It never occurred to me you'd need to be mates with your boyfriend as well as fancy them, but it's right, isn't it? You need both things, otherwise what's the point?

'Penny for your thoughts?' asks Duncan, coming to lie next to me.

'I was just thinking that I should ask my mum if we can have a party at mine,' I tell him. 'As a fun thing we can all do, out of school.'

'Oh,' Duncan says. 'Wicked. If she says yes, I can help you if you want.' He gives a cheeky smile and adds, *'New friend.'* It makes me smile. Duncan Higginbottom has jokes! I poke him in the ribs and he pretends it has hurt way more than it has. I roll my eyes, but in a nice way.

A bunch of people file from around the corner on to the field then, Lucy and Star and their partners, and Tommy Tsao with his team. They look disappointed we're there first and have won, but they're all laughing like friends so it looks like the icebreaker worked for them and everyone is having a good time.

'I'm going to ask Mum if I can throw a party for us,' I tell the girls, propping myself up on my elbows as they settle down beside us. Before either of them can respond, Tommy Tsao says: 'I'd best be getting invited!' I hadn't even realised he was listening.

'Errr, yeah,' I say. 'Of course. Everyone will be invited!'

More people finish the hunt and Tommy tells everyone,

'Taylor's having a party, guys!' so even though five minutes ago it was just a thought, everyone thinks it is definitely happening now. God, it will be *so* embarrassing if Mum stops being cool for a second and says no!

'Yeah!' I find myself saying, even though I haven't checked. 'I'll email you all!'

I cross my fingers once I've said it, for good luck, and try to meet Axel's eye to check he's noticed what's going on. He hasn't. He's still talking to Pierre.

'He's cute,' says Lucy, noticing me notice him.

I give her A Look.

'I know what you're thinking,' she teases me, and I tell her to shush.

'It will happen,' she whispers, taking my hint. 'He's been looking at you too, you know.'

My heart soars at the thought. 'Has he?' I say, louder than I mean to. Axel looks up. I smile at him, and he smiles back. Who'd have thought I could go from NO smiles from boys to two different boys making eye contact and giving shy grins in a mere matter of days?!

'Told you,' whispers Lucy, and I could die of happiness. My emotions have been all up and down since yesterday and Axel's arrival, but Lucy's encouragement makes me feel loads better.

'Thanks,' I whisper back, beaming, and it is immediately

crystal clear to me what's going to happen. The party …
stepping outside for some air (his suggestion) … fingertips
brushing … lips locking …

PARADISE!

PURE KISSING BLISS!

9

Members Only

Me: *I can't stop thinking about Axel*

Lucy: *Because he fancies you?*

Me: *It's made me so happy that you think so!*

Me: *I just wish I was better at this sort of stuff ...*

Star: *Have you asked about the party yet? What's Erica said?*

Me: *Not yet, just thinking about to how to guarantee a yes ...*

Lucy: *Tell her we'll be there and will help you keep things in order!*

Me: *She does really trust you two ...*

Me: *And she's always said she'll trust me until given a reason not to, to be honest*

Star: *So cool*

Lucy: *My mum won't even let me get the bus on my own still! She's soooooo protective*

Star: *It's because she's a teacher, babe*

Star: *She's seen the worst of teenagers and hasn't realised you're not that bad!!*

> **Me:** *Or she doesn't want you to get that bad!*
>
> **Me:** *Anyway, I'll ask about the party*
>
> **Me:** *And today I'm just going to be even friendlier than normal. Axel said yesterday how important he thinks friendship is, soooooo*

Star: *When are we going to find time for the fanfiction story this week? We need a plan!*

Star: *Also, how's the spot?*

> **Me:** *Slept with toothpaste on it like you said!*

Star: *Good!*

> **Me:** *You're my beauty queen. Thanks for the advice!*

Star: ☺

Star: *Wear some clear mascara and lip balm today. Then your eyes will look bigger and lips more kissable, for Axel!*

> **Me:** *Operation Kiss is a go!!*

Except … Nooooo! I've just gone for a morning wee and Axel has seen me! *Toy Story* pyjamas and toothpaste on my face – full troll!

'Good morning,' he croaks, raising an eyebrow at me. He's already dressed and heading downstairs.

'Morning,' I mumble, slamming the bathroom door behind me and dying of shame in private. That is NOT the state I wanted him to see me in! Tomorrow I'll have to get up earlier and be ready before he is, to avoid this EVER happening again. I try to breathe deep. Maybe he didn't see the toothpaste on my spot. Maybe he didn't notice Buzz Lightyear on my T-shirt … maybe?

Oh god, who am I kidding? He totally did. I wish I had a time machine and could dial it back five minutes. If I had come out of my room even ten seconds later, this whole mortification could have be avoided! Damned universe!

By the time I'm dressed and ready for the day, I can hear Mum and Axel chatting in French downstairs. I try to linger outside the kitchen door to get an idea of what they're saying, but it's too fast for me, I can only understand about every tenth word, and that's normally *c'est* or *oui*. A baby could catch that drift.

'Darling!' Mum says, as I make my grand entrance. She's showing him something on her phone— God! If it's her social media I'll kill her! 'Axel was just saying how you

117

want to invite the French exchange people over for a bit of a party!'

I shoot Axel a look, and he just grins at me. Has he blown this for us? Mum needs asking things in a very particular way. I've spent fourteen years honing the skill of getting her to say yes. I find myself holding my breath, waiting to see if Axel's request has landed well.

'It's a very good idea!' Axel says, pouring himself some black coffee from a cafetière I've never seen in my life. Mum is certainly pulling out all the stops for him. There's even fresh *pain au chocolat*! Yum.

'I agree,' smiles Mum, gesturing for me to sit down and eat.

'Really?' I say, because can it honestly be that easy? I stuff some croissant into my mouth. It's delicious. The French really do know how to live.

'Sure!' Mum insists. 'I trust you, Taylor. I've always said, I will continue to trust you until I'm—'

'Shown otherwise, yeah, I remember,' I interrupt. 'I'm really shocked you've said yes, Mum. Thank you.' Mum looks happy that I'm happy, and it makes me add, 'I love you.'

I shoot her a massive smile, and end up locking eyes with Axel whilst still grinning and so he treats me to a huge smile too. Then we're just three people, surrounded by pastry crumbs, smiling at each other like goons. And just like that, a bad morning has become a magnificent one!

There'll be rules, of course,' Mum says, standing up to clear some of the empty plates and cups. 'I'll help you set up, and you can have exactly two hours of unsupervised fun.'

'Two hours, got it,' I say with a nod.

'Nobody can go upstairs or into my writing studio,' Mum continues. 'Absolutely no alcohol or smoking …' I don't mean to look at Axel when she says *smoking*, but I can't help it. 'You'd better not smoke, Axel,' Mum says, wagging a finger at him. '*C'est dégoûtant!*' she says, which I know means *disgusting.* Axel nods and looks at his coffee cup.

'Anything else?' I say, already finishing my breakfast and standing up to go and text Members Only. They'll be so excited too! None of us has ever had an unsupervised party before! This is *so* grown-up. I think I'm the first girl in our year to throw a party! An! Un! Supervised! Party!! How majorly awesome.

'Yes,' Mum says. 'I want confirmation from everyone's parents that they know it's unsupervised. OK?'

'OK!' I say, with a squeal, and even Axel claps his hands. 'Thank you, thank you, thank you!' I cry, wrapping my arms around her and giving her a big kiss on the cheek.

I run to the computer and fire up my school email account. There's a thread with the email addresses of every-one in the exchange group, so I copy and paste it and then

119

get stuck, because I want my invitation to be a good one and it's hard to hit the right tone.

I type, *hey everyone*, and then delete it.

I try: *What's up guys!*

… and then delete that, too.

Hi all, I type, but that sounds like something a teacher trying to be cool would say, all unnatural and try-hard. Hmmmm. Eventually, I settle on:

Hey! Party at mine on Friday. 6–8 p.m. Lame, but your parents need to text my mum confirmation that they know it's unsupervised. There will be dancing! Taylor xxx

I save it to drafts, so I can ask Lucy and Star to help workshop it – or maybe I'll even ask my new friend Duncan. He's a copy editor, after all! Squee! I'm on cloud nine about all this. In fact, in a surge of euphoria, I find myself grabbing Axel's arm so we can go to school. He seems just as excited as I am! *La vie est belle! Ooh la la!*

'How does Buzz Lightyear say?' Axel asks as we step out of the door. 'To infinity, and beyond!'

OK. He definitely saw me in my pyjamas then.

Damn!

Before English class with Ms K, I get five minutes with Duncan to ask him if he thinks my invitation is any good.

'You're asking *me*?' he says, wide-eyed, and I think he

even blushes a bit. I hand him my phone with the draft open.

'It's no different from showing you an article, is it?' I say, suddenly a bit embarrassed to be asking for help. I didn't think it was a big deal.

'No, sure, you're right,' Duncan says, taking my phone and squinting at the screen. He reads it, mouthing the words under his breath, and concludes: 'Send it. Maybe add in your phone number too? But yeah, all the relevant information is there, isn't it? And if people have questions, they just hit *reply*.'

'OK, yeah,' I say. 'Thanks.' Duncan shrugs, like it's no big deal, and for some reason it makes me want to tease him. 'New friend,' I add, and he pulls a face, but I think he likes the banter really.

'Your Year 9 article was great, by the way,' he says, as I make my way to my desk. 'Thanks for sending it. Ms K should see it!'

'Ooooooh!' Bobby Hasstlehoff says, as he hears what Duncan has said. He's talking in a stupid high-pitched voice. 'Ms K should see it!' he mimics. Duncan flushes pink again. Bobby Hasstlehoff is a renowned idiot – the kind of kid who thinks being a bully makes him cool, when really it just highlights how he's barely got a single brain cell.

'Sit down,' I snap at him. 'And pop a Tic Tac,' I say, wafting a hand under my nose like his breath stinks. It makes everyone around us burst out laughing and has the exact desired effect of making Bobby scamper to his desk. Duncan shoots me a grateful look. I stick my tongue out at him. He shakes his head, like *I'm* the fool.

'Cow,' Bobby Hasstlehoff whispers in my direction, but I pretend not to have heard him.

Ms K comes in and starts talking about the homework we did, and where to pick up for the start of this class. As she's talking, I get a text. I didn't even realise I still had my phone out – there's rules about keeping it in your bag in lessons. I wouldn't normally pick it up but I can't help it, because … it's Tommy Tsao!

Cool about the party, it says. *Thanks for your number, was gonna ask for it anyway. Tommy* ☺

'Whoa,' Star says, impressed, when we set off on some group work. We have to decide what *Of Mice and Men*'s five main themes are, with quotations to prove it. 'So, do you fancy Tommy, or Axel?'

'Shhhh!' I say, shooting a look over to where Axel sits with Pierre, just behind Duncan's usual spot at the front. It's a tight squeeze, having extra bodies in class. I can't imagine it's much fun for all the Frenchies to be studying American classics alongside us, but part of the exchange is that they do our lessons with us. There wasn't room for Axel on my table, hence why he's over with Duncan et al.

'You literally just sent the email with your number on it five minutes ago, and Tommy has already texted?' clarifies Lucy, sounding impressed. She writes down *the difficulty of the American Dream* on the piece of paper we're brainstorming on and then hands the pen to me.

'He's so into you! You should definitely go for it,' Star says, as I write down: *male friendship*.

'I like Axel,' I say. 'And Lucy thinks he might like me too.'

Lucy writes down *fear*.

'I do,' she says, with a nod. 'I mean. I want for you what you want for yourself. Tommy *is* a Year 10. But I get the French boy thing. Just don't worry about him seeing you in your PJs. Even French girls get spots – I'll bet it's nothing he hasn't seen before.'

'Hmmm,' I say. I know Lucy means well, but I wonder if she 'gets' how complicated it is with girls and boys. Grandma says men are from Mars and women are from Venus, and sometimes I think I agree. I know being queer isn't *easier* – god, of course it isn't! OF COURSE! – but … I just mean … well … I wish I could talk about all this with somebody who also goes through it too, you know? Another girl who likes boys. But who would that be? Mum? Ewww. No thanks.

'Taylor.' Ms K suddenly appears by my desk. I stuff my phone into my bag guiltily. She smirks, and says, 'I'll pretend I didn't see that.'

123

'Thanks, miss,' I say. 'Sorry.'

'It's OK,' she says. 'I wasn't coming over about that. What's all this about a fantastic column for the paper? Duncan has been singing your praises.'

'Has he, miss?' I say, shocked. Then the shock gives way to feeling a bit annoyed, to be honest, because that wasn't his column to talk about, and he's only seen a first draft. It's my article to shout about!

'Don't be mad at him,' Ms K says. 'In his capacity as copy editor, he wanted to make sure you have the courage to send it me. So, when it's ready I'm excited to see it! And your competition entry, of course …'

'Talk about piling it all on my plate, miss,' I say cheekily, but Ms K, as ever, gets the joke, and she simply lifts her palms like *What can I say?* And then tells me: 'If anyone can handle it, Taylor, you can.'

OK, so maybe Duncan has done me a favour, telling Ms K about the piece. Would I have sent it her? I'm not sure. I just know how hard it is to get space or opinion pieces in the *Register*. And I like the encouragement. With the exchange and whatnot it could be really easy to forget about writing, but this has been a reminder to stay on top of it. I make myself a silent promise to write another piece today. Or tomorrow. Soon, anyway.

When the lesson is over I get up and wait by Axel's desk,

where he's got his notebook open to a sketch he's done. It looks a lot like his best friend, Pierre, which is so cute. I wonder if he might draw *my* picture one day.

'*Très bon*,' I say, pointing at it, and Axel quickly covers it up before Pierre can see. Once it's safely in his bag he whispers, '*Merci*,' with that sexy French shrug he does. I like seeing him be coy, it reminds me that he's human too. It can be very easy to think that because he's so handsome he's somehow not a real person. But he is. A very handsome, but real, person.

'Do you like art?' I ask. Axel nods.

'My father is …' he says, like he's searching for the word. 'I don't know how to say, he makes the cartoons? For the newspaper?'

'Oh!' I say. 'He's a cartoonist? Like, drawings for children?'

Axel shakes his head. '*Non*,' he says. '*Politique?*'

I try to think what that word means in English.

'Oh!' I say. 'Political? He draws … political cartoons?'

'*Oui*,' says Axel, satisfied that I have understood. I'm pleased he thinks I have, although I have no idea what political cartoons are. I'll google it later.

'I would like to study art, in Paris. And then make *animation*. I will go to Parsons Paris?'

I nod again, adding yet another thing to my Google list.

'I want to live in Paris too,' I say. 'Like my mum used to.' I try to say in French, *We went a few years ago and I loved it!*

But I'm not sure I get my tenses right. In English, I add, 'When we both live there, maybe we will meet for coffee!'

'Ah, yes,' Axel says. 'And you will study there?'

I shrug. 'Maybe. I want to be a journalist. A culture writer, maybe? With a column about my opinions.'

Axel looks impressed by this. '*À cause de ta mère?* You write because of your mother?' he says, and I shrug. I don't think I've ever really thought about that before. I suppose growing up in a house with papers Blu-Tacked to the wall with plotlines all over them might have influenced me a bit.

'Urm,' I say, trying to decide on what my answer is. 'Well, I write real life, and she writes novels. But I guess she's always read to me loads, and encouraged me. I read her novels before they're published, too.'

'Not so many parents are this way, I don't think,' Axel suggests, and his accent is so sweet I could honestly squeal. 'We are lucky, *non*?'

'The luckiest,' I reply with a smile, and I feel like we've bonded that tiny bit more. Yay!!

As we leave for assembly, he holds out an arm for me, and I take it. Holding on to him as we navigate the corridors of Crickleton High makes me feel like the swankiest woman in the world. Don't mind me! Just walking arm in arm with a French boy on the way to the main hall! I swear some of the

Year 10 girls nudge each other as we pass by, even horrid Anna who was mean about me 'only' being in Year 9. Ha! Take THAT, Horrid Anna!

'It's very serious, English school, *non*?' says Axel as we cram into the hall, everyone elbow to elbow on chairs that are way too close together.

'I suppose so,' I say. 'Is your school not like this?'

Axel laughs. '*Non*,' he says. 'It is ... how do you say ... a madhouse?'

I laugh. 'Good English,' I giggle. 'A madhouse, yes.'

'Your grandmother taught this word to me yesterday,' Axel says. 'And also, *palaver*. This also means a crazy situation, yes?'

'It does.' I nod. 'If something is a bit of a mess, you can say, *What a palaver!*'

'Well, my school,' Axel tells me, 'is a palaver!'

Mr Logan, the head, stands up at the front and we all have to go quiet before I can explain to Axel why that sentence doesn't quite make sense, but I suppose I've been saved from myself because I don't know *how* to explain it. I'll leave it to Grandma. Trust her to be teaching Axel useless 'old people' sayings. It reminds me of when I was five and my friend Lala was late for a playdate. When Mum told me they were stuck in traffic, apparently I threw up my hands and said, 'There's nothing as rude as lateness! Don't they know that!' An eighty-year-old trapped in a five-year-old's body.

Assembly today, Mr Logan announces, is about why more girls should get into STEM – science, technology, engineering and maths. I'm off in a bit of a dreamland as he introduces a guest speaker, thinking about the party and how much there is to organise. But then this Ms O'Leary from a charity called GIRLS SAY YES! starts to give us a presentation on why traditional boys' subjects *have* to be explored by girls, too (gender binary much, Ms O'Leary?), which doesn't seem right to me and snaps me back into the room. I thought feminism was about choice full stop, not telling girls they're making the *wrong* choice. Ms O'Leary tells us her mum was an airline pilot, and so she was lucky enough to see what was possible for her career and became a pilot herself.

'But I know other girls aren't so lucky,' she tells us. 'They think they have to stick to what we call "soft" subjects, like English and art.'

Well. I've never heard such rubbish! Soft! Has Ms O'Leary ever tried to write an article or get a byline in the *Register*?! It's not for the faint of heart! You have to be creative, and resourceful, and resilient. That's not SOFT.

By the time it gets to her taking questions, my hand is the first in the air. I'm full of things to counter what she's said, and I don't want to seem impolite or like I don't agree with *some* of what she's said ... but also, she can't offend all of us girls who *don't* want jobs in STEM!

'Yes?' Ms O'Leary says. 'The girl at the back? Do you have a question?'

'Hi,' I say, and Mr Logan gestures for me to stand up so they can see me all the way at the front. Gosh. My mouth feels very dry. I don't think I've thought this through …

'Urm …' I say, trying not to let my heart beat out of my chest. Public speaking is so embarrassing. 'Everything you've said is really cool,' I begin, and the woman squints and says, 'Sorry, could you talk a bit louder? I can't quite hear you!'

I clear my throat and feel myself blushing, but I'm standing up now. I can hardly sit back down and mumble that it doesn't matter. It does matter! I need to find my courage and say my piece!

'Go on!' says Lucy, on my left, smiling encouragingly. I look at her. Beyond her, in my eyeline, is Duncan. He gives me two thumbs up. I take a breath. I can do this.

Louder this time, I repeat: 'Everything you've said is really cool,' and the woman says thank you. 'But,' I say, and I can feel her energy shift and watch her eyes narrow. 'Isn't everything you've said a bit … anti-feminist?'

I feel loads of people turn around to look at me, so try to just focus on the speaker.

'How so?' she says, with a wry smile.

'Well …' I say. 'I understand why it's needed, but on the other hand, you've sort of made out like girls aren't being good enough if they don't do more science or tech or whatever. I want to be a journalist. Does that mean I'm not feminist enough? Am I letting the side down?'

Mr Logan looks at his watch and pipes up, quite meanly if you ask me: 'Well, I'd certainly say that question has been posed like a journalist, Ms Blake! So you're obviously well on your way to being whatever it is you want to be. As for today, please join me in giving Ms O'Leary a big applause of thanks!'

And just like that, I don't get my answer. I'm left feeling like an idiot for daring to think for myself. Oh, the audacity of being a teenager with an opinion!!

'You are very intelligent, I think,' Axel whispers to me as we file out of assembly. I look up at him. I'm *reeling* from what Mr Logan said – he acted like my opinion didn't matter, that what I said was silly and inconsequential. I'm so mad at him! Should I not have spoken up?

'Yeah?' I say, a bit sadly. 'You might be the only one.'

Axel pulls on my arm, so we go off to one side. 'No,' he says, in the quiet corridor off from where everyone else is headed for lunch. 'That teacher – it wasn't right, how he spoke. To you.'

I look at him. His English really is very good. He must understand more than I thought, especially if he got what I was saying in there.

Axel tips my chin up so that I have no choice but to look at him and accept what he is saying. He looks at me, and I have this thought: *IT. IS. HERE.*

The moment has arrived.

I think he wants to kiss me! I'm not even going to have to wait until the party!

Suddenly, I forget all about Mr Logan, and Ms O'Leary, and feminism, and I look deep into Axel's eyes.

'You are a wonderful person,' Axel tells me. 'Full of so much … passion!'

And so I do it. I close my eyes, and I lean towards him, and I wait for his lips to meet mine, because surely this is all a prelude to a kiss. Surely!

And then Axel claps, and barks: '*On y va!*'

The sound shocks me into opening my eyes again. No kiss? Axel holds out his arm in the way that is becoming usual for us, and gestures to the lunch hall. Right, then. Definitely no kiss. Probably for the best, though – who wants their first kiss at school? At the party there will be soft lights, cool music, the excuse of finding time together alone … it's much better.

(OK, fine, I would totally have had my first kiss at school. But maybe Axel lost his nerve. I still have hope! Roll on, party time!!)

* * *

In last period we have ICT, but because Mr Pollock is off sick we have a substitute teacher who tells us to just use the computers to quietly do any outstanding homework, because she can't find the instructions Mr Pollock left for his absence. I take the opportunity to write a column on what we talked about in assembly, because I can't stop thinking about it – not only how wrong the speaker was, but about how to find a way to make Mr Logan understand that I totally have a point. The words flow out of me really easily. I end up writing:

You Don't Have to Go into STEM!

Knowing that the sky is the limit is important for any student, not matter what their gender. Anyone can become a lawyer, an entrepreneur, a nurse or a stay-at-home partner. This is a time of equality!

But, that said, to redress the balance of some traditionally 'masculine' jobs, us girls get told to chase after them. We even had an assembly about getting girls into STEM.

However, it can make girls feel inadequate if we don't love STEM, like we're not competitive leaders or giving the boys a run for their money. It's not our fault STEM is where the high-paying jobs are. It feels like the teachers are afraid to tell us it's OK to want to take art or media studies instead of an extra science at GCSE.

Last year, 76 per cent of female-identifying Crickleton High school leavers who were headed to university said they were going to study science, technology, engineering or maths-based subjects. And school talk about this like it's a win for feminism! But if school makes being a 'good' student synonymous with being a science kid, girls will then conform to that expectation, whether they are or aren't interested in STEM. And that is not feminism!

I want to be able to explore what naturally interests me without worrying about whether it makes me a 'good' student or not on paper. I might want to take a woodwork GCSE, but also art, or choose drama club after school instead of coding club. That doesn't make me a bimbo or unambitious! And a girl who does science club isn't more intelligent or more driven than me if that's where her interests lie!

Everyone should be able to do what they want to do, because that's true equality. Yes, make it easier for the people who traditionally feel pushed out of STEM to get a chance if that's what they want. But equally, don't make those who don't feel guilty, either!

I decide, before I can change my mind, to send it to Duncan to see what he thinks. I attach it to an email that reads: *OK, now you have to show me something you've been working on too! From, your new friend x*

Once I've done that, I google 'political cartoons' and 'Parsons Paris', as per my 'Must Google' list. Turns out political cartoons are basically an artist's version of a column, a way for an artist to convey their opinion about what is happening in the world. That's very cool that Axel's dad does that! Maybe he can get me a job at his newspaper one day! I'd have to improve my French though – or maybe they have an English section to their paper! And Parsons Paris is, apparently, the Paris outpost of a very famous New York art school. It looks *very* fancy. So Axel is *très* international! Yet another thing we have in common!

I go to bed content, feeling like I've accomplished something really, really good today. Writing my articles makes me so happy. As does nearly kissing Axel …!! I read the last few chapters of my book and go to sleep dreaming of his soft-looking lips, his lazy half-smile and the party that will kick-start my new life. Mmmmmm. Lovely, lovely Axel …! I'll be wearing something floaty and cute but not try-hard, and probably he'll see me dancing and laughing in my living room, and stare at me, knowing he has to take his chance because he's never fancied anyone this much in his life! I'll excuse myself to go and get some more drinks from the fridge, to keep everyone topped up and hydrated, and he'll follow me, and suddenly we'll be alone, and then …

Well. You know the rest!

10

Emails keep popping up on my phone over breakfast, loads of people saying they're coming to the party. I can't believe it's making me this popular!

This is so cool! says Rebecca Addington. *Yes!*

OMG YES! writes Trevor McGregor. *Wicked.*

Count me in! sends Calum Maggiore.

'That is a *lot* of beeping for this early in the morning,' Mum says over breakfast. Axel is still upstairs getting ready, so it's just her and me.

'Party invite replies,' I explain. 'Everyone is saying they're excited.'

Mum smiles her crinkly-eyed smile.

'I'll give you a drinks and snacks budget,' she says.

I look at her. 'Really?!' I ask.

She nods. 'Really. You're a good girl, Taylor. I'm excited for you.'

'I have to text the girls!' I shriek, going back to my phone and opening up Members Only. There's a message from Star with ideas for the next chapter of our Harry Styles/Tom Holland fanfiction, but I don't have time for that.

MUM IS GIVING ME MONEY FOR DRINKS AND SNACKS FOR THE PARTY!!!!! I type, but they must be busy because they don't properly reply, just give it a love heart 'like'. Well. I love it too!

It's 'English Countryside' day for everyone on the French exchange today. I was on the planning committee, and not to brag, but it was my idea to do something quintessentially English like taking a picnic into the woods. I mean, I know anyone can do that, anywhere, but I suppose in my head I was all wicker baskets and 'If you go down to the woods today …' and 'Teddy Bear's Picnic' and whatnot. Anyway. Yup. Me! My idea! This is going to be so cute and romantic!! I've got a glass bottle of lemonade for me and Axel, and tuna sandwiches in the special brioche rolls from the baker's, not normal boring bread. I made a fruit salad, chopping up banana, orange, strawberries and grapes and covering it in juice, too, which I thought was very *How to Be Parisian When You're Not from Paris*:

Hosting

No Parisian woman has to be a gourmet chef.
It is more than enough to prepare a few simple
things well, with fresh ingredients and a sprinkle
of love. Portions should always be generous,
and never worry about matching your
linens – a little disarray is très chic.

And I found linens! Linen napkins at the back of a cupboard! It's kind of bulky to carry a picnic basket, but we shouldn't be walking far. It would be easier to carry everything in a rucksack, but way less in keeping with the theme. I wanted the picnic basket vibe!

Anyway. The thing is, as Axel and I approach the front gate to school – talking about art again, if you can bear it! Like, how sophisticated of us!! – I can see Monsieur Brown in full hiking boots and waterproofs. He seems to clock me at the exact same time, because we both look each other up and down and frown. He is very much *not* the vibe. Huh.

'All right, sir?' I say, going to stand by Lucy and Star. Axel makes his way across the group to go and say hi to Pierre, our conversation about Frida Kahlo terminated. I only know about her because Mum has a little postcard framed in her study, a self-portrait of the artist. But it was enough information to impress Axel! I'm doing very well!! I'll have to read up on some more conversation topics to keep this chatty streak going. As I look over, Duncan gives a little wave. Tommy sees and imitates him, waving his hand at me with a floppy wrist. I shake my head, because making fun of people isn't very interesting to me, and I'm disappointed Tommy has done it. Like, shouldn't he be more mature than that? As a Year 10? And yet, he's still so handsome. It's not fair that a handsome face can be forgiven quicker than a less handsome one, but I fear it might be a true thing.

I wonder if there's an article in that?

I focus back on Monsieur Brown.

'Taylor,' he says. 'Why do I get the feeling you didn't get the memo about today's adventures?'

Bit rude, I think, but I can't very well say that to his face, can I? Instead I say, 'What do you mean, sir?'

'Jeans and trainers for a woodland hike?' he says. 'I'd have thought you be more prepared.'

I look around at everyone there. The French kids all have on jeans too, which is a nice boost because I deliberately tried to be continental-looking today. I've got on faded blue jeans that I've rolled up twice at the ankle, a black T-shirt and the black Converse I got off Grandma and Grandad for my birthday. (Well, they gave me their bank card and I ordered them online in front of them because they weren't sure about my size. They were shipped to their house, though, and they still wrapped them up for me so I had something to open. Plus, they got a proper M&S Colin the Caterpillar cake too. I get one every birthday! Yum.) I've also got on my pretend leather jacket – my *pleather* jacket, if you will – which does, if I'm honest, make me sweat, but Mum wouldn't spend all that money on a real leather one and said anyway, leather is unethical. I said her best winter boots are leather, though, and she said crossly that that's beside the point. Anyway, whatever: I have a whole Pinterest board dedicated to French style and really tried my best to copy it. To see the actual French girls in similar stuff today makes me feel like I nailed it. Yas!!!

Some of the British kids have walking boots on, though, like they know something I don't. Not all of them, but some. Duncan does. Lucy does – I mean, she's Ms Practical, so that tracks – but Star doesn't.

'Woodland hike? I thought today was a woodland *picnic*,' I say to Monsieur Brown, making a quick inventory of everyone's footwear by glancing downwards.

'Ah, of course,' he says. 'You missed the last four meetings, didn't you?'

Monsieur Brown says it like I missed the last four French exchange planning meetings because I was drinking Coca-Cola on the rooftops of Madrid, not because they clashed with meetings for the *Register*.

I blink.

Monsieur Brown continues. 'The plan evolved somewhat, Taylor. It's not a woodland picnic. Madame Jones and I thought it more appropriate to give it a more British spin, so it's Duke of Edinburgh taster day. Give the French a sample of our rustic, outdoorsy spirit!'

'Duke of Edinburgh *taster* day?!' I say. 'But … but …' I can't believe I missed this. I blame the French exchange emails: they're always so *long*. I do normally skim-read them, to be honest. Duncan Higginbottom needs to get a job copy-editing them, starting by cutting their length by half! Then maybe I'd keep up to date!

Again, though, I do not say this out loud.

Instead I say: 'But I have a picnic basket, sir!'

A few people burst out laughing, and I feel myself blush.

'I have a spare backpack you can borrow, Taylor. Although I'm unsure what can be done about the shoes. Let's just hope the rain keeps off.'

'Thanks, sir,' I grumble, thinking: *Duke of Edinburgh day?! What the heck!*

'So what it is, *Duke of Edinburgh*?' Axel asks as we make our way through town, towards the woods. It's quite pretty at first, quite like I'd had in my head when I first suggested it. At the edge of the forest there's load of trees that make the sunlight dappled, and the birds are singing like they've had sugar for breakfast and are now hyper. But the further up the path we get, the sludgier the ground becomes, and the colder the air because we're hidden from the sun.

'Urm,' I say, holding on the straps of Monsieur Brown's rucksack, noticing how they smell of damp. 'It's an award that you can get. When Queen Elizabeth was alive, it was set up by her husband – Prince Philip – to get everyone out and about. You know, active.'

'In the woods?' clarifies Pierre, who, annoyingly, just like Axel, has giraffe-like long legs that mean neither of them are scuttling along and getting out of breath like, say, I am. I'm going to have to take off my jacket in a minute because it is sweat city under my armpits and all down my back, but I don't want to do it right now because I don't want to stop walking and end up bringing up the rear with Madame Jones, who is insisting on speaking nothing but French all week.

'Yeah,' Lucy says, equally as flustered as me, despite her 'appropriate' footwear. This is less of a country walk and more like a cross-country jog. Monsieur Brown is practically channelling Usain Bolt, the way he's bounding away so fast! 'He liked the idea of teenagers learning to use maps and starting fires, that sort of thing. Survival skills.'

'Hmmm,' says Pierre, in such a way that Axel bursts out laughing.

'Hmmmm!' says Axel, and then we're all laughing, because this is ridiculous. All the French girls are complaining and all the English boys are showing off at the front and then there's just us, in the middle, already eating Star's snacks because hers are easiest to get to. I break off a finger of KitKat and pass it to Axel, who takes it with a grin. Lovely, dreamy Axel. He looks at me all happy and smiley and it makes me feel all warm inside.

'So this is OK?' I say to him. 'The woods?'

He shrugs, in that very French way that he has. 'It's an adventure,' he says, and it makes me try to be more positive, too. Yes! An adventure! A bit unusual, but still. When else would I hike through the woods like this?

'You have a very positive attitude,' I tell him, and he jiggles his shoulders.

'Life is ...' Axel says. 'Short. Do you say, YOLO?'

I laugh. 'How do you know YOLO?!' I say.

'You Only Live Once!' Axel says dramatically. 'I hear this in a song, I think. I like it!'

'Taylor!' Star says, from just behind us where she's walking with her partner. 'Sophie writes for her school newspaper too!'

I turn around and nod politely. 'Oh!' I say, with a quick smile. 'That's cool!'

I turn my attention back to Axel – I cannot get distracted from my task of making him comfortable with me!

'Do you feel homesick at all?' I ask. 'Being away from home?'

Axel shakes his head. 'You mean, is missing home bad for me?' he clarifies. I nod. '*Non*,' he says. 'Travel is important. I like to visit new places.'

'Me too!' I cry. 'We went to Italy last summer and I could have stayed forever.'

'I went to Seoul with my family last year. It was … *incredible*.'

I daren't ask where Seoul is (is it Japan?) because I don't want to seem ignorant, but it's exciting to me that Axel likes to see the world too. Yet another thing we have in common! Score!

We walk for about an hour, which feels like two, and despite Axel's positivity, I do feel guilty that I wasn't at the rest of those meetings. If I was, I could have objected to this! But, *c'est la vie*, we're here now, at a clearing in the woods by the river, with logs we can sit on and an instructor in a bright red vest and cap who is going to teach us a few tricks, apparently. And Axel is here, sitting next to me, laughing. Things could be worse.

'I'm sorry, but *merde*! *Non*,' says Axel, holding on to a frankfurter sausage with his thumb and forefinger. The instructor – Earl – has built a fire, and we've all had to forage for a big stick to put a sausage on and roast in the fire. Axel is eyeing up his food like he'd rather go hungry.

'It is dog food!' he says, barely able to conceal his disgust. I got quite excited when I learned we were going to do this – I love a frankfurter, and only ever have one when we go to IKEA. 'This is not food for humans, I don't think,' Axel insists, and it makes a squelch as he puts it on his stick. Pierre laughs at him, which frees me up to laugh at him too. Slowly, I feel like the boys are letting me into their little gang. Making room for me. I like it!

We all take turns cooking our food, and because Axel refuses to eat processed sausage, when it's my turn Duncan stands on one side of me, and Tommy on the other.

'Are you having a nice day?' Duncan asks, and I shrug.

'I've got wet socks,' I say. 'I was on the planning committee and didn't even know they'd switched today from a woodland picnic to a Duke of Edinburgh day. How lame is that?'

'Not lame,' says Duncan. 'A woodland picnic would have been nice too.'

I give him a grateful smile.

Tommy says, 'Both are stupid, to be fair. Who wants to be out in the cold this way? Your idea for a party is the best thing, Tay. I can even see if my big brother will get us some beers in?'

'Beer?' I say. 'Oh.'

Is it uncool if I say no? Do I seem babyish if I say that?

'My mum wouldn't like it,' I settle on saying. 'And I want to stay on her good side, you know? So I can do it again one day?'

Tommy nods. 'Yeah,' he says. 'Got it. Fair play.'

It's so embarrassing, but all that walking and all that snacking – I realise as I'm talking that I kind of need to poop. I didn't have time for one at home this morning because I spent so long putting my outfit together ... but yup. I can feel my tummy gurgling. I try to focus on the sausages, arranging my face into something calm and serene. But on the inside, I am *dying*, because not to be gross but there's some poops you can make go away, aren't there, and other poops that you just know you can't. And I can feel it – this is not a poop that will be going away.

'Do you mind holding this?' I ask Duncan, who happily takes my stick and says he'll finish roasting it for me.

'Lucy!' I hiss, looking all over for where she's gone. 'Star!' I find them over on one of the far logs, with their partners.

'Hey, Taylor. Have you eaten yet? These sausages are actually really good! And they're going to show us how to make Angel Delight in the river – apparently the water cools the bowl to make it set!' Lucy says, before clocking he look on my face and dropping her voice. 'Oh my god,' she says. 'Are you all right?'

'I have to poop!' I whisper. 'Like, so badly!'

'Oh,' she says, eyes wide in fear for me. 'Crap.'

'Exactly,' giggles Star in her sing-song voice, and Lucy hits her arm.

'I think you'll have to go in the woods ...' Lucy says, horrified, right as Earl the Instructor comes over and asks, 'Are we all OK here?'

Everyone falls silent and looks at me.

'OK ...' says Earl. 'What's wrong?'

I can't say it. The words just won't come out of my mouth. I look at him, and he looks at me. He cocks an eyebrow, as if to say, *Go on, it can't be that bad.* But it is. Because I've obviously already done the mental maths: There is no toilet out here.

'She needs the loo,' Star says for me.

'Oh, OK.' Earl nods. 'That's no problem. Number one, or number two?'

I wish I could wade out into the river and sink to the bottom and go and live like the Little Mermaid for the rest of my life.

'Number two,' I grumble, looking at the ground.

'Absolutely no problem!' says Earl, his voice bright and too loud, like this isn't the worst thing to ever happen.

Although, as I quickly learn, needing to poop in the woods isn't the worst thing.

148

The worst thing is Earl disappearing and then waving a spade around saying, 'Who needed this? Who needed the poop spade?'

EVERYONE turns and looks, Crickleton kids *and* the Frenchies, and I don't put up my hand. I try to hide my face but it's no good. Earl spots me, marches over, and as everyone stares he says: 'You just dig a hole with this, use this bamboo toilet paper – it's biodegradable, you see – and then cover the hole back up again, OK?'

It's like everyone holds their breath as Earl dangles the spade in front of me, waiting to see if I will take it. I don't look up. I stand there, feeling the poop get more and more desperate, and then I realise my choices are horrible, and even more horrible: If I don't take the shovel, I'll end up pooping myself in front of the whole class. And that is in *no way* happening. Oh my god. I'm going to have to accept the poop shovel!!

'Thank you,' I mumble, and I honestly could cry it's so humiliating. Star must feel sorry for me because she takes my free hand and guides me through all the people towards the direction Earl pointed in, meaning I don't have to look up. But I can hear them sniggering and talking about me, nudging one another and saying, 'Taylor is going for a poo in the woods! Look! She has the poop shovel!'

'You're OK,' Star tells me flimsily, like she doesn't even believe that herself. She scrambles to back up her point, saying: 'After we've finished eating somebody else is *bound* to have to do the same. You won't be the only person who needs the poop shovel. In fact, that's why they have it! Because people often have to do this!'

'But why am I the person who has to use it?!' I complain. 'Out of the fifty people here, why is it me who has a bowel movement at an inopportune moment?!'

Star offers me a weak smile of condolence and tells me she'll keep guard, and then I traipse further into the woodland in my best trainers and pleather jacket, and do exactly what Earl instructed me to do.

I hate it. It's the most unnatural thing in the world to poop in the wild. I keep thinking somebody is going to pop up and take my photo to print in the school paper or something. I wish there was a way to wipe moments from our memories, like how you shake an Etch A Sketch to clear it. I do not want to remember this. Not ever.

When I'm finished, I feel dirty and unclean, like I've just done something I shouldn't. I wish I could wash my hands somehow.

'Here,' Star says, handing me some antibacterial gel from her bag before we scurry back. 'Dad said I'd need this ...'

I take it, and as we near the group, I try to hide the shovel and give it back to Earl without everyone noticing. But they do. One of Tommy's friends is making chocolate

Angel Delight in the river, and when he spots me yells, 'Taylor! Is this yours?!'

I swear, I'm going to hear that laughter for the rest of my life, in my nightmares. When Tommy comes over later to say sorry for his friend, I can't even speak. I am so ashamed by what has happened, that I am mute. I don't trust myself to open my mouth. If I do, I think I'll cry, and then I'll be the crying pooey one.

In fact, I don't speak for the rest of the afternoon, or the whole way back to school, or on the way back home. I don't care about Tommy's stupid friend or Tommy's stupid apology for him; and I don't care about being chic and alluring for Axel; and I don't even want to talk to my new friend Duncan, who tries; or the girls, who both know to stay close but give me space.

When me and Axel get home I just want to take off all these ridiculous clothes and get in a hot shower that lasts for half an hour so that I can feel clean again. I kick off my Converse and go straight to the bathroom. On the way I hear Mum come through from her writing studio and say to Axel, 'Is everything OK?'

Axel says, 'She made a *caca* in the woods.'

Mum gasps, and then says, 'Oh! Oh. I see. Well. Tomorrow is another day, isn't it. Now she really needs to host a great party – she can't be known as the *caca* girl!'

Ohmygod.

CACA GIRL?! Nobody will come to my party now! Everything is RUINED!

'Mum!' I scream down the stairs. 'Shut up!!!'

I cry and cry and cry in the shower, scrubbing myself clean and then sitting in the bath as the hot water beats down on me. I feel like I'm in a scene from a movie, the bit where the main character is so sad she doesn't know if she'll ever be happy again. It was all going so well with Axel – we were joking around, laughing, making the best of it ... and then I went and humiliated myself. Everybody poos, literally even the King. Even Harry Styles! But I just feel like now that Axel knows that *I* poo, it's ruined the image of me as chic and fabulous. He'll probably never fancy me now, *never* want to kiss me, and that is just so so sad because we could be so happy together! Every time he looks at me, even if he's tipping my chin up towards him gently and saying I'm wonderful, he'll also be thinking: CACA GIRL! And probably trying not to be a little bit sick in his mouth at the thought of me squatting behind a tree!

When I go into my room, Mum has left *Isla and the Happily Ever After* on my bed. She said she'd collect it from the library for me, and she has – but not even sinking into a good book can help me now, because I don't know how I will ever fix this!!

It's not like I can google it, like other people will have had this problem, is it?!

Urgh!!

My life is OVER!!!

I WILL NEVER BE KISSED NOW I AM CACA GIRL!!!!!!!!

11

I'm just tying one of Mum's silk scarves around my neck when there's a soft knock at my bedroom door. I know what Mum's knock sounds like, because she's my mum, and this isn't it. Which must mean …

'Taylor? It's Axel.'

Axel is knocking at my bedroom door! Oh my gosh. OK. Don't panic. He probably just wants to let me know I am so disgusting that he's going to stop being my partner and go and sleep on Monsieur Brown's sofa bed.

I look around my room nervously. Is there anything else foul and gross lying around that will further prove I am totally un-fanciable?

Hmmmmm.

'Hold on!' I screech.

Luckily my bed is made, and I'm already dressed. Lucy messaged me last night, right before bed as I was trying to finish one last chapter of *Isla and the Happily Ever After* (it's so good!! Good enough that I stopped crying long enough to lose myself in another reality for half an hour!!). She said that Veronica Sellers got pooed on by a pigeon at the park last night, when a few people were hanging around after school. I asked her what that had to do with me, and she said *my* poop story was old news – Veronica Sellers is the new *caca girl*. Obviously that sucks for Vee, but I woke up feeling like if that's the case, if there's a new caca girl in town, I need to put my best foot forward today and act like I don't even *remember* yesterday, you know? Scrub it from my memory, and hopefully everybody else's, too. Veronica's misfortune has made me feel like maybe I will live through my own. Hence, the silk scarf. I'm also wearing black boots because my Converse are still wet from yesterday, with my other jeans and another T-shirt that's tucked in. I'm really trying my best with this whole *is she French or is she just really stylish* schtick.

All this to say: I'm surprisingly put together for receiving this unexpected visitor. But. I am suddenly doubting if I can confidently pull off this change in my attitude. I suspect not. Axel knocks again. Urgh! I'm going to have to face him! I open the door.

'Hey!' I say, trying to sound bright and enthusiastic (and not confused or a bit worried about why Axel is standing in the hallway, dressed all in black and smelling like mint body wash).

'Hey,' Axel parrots, and I like when he says something 'proper' English in his accent. It's soooo cute. I melt in spite of myself. 'Can I …?' he says, gesturing.

Mum and I didn't really cover if Axel was allowed in my bedroom, but I figure that it's before 8 a.m. and I can keep the door open – what's the worst that could happen? Lucy and Star are in my room all the time, right? I kick the doorstop under the door with a flourish and Axel sits on my bed.

'Nice bedroom,' he says, taking in my Tom Holland and Harry Styles posters and collection of moisturisers from the Body Shop. I like to keep them out on display. It makes me feel fancy.

'Thanks,' I reply, leaning against the bedroom wall in a way I think *How to Be Parisian When You're Not from Paris* would agree is 'relaxed' and 'casual'. I wait to see what Axel wants. Surely he's knocked for something? If he wants to let me know he's moving out, I wish he'd get on with it. Like, just rip the Band-Aid off, dude! I can take it! I am a disgusting human who poos in the woods, I get it!!!!

He keeps looking around, and I think how I've never had a boy in my room before. He's very handsome, sitting there with the morning sun streaming through the curtains behind him, making it look like he's got a halo of light all around his head, like an angel.

My phone beeps. Instinctively I pick it up. It's Tommy Tsao.

'Popular girl,' Axel says, and I shrug.

'It's Tommy, you know the guy in Year 10?' I tell Axel, opening the message. 'He wants to know how the party planning is coming along.'

'Strange boy, I think, Tommy,' Axel says. 'Like a puppy in the body of a teenager.'

That makes me laugh. 'I know what you mean,' I say, and somewhere in the very back of my mind I'm aware of a thought: *Axel doesn't like him.*

I scribble back to Tommy: *OK! Mum's getting loads of nice snacks!*

Then I feel a bit stupid for talking about something as silly as snacks. He sends back a thumbs up. I put my phone down. What a strange exchange. We've talked, but not really said anything.

Axel doesn't speak, so I figure now is the time to practise this confidence thing I've concocted. OK. Here goes nothing!

'You ready for another exciting day?' I ask Axel, picking out a lip balm to take in my bag. 'The exciting world of Crickleton!' I say, waving my hands about like I'm doing a dance. It makes Axel laugh, AND I REALLY LIKE WHEN I MAKE THAT HAPPEN!! It gives me a jolt to the heart, and the encouragement makes me add in more stupid faces and a bum wiggle. 'And,' I add, 'you're in luck. It's tea at Grandma and Grandad's tonight! WHAT A TREAT!!'

'That is a treat,' Axel says, and I think he means it. 'I have questions for your grandfather about the garden. It is the best garden I have ever seen!'

'Tell him that,' I say, 'and you'll have a friend for life.' I do another little dance, just to see if I can make him laugh again.

'I am very happy to be your exchange partner,' Axel says, when I'm done dancing around like a moron. I don't know what came over me. I think, when you feel like you have nothing to lose, it's easier to just be free and silly. 'It would be very boring to be with somebody else.'

AXEL LIKES BEING HERE!!!!!!!!!!!!!!

This is amazing. I do another little dance and then freeze.

'You're OK,' I say dramatically, scrunching up my nose so he knows I'm teasing. He throws a pillow at me. 'Hey!' I screech. 'You can't be nice and horrible at the same time!' I throw the pillow back at him.

Mum's voice floats up the stairs. '*Le petit déjeuner!*' she shouts. '*C'est prêt!*'

'*On y va,*' Axel says, holding out a hand for me to pull him up. I grab hold of him, and his grip on my hand is firm.

My heart lurches up to my throat as he looks at me seriously, like all of a sudden he *sees* me and feels brave enough to make a move. I can literally see him gathering his courage. I swallow hard, and tell myself to stay present. He's going to do it! Scoop me up in his arms and give me a passionate, meaningful kiss, and then we'll go and eat croissants! All my troubles will fade away, and my future will be his lips. *Quelle joie!*

Except then his expression changes into one of total trouble, and before I know it he's yanked my hand and pulled me on to the bed beside him, leaping up out of my way as I get a face full of duvet, almost swallowing a feather. Urgh!

… But then there's that sound again: gleeful laughing. It's too beautiful a noise to feel embarrassed or mad. I flip over and narrow my eyes like I am about to extract my revenge.

'Butthead!' I squeal, leaping up to chase him down the stairs.

But we're both laughing.

I think … I think Axel is *flirting* with me?!

And I think I might be quite good at flirting back!

No kiss yet, but what a turn-up for the books!

12

Members Only

Me: *OH MY GOD, I NEARLY JUST KISSED AXEL!*

Lucy: *Again?!*

Me: *What do you mean?*

Lucy: *This is a lot of nearly!! Just do it already!*

Me: *Hey! The conditions must be perfect, OK?!*

Me: *How to Be Parisian When You're Not from Paris says build-up can be everything ...*

Star: *How's Amelie's tummy today Lucy? Is she feeling any better?*

Lucy: *She says yes, thank you for asking!*

Lucy: *Does Sophie want that T-shirt bringing today? I said she could borrow it?*

Star: *She says yes please!*

Star: *Thank you!*

Me: *Guys? Hello? back to the almost-kiss?*

Star: *Go on then ...*

Me: *Well, that's it really. He was in my room and we were messing around and there was A MOMENT*

Star: *That's good!*

Me: *IT IS MORE THAN GOOD!!!!!!!!!!!!!*

Lucy: *Does anyone have a beige jumper they can bring today?*

Lucy: *I want to try draping it over my shoulders, like Amelie does*

I put my phone down. Honestly! These girls cannot stay on subject! It's like they don't even care about this kiss!! Urgh! I do have a beige jumper, but I'm not telling Lucy that. Not if she can't even act interested in my kiss! I want to text some more to ask their advice about the party – I want to know what I should do if people break any of Mum's rules. Like, how should I enforce them but still be super chill? But it's going to have to go on the Google list instead.

Today is a 'cultural tour' of the town, with us all taking a walk around the local history museum to learn some more about Crickleton. I'm not sure how much there can possibly be to learn. I mean, Crickleton can be OK when the sun is out and when it's local Pride or the big winter lights switch on, but surely these people don't want to look at old black-and-white photographs of how the place used to look? It's a bit embarrassing really – I'll bet French history is way chicer – but I suppose what I'm learning is that if the company is good, whatever we do is at least a bit more bearable. Look at yesterday – we actually all bonded quite a lot! Poo aside.

Urgh.

Will I ever not be haunted by that?!

We all meet at the big clock tower on the marketplace, and Axel makes a beeline for Pierre and Duncan. I follow him, because the girls haven't arrived yet, but a big shadow looms over me that makes me stop. It's Tommy, with his broad shoulders and hockey shorts and flippy-floppy hair. I think about what Axel said before, about him being like a puppy dog. I think he meant that Tommy is, like, immature. I guess he is a bit, but that doesn't stop my breath from catching in my throat and my tummy lurching. Is that an excited lurch or an awful lurch? I can't tell the difference. Why does he have this effect on me?! At least with Axel I can control my emotions, even when he's making me weak at the knees.

'How do,' Tommy says, tipping his chin up at me.

'Hi,' I say, not quite knowing where to look.

There's a strange pause.

Is that it? Are we done talking?

'I just wanted to tell you that you look really nice today,' he says, and I'm so surprised by how gentle and sincere he sounds that I look up in shock, meeting his eye – and Tommy BLUSHES! Tommy Tsao is blushing!!!

'Oh,' I say, half smiling and half trying not to have a heart attack. 'Yeah, urm. Thanks. You're very sweet.'

'Sure,' Tommy says, and I swear a couple of French girls nearby are nudging each other and giving Tommy the eye. But it isn't them he's complimenting, is it? It's me. I feel all funny in my pelvis, like there's a fire in my pants. It's something to do with how Tommy deliberately came over here, deliberately sought me out. Me! *Caca girl!* Lucy must be right. Everyone has forgotten already! Praise be!

'I'm just glad you've not worn that beret again. You looked like a French detective on the run!'

… Aaaaaaaand he's ruined it, like all English boys seem to do. Typical Tommy!!

'Thanks for the feedback,' I say, arching my eyebrow. I won't let him make me feel small! No way! HE came over to ME! 'I forgot you're the fashion expert of Crickleton.' I look at his hockey shorts and then back to his face. '*Not.*'

'Hey!' Tommy says, and he sounds like I really have hurt his feelings, but if I have then GOOD. He was mean first! I see that Lucy and Star have arrived and saunter off to them, leaving Tommy and his comments about my beret to it. He just really blew it.

'What was all that about?' Lucy says, pretty face creased in curiosity and wiping her fringe from her eyes.

'Nothing,' I say, feeling really confused. Tommy was nice, and then he wasn't, but then he acted like I was the mean one? What the heck?!

'Hey – whilst I remember, Amelie was asking what the dress code is for the party?' Star says. 'Are we going fancy, or *fancy*?'

'Hmmmm, yes,' Lucy observes. 'Two very different styles of dress. Fancy or …' She adopts a silly accent: '*Fancy!*'

'I know what you mean,' I tell Star. 'Like, we want to look nice, but we're not doing ball gowns and tiaras.'

'Dammit,' quips Lucy. 'I shall have my maid put my jewels away then.'

I playfully jab her in the ribs with my elbow.

'I was thinking nice trousers and a top, and, like, a smoky eye? Not as smoky as the other day, of course …'

Star frowns. 'Too soon,' she jokes. 'I'm still not over making you look that way. It's like I lost my magical make-up powers that morning!'

165

'Bygones,' I say, waving a hand. 'Apparently it has done me and Axel no harm …'

'You nearly went five whole minutes without bringing him up then!' Lucy jokes, but she's got an edge to her voice that hurts my feelings a bit, especially after this morning on the group chat where she didn't seem very interested.

'Hey!' I say, and she shrugs and replies, 'I was just joking!'

'Are you coming to the cafe at lunch?' Star asks, changing the subject as she gets a pair of sunglasses from her bag and puts them on. With her short hair and wide smile, she looks like she could be in a movie. 'We're going to that one on the corner with the chairs. The posh one, like we said we would.'

'Oooooh,' I say. 'The one off the "Must Do with the Frenchies" list?' It's funny, I haven't thought about our list since the exchange started. I've been kiss-distracted! We've not even done any of our Tom Holland and Harry Styles fanfiction, either, which is strange for us. We normally send each other paragraphs every day! 'Yeah!' I say. 'Mum gave me a tenner earlier, so I've money, baby!'

The girls laugh. 'Great!' says Lucy, and she seems genuinely pleased. It's touching! 'It's silly, but I feel like even though we see you every day at school, we're not hanging out like normal, you know? And texting isn't enough! I miss you!'

'Yeah,' I say. 'Same.'

'It's because you got a boy,' Star says. 'And so he wants to hang out with his boy friends, doesn't he? Not coming over to my house and doing face masks.'

'You guys have been doing face masks?' I say. I get an immediate sting of FOMO. 'I didn't know that.'

Star looks sheepishly at the ground. 'Well, yeah,' she says, and she really does sound sorry that I've missed that. 'Amelie and Sophie are friends too, so it's worked out for us. We get to hang out as a four. Sorry.'

I stick my bottom lip out and give an exaggerated pout. 'I feel left out,' I say.

Star hits my arm. 'No you don't,' she says with a wicked grin. 'You've got your own thing going on!'

I see what she means. I wouldn't be getting to know Axel like I am if I was at hers with cucumber over my eyes.

'I can see how handsome Axel is and I don't even like boys,' Lucy offers, and I perk up that she's brought the conversation back around to my favourite topic. 'You do seem to be really getting on. Tommy who, right?'

'Lol,' I laugh. 'Axel has the edge because he's French! What can I say! And yeah, we are getting on. Like, I want to kiss him but also I do just like talking to him. He talks about, like, art, and living to the max. We've got stuff in common! Hopefully you can chat to him properly at lunch, at the cafe?'

'Great,' says Star. 'I need to check he's suitable for you, you know!'

That's funny to us, because Star likes and approves of everyone: It's just who she is.

'Yup!' laughs Lucy. 'Obviously I've got questions too! Like, a whole list!'

I roll my eyes and tut like *they're* the ones being extra, but I'm pleased we've made a plan. I'm loving Axel being here, but I hate knowing the girls have been hanging out without me. I suppose I thought maybe Axel and I could slip off together to a little cafe by ourselves at lunch, maybe sharing a bowl of spaghetti like Lady and the Tramp, giving way to that kiss *finally* happening ... but lunch with the girls is good too. I want him to know my friends!

OK. We have survived our boring 'cultural' morning – so boring it doesn't even bear repeating – and it turns out Axel wants lunch with Pierre and Duncan in the museum gardens. Urgh! And because I'm such a good host, obviously I've said yes, of course, whatever you want!! I watch forlornly as Lucy and Star head off with their partners, everyone linked at the arm like they're in a music video for a girl band. Meanwhile, I get sandwiches with the boys from the museum cafe and we trundle off to a small clearing by one of the big oak trees, where Axel and Pierre start chatting away in French and I'm left to talk with Duncan. Again.

'You can't blame them really, can you?' Duncan says,

offering me a Hula Hoop and gesturing in their direction. 'Axel and Pierre? It must be hard speaking in English all the time. This is their time to relax, I guess.'

I take a Hula Hoop and look at him. 'You're oddly understanding. Have you ever been told that?'

'Not as a criticism,' Duncan bats back. I make a face.

'Ha, ha,' I say. 'Duncan and his deadpan humour strike again!'

Duncan raises his eyebrows like he's considering this. 'Deadpan humour,' he says with a nod. 'I didn't know I was capable of humour at all. I'll take it!'

'All these skills, just bubbling to the surface,' I joke.

'And always in the presence of you,' Duncan jokes back.

I don't know what that means. Is that ... a good thing? Duncan keeps crunching on his crisps and taking in the peace and quiet of the gardens, and I see Pierre offer Axel a cigarette. Axel shakes his head no. Good! What Mum said landed with him! It IS disgusting! Pierre puts them away.

'Been editing much lately?' I say, flicking the crumbs from my cheese roll off my lap.

'A bit.' Duncan nods. 'Hard when all this is happening. I've not even really had time to read, either, and I'm always reading! I *have* been working on my submission for the competition, though. For Ms K?'

I feel a flush of shame that I haven't even thought about that yet. I don't want to let her down! But as much as it's awesome being in Year 9, there's also soooo much happening. It's hard keeping up with everything! The exchange, planning the party, getting kissed ...

'It's a poem,' Duncan offers. 'Which is new for me. But it just ... I dunno. Sort of came out. Does that ever happen to you?'

I think about it. I hadn't expected Duncan to be a poem guy. In fact, there's a lot about Duncan that is unexpected. Like how he looks at me really intently when we talk, which makes me feel a bit self-conscious. And he asks a lot of questions, which is sometimes like an interrogation, even if it is nice that he shows an interest. Almost like Lucy and Star do, really – I don't know him very well but he's definitely more like talking to the girls than the boys, if the inane things Tommy Tsao says are anything to go by. He's nice, Duncan. A bit of a background boy and not a main character ... but nice. And nice can be good!

'I know what you mean,' I say. 'I wrote that thing about girls in STEM the other day, the piece I sent you, and that just sort of ... well, it flooded out of me, you know? It's a nice feeling!'

'Yeah,' Duncan smiles, 'it is. And it was a great piece. One of your best!' He's so earnest, Duncan, that sometimes I don't know where to look. When I don't say anything else he presses, 'Well, I'm sure whatever you submit for the comp will be great.' He smiles at me and then puts on a funny voice to say: 'And will you succeed? Ninety-eight and three quarters per cent guaranteed!'

My face must say it all because he throws up his hands and says, 'Dr Seuss? *Oh, the Places You'll Go!*?'

I shake my head. 'I don't know it …' I say, but the way he's acting makes me feel like I should.

'Oh, Taylor! I'll get you a copy! It's supposed to be for kids but I think it's for everyone. It's, like, my favourite book, I reckon. About how we'll move mountains, but sometimes there's ups and downs. It's fun. It's a good, fun, hopeful book.'

And he's so intense when he says it – when he says he will BUY ME HIS FAVOURITE BOOK! – that I don't know where to look. And it must come across as rude and dismissive because suddenly he's saying, 'Or not. Sorry. I didn't mean to make out like you're stupid for not having read it or whatever …'

Oh, Duncan! He's just so … well. It's concerning that he's so interested in me. That he's so kind! Aren't boys supposed to be dismissive and aloof?

Like Axel. We get on, but he's still a step removed, somehow unreachable …

I steal a look at him, laughing and joking with Pierre just a little harder and louder than he laughed and joked with me this morning …

Oh, Axel. Sexy, sexy, Axel …! How I want thee!

'Taylor?' Duncan says. 'Helllllllo?'

Oooooh. I must have got distracted. Duncan is waving a hand in front of my face.

'Yes?' I say, but Duncan shakes his head.

'Never mind,' he says, picking up the second half of his sandwich.

13

We head off to get the bus from town to Grandma and Grandad's, and I am delighted when Axel offers me his arm again. Several people from school see us, people not even on the exchange, and I'm not being big-headed when I say we turn some heads. I mean, if I saw somebody like Axel walking with a Year 9 all through town, I'd be curious too! It's nice to have his attention back, because it turns out that whilst I've been in the museum gardens with two boys who ignored me and one who ... well. I don't know what to make of Duncan. I really don't! Anyhoo, whilst I was there, the girls had a whale of a time at the fancy cafe they took *their* Frenchies to.

Members Only

Lucy: *OH MY GOD, STAR AND AMELIE JUST SANG A LIZZO SONG AT THE TOP OF THEIR VOICES IN THE MIDDLE OF THE TOWN SQUARE!*

Star: *The time was right! Who doesn't love Lizzo?!*

Me: *Oh! Send pics!*

Star: *We miss you! Can you come for the bbq later? At my mum's?*

Lucy: *Come! Come! Come!*

Me: *Oh! We'd love to!*

Star: *Yay!!*

Me: *... but Grandma and Grandad are expecting us*

Me: *Grandma even got some Milka in that she found in the 'world' section of the big supermarket*

Star: *Cute!*

Lucy: *Boo! Hiss! But also, tell David and Rachel we say hello!*

Me: *OK! Don't keep having too much fun without me!*

Lucy: *No promises!*

Lucy: *Do you need any party help? Let us know!*

I wish we could go to the BBQ. Star's mum has this massive back patio with all these swinging egg-shaped chairs and always gives you second helpings. But Grandma and Grandad are *really* excited to host us – Mum told me so this morning. I mean, Grandma said *I* get all passionate and throw myself into things, well, look at her! Going bananas because a French boy is coming for tea! We're having omelettes – but she's cooking them this time. It's safer that way.

Right before we were all dismissed from the 'Culture Day' Lucy said *obviously* she supports my love affair with Axel, but she told me not to get too first-kiss obsessed. It was quite abrupt! I said, 'What does that mean!' and she just sort of shrugged and said, 'Nothing.' So now there's that to worry about, that she and Star think I'm *abandoning them* somehow, putting a boy first. But he's my exchange partner! Even if I didn't fancy the pants off of him, I'd still have to take him to Grandma and Grandad's!

'I enjoy where you live,' Axel tells me, when we're on the bus. 'It is …'

I hold my breath as I wait for him to find the word.

'… authentic, *non*?'

'Hmmm,' I say. 'That's one way of putting it!'

Axel cocks his head like he doesn't understand. We're sitting next to each other because the bus is quite full and so my leg is touching his leg. I wonder if he's noticed? He must have noticed. I don't think I've ever sat so close to a boy before, now I think about it. But if I don't want to move my leg, in order to look at him properly I have to move my head at a really uncomfortable angle. Axel sees me struggle, and shifts in his seat. Dammit. He feels so far away now! Although it's better for my neck this way.

'I'm serious!' Axel says. 'You are a journalist, *oui*?'

'*Oui*,' I say, not sure where this is going.

'Then this is what you need! Real life!'

'Urm,' I say slowly. 'But what about London? Paris?'

Axel waves an arm. 'I think if you pay attention, everything you need to become the person you are supposed to be is right here …'

Everything I need to become the person I am supposed to be is right here?! Gosh. French boys are soooooo deep. No English boy would ever say anything so profound. Obviously I disagree, but still. It's like riding the bus with an ancient philosopher.

We get off the bus, and I take in Grandma and Grandad's bungalow, on this street where every house looks the same, in this boring town where we've just made everyone spend the day in a museum of black-and-white photographs, and I think, *Seriously, Axel?!* The home of overcooked eggs and lack of chocolate sandwiches? *This* will be the making of me? I think he's just being kind.

Isn't he?

Or does he understand something that I don't?

176

… Nah. He's definitely just being kind.

'Axel, *bonjour*! *Bonjour*!' Grandma says, waving at us from the doorstep. 'Taylor! *Mon amie*!'

I laugh. *Mon amie*. She's been doing her homework!

This time, there are no berets and striped T-shirts … but as we take off our shoes and drop our bags, turning the corner into the sitting room, it becomes apparent that there are … several French flags, and as we walk in Grandad hits *play* on his phone so that it blasts 'Non, je ne regrette rien' by Edith Piaf at full volume.

'What the …' I start to say, my eyes wide, before Axel bursts out into a round of applause!

'*Fantastique*!' he cries, before closing his eyes and putting his hands in the air and singing along. '*Non, rien de rien* …' he trills, and Grandad says, 'That's my boy!' and on the next bit he joins in so that they're both belting out: '*Non, je ne regrette rien! Ni le bien qu'on m'a fait!*' except Grandad's words sound a bit more like, 'Ni-le-beeeeeeen!!!!' but Axel doesn't seem to mind. In fact, it looks like he has tears in his eyes.

'My grandmother!' he tells us as Edith gets, unimaginably, even more passionate, even more theatrical. 'She loved Edith Piaf!' He kisses two fingers and holds them up to the sky, in a gesture we all understand means that she died, and he misses her.

'Oh, love,' Grandma says, pulling him in for a hug, but because Grandad already has an arm around him it ends up in a three-way cuddle, and my choice is either stand and watch this bizarre, unexpected scene unfold, or … join in?

I join in, reaching around all of them as Axel has a little cry, which makes Grandma have a little cry, which makes my bottom lip start to wobble but then the song finishes and there's a sudden silence and it's so jarring that instead of sobbing we all ring out in laughter.

'What a welcome that was!' Grandad says, wiping tears – of laughter or from something else, I'm not sure – from his eyes. 'Goodness me!'

'Come on, let's get you all a drink,' Grandma says. 'Axel – cuppa tea? Coffee?'

Axel rubs his palms together. 'Can I make a *cuppa tea* with you? In the real English way?'

Grandma points to the kitchen and says, '*Absolument, mon chéri!*' and then giggles, proud of herself. She's speaking French, but with a thick English accent. I wonder if that's how I sound when I try, too … I hope not!

They busy themselves in the kitchen, and I settle down on the sofa next to Grandad's chair.

'How's it all going, then?' he says, tipping his head towards the laughter in the kitchen, where, whatever Grandma and Axel are doing, they're having a laugh at the same time.

'Yeah, cool,' I say. 'He reckons he really likes Crickleton.'

'You say that like you're surprised!' Grandad says.

'Well, it's no Champs-Élysées, is it?'

Grandad tuts. 'Doesn't have to be,' he says. 'It's good enough here to have tempted your mother back after all those years she was away ... don't write it all off just yet! It's a nice community you're a part of here.'

'Yeah,' I say, sort of seeing his point. I guess. Maybe. 'You're right.'

'Of course I am,' he says with a smirk. 'And your fancy man? How's all that playing out?'

I freeze for a moment, because WHAT! Grandad can tell I fancy Axel?! God, that is sooooo embarrassing! I try to think fast, to say something that could throw him off the scent. We're close, me and Grandad, but not *talk-about-your-love-life* close.

'You know,' he says, waving his hand, 'your boy off the bus last week.'

'Oh!' I say, suddenly relieved. 'Tommy!'

'If that's his name,' Grandad smiles. 'Is he treating you well? Gosh, when we were young and I was courting your grandma, I really had to learn to stand out from the crowd! Hordes of fellas after her, there was. Hordes!'

Grandad loves to talk about how Grandma was the belle of the ball, the one everyone was after. He's so proud that she chose him, out of all the men she could have had. It's really cute.

'And all these years later,' I grin, 'it's you I get as my grandad.'

'Exactly,' he grins back. 'Gosh though. There was this one fella. Tall. Handsome. Sporty. Hopelessly in love with her, he was. He was a catch, by all accounts. But he was flashy. He could do the big romantic gestures but he couldn't just sit, you know? And that's what love is, really – me and your grandma could be sitting in an empty room and still have the time of our lives. I used to love spending time with her, even just going to the shops. Still feel that way.'

There's more laughter from the kitchen. I can hear the faint beats of some French rap music – I think Axel is teaching Grandma French swear words?! Grandad notices too, and shakes his head fondly, like, *Ah yes, my wife is learning French profanity from some hip-hop music, of course she is.*

'You really love her, don't you?' I say, noticing his expression.

'I really do,' he says. 'Who wouldn't?'

'So what happened to the flashy guy? You've never told me about him before …'

'Well,' Grandad says. 'That's because nothing happened! But I played the long game. I became her friend. Slow and steady, we got to know each other, and over time it meant all the fools just faded away. That's what wins the race. Friendship. And that's what keeps love going, too. That's what I reckon, anyway. The thoughts of an old fart.'

'A funny old fart though,' I counter, and he smiles.

'Oh well,' he chuckles. 'As long as I'm funny.'

Grandma and Axel bustle through from the kitchen, both carrying mugs of tea, and Grandma says, 'Poor boy, he's tried his best here but he's still got a way to go before they'll meet my standard!'

Axel offers me a cup and I take it gratefully. I actually like it weak and milky, but I can tell by the looks on Grandma's and Grandad's faces that they're only drinking theirs to be polite.

'Oh, David,' Grandma says. 'Axel was admiring your begonias!'

Axel slurps his tea noisily, also looking unimpressed with his handiwork, and then nods. 'You have a very beautiful garden,' he says, and Grandad takes the opportunity to put his awful cup of tea down and take Axel into the garden.

'You're done for now, lad,' he says, as Axel takes his lead and follows. 'Don't get an old man on about his garden!'

I watch them through the sliding glass door that looks out over the patio, noting how kind Axel is to Grandad – and how kind Grandad is to Axel. I can't believe he was asking after Tommy, though. We're going to have set up some boundaries around all that talk! My love life needs to be off limits.

Although … hmmmm.

Tommy.

Grandad said it drove him mad that other boys were interested in Grandma back in the day. *Perhaps* … maaaaaaaybe … is it possible? What if Axel needs a little shot of jealousy to realise that he needs to act on whatever is happening between us?!

Grandad is a GENIUS!

Since Tommy keeps chatting to me, even if he is a bit immature sometimes, what if I ramp it up a bit with him, and then Axel will realise he needs to swoop in and shoot his shot!

Grandma goes to make a start on tea, and so I pick up my phone and text Tommy: *Hey.*

He texts back right away (!!): *Hey!*

Bingo.

What u up 2? I say.

Tommy tells me nothing much, just hanging out. I tell him, *cool*, and that I can't wait for the party. *Same!* he replies, and I send back a love heart emoji! It makes me feel really bold!

When Axel comes back in, I say, 'I'm just texting Tommy.' I wait to see his reaction.

'Oh,' he says, with his French shrug.

Hmmm. I was expecting a bit more.

But then, when we eat our tea, Axel keeps smiling at me loads, and on the way home we walk arm in arm again, and I don't think it's my imagination that he's clinging a bit tighter. It makes me feel confident enough that as we say goodnight, before bed, I lean up on my tippy-toes and kiss his cheek. And Axel looks thrilled about it! He flushes pink, and puts his hand to the spot I've kissed with a smile.

'*Bonne nuit,*' he says, leaning in to kiss my cheek, too.

I could die! As I close the bedroom door I flop down on my bed, and it feels like cloud nine.

Axel kissed my cheek! Ahhhhhhhhhh!

It's not a real first kiss, but it's something! All the blood is pulsing around my body and I feel like I could run around the town twenty times and still have energy! It's such a fun, thrilling feeling! My heart is beating so so so so fast. I mean, god, if this is what a kiss on the cheek feels like, imagine what a real kiss will do to me!

OMG!!!!!!!

OK. I am so pumped that I have to do something with this energy. I think about how I still haven't done the piece for Ms K, for the competition, and so sit at the computer and just let myself write. I find myself typing at the top of the blank page: *Moving Mountains.*

Moving Mountains

He sees me. It came as a surprise.

Kindred spirits, he and I.

I like my laughter more now.

To make him smile is to win gold.

And silver.

And bronze.

He believes in me, and it makes me strong.

He knows what I can do.

I didn't know that's what I was waiting for.

But all along it was you.

I'm not saying it's, like, a *love poem for Axel*, but yeah. I guess he just really inspired me! I reread it, decide that it's perfect as it is, and then I load up my email to send it to Ms K, along with the column Duncan told her about, the one about Year 9 being the best year of your life. And then, just because I can, I add the column I wrote called 'You Don't Have to Go into STEM!'

I hope Ms K thinks it's OK to send her so much, but I'm just suddenly feeling like I should go for it, you know?

I hit *send*, and feel a flutter in my chest that I'm learning goes hand in hand with sharing what I write. It's like a mix of being proud and feeling scared the person who sees it will hate it and tell me I'm a joke. Is that weird? That I can feel both things?

Well, never mind. It's sent now!

I slide under my duvet and flip out my bedroom light. I'm so pleased with how today has gone I fall asleep with a massive smile on my face, like a cat who has just found all the cream. And inevitably, I fall into lovely, lovely dreams about how it will feel to finally be kissed …

The thing is, in my dream I can't tell who I'm kissed by. It's a boy with no face! And I can't quite decide who I think it should have been … Huh. Weird!

14

I wake up to a reminder on a Post-it note by my bed that I wrote to myself. It says, *Ask the girls how the BBQ was!* It's my way of checking in, of making them know I haven't forgotten them and I can still be a good friend even whilst pursuing my first kiss. It's been lingering on my mind that Lucy commented on it, as if she'd only just found out my plan and didn't know this was what I wanted all along. Add that to the joke they made about me only hanging out with them until I got a boyfriend, and I just want to make sure I don't stop being a good friend because of first-kiss fever! Because a girl can have it all! Also, I don't want to start being left out. I already feel like I missed out on the face masks, the posh cafe, the BBQ and anything else they've done with their French exchange partners, so I want to stop that happening even more. Can you imagine if after the exchange we suddenly weren't best friends any more because they'd forgotten about me? Nightmare scenario!

I'll text them later, though – because I am indeed chasing that kiss, and today is the first day of Operation: Make Axel Jealous!

Wait. No. That sounds meaner than it is. It's more like ...

Operation: Make Axel Aware I'm a Catch!

Or ...

Operation: Make Axel Want Me!

Or ...

Operation: Friends to Lovers!

Axel has said friendship is important, and Grandad has said friendship is important, and I think everyone can agree Axel and I have become firm friends ... Well. Now it's time to be brave and take the next step. Here I come!

In a bid to avoid *Toy Story*–gate like the other day, I'm up early to take an extra-long shower and straighten my hair and put on some clear mascara and lip balm. By the time Axel comes down to breakfast, in his usual all-black outfit and pouty gorgeous smile, I'm already at the breakfast table, sipping black coffee (disgusting, but chic). I am also pretending to read a newspaper from the weekend, as if *oh! You just happened to find me being fabulous! Excuse me, Axel!* Pahahahaha.

Axel grabs a Sunday supplement and flicks through it as he eats a croissant, and I keep pretending to be interested in *The UK's Top 15 Coolest Towns to Live in Now!* whilst actually just sneaking looks at Axel and trying (and failing) to come up with amusing things to say. It's harder than you'd think. I could try and say something funny about Crewe or the Norfolk coast, but I think it would be lost on him. Ditto if I try to be witty about something topical in the news, on account of me not really following the news. Does he? Hmmmm. Must investigate. He *is* very clever. Axel looks up at me and catches me staring. I give a little smile and get back to my 'reading'. At least I look quite cute today.

'Shall we …?' Axel says, as he finishes his coffee. Ooooh! It's my favourite time of day already: the walk to school, where I get to hold his arm. Squee! It's even better than holding hands, if you ask me. It's more mature. I can tell by the way even Tommy Tsao looks at us when we pass that everyone thinks so.

'Morning, Tommy!' I say, remembering that I'm supposed to remind Axel that there are plenty of other fish in my sea by being as flirtatious as I dare with other boys. 'Y'alright?'

(I thought *Y'alright*, like 'you all right?' but as all one word, was cooler than saying, like, *And how are you this fine morning, sir?* Do you know what I mean?)

(Am I overthinking this?)

(I don't reckon I am …)

'Morning, Tay,' Tommy says, and I have to admit that it feels really good to not only have the confidence to talk to a Year 10 first, rather than just responding when they deign to speak to me (!!), but also I'd be lying if I said I didn't notice Tommy's crooked smile. His eyes light up when I wave at him, and he falls into step with us to say, 'Hey, I was thinking – save me a seat at lunch?'

'OK,' I say, getting that increasingly familiar feeling in my stomach, that roller-coaster-meets-throwing-up feeling. Everyone knows who Tommy is, and half the school fancy him – when he talks directly to me it makes me feel special and chosen, but also a bit … scared?

As we head off to registration Axel says, 'So we eat with the puppy today?'

I playfully slap his arm. 'Stop!' I say, my voice all high-pitched and girly. 'He's not so bad. I like him. He's funny.'

'Hmmm,' replies Axel, and I feel guilty to be playing two boys off each other this way, but I can tell by the way Axel crinkles his eyebrows that I've planted the seed of competition for him. Like yeah, dude, make your move before I get snapped up! 'Not as funny as you,' Axel concludes, and I roll my eyes playfully whilst secretly feeling over the moon at the compliment. Axel thinks I'm funny!!!!

'Funny-looking,' I joke, but Axel doesn't get it.

'*Non*,' he says, suddenly serious. 'Taylor, you are beautiful!'

His seriousness nearly knocks the wind out of me.

'Oh,' I say, pulling a face. I try to add a qualifier to that, to say something else that's smarter or more gracious. 'Oh,' I say again. It's all I'm capable of.

I'm beautiful? Nobody not related to me has ever said that before! Mum and Grandad and Grandma say it, but they are contractually obliged to, aren't they!

AXEL ISN'T!

AXEL JUST CALLED ME BEAUTIFUL!!!!!!!!!!

Be right back, just gonna go die of happiness!!!!!!

Despite thinking *I'm* the beautiful one, Axel spends all of our maths lesson with Mrs Bates doing line drawings of Pierre in his notebook again. He sees me notice, but doesn't try to hide them or anything like he did last time – I guess because Pierre isn't here. I'm a more objective eye, what with it *not* being of me, and so I give him an encouraging smile and thumbs up in between algebraic equations. I still can't help but wonder why he isn't drawing *me* though. Maybe he draws Pierre when he's with me, and me when he's with Pierre? For privacy?

Yeah. I'll bet that's it.

Anyway, the morning passes in a blur and before I know it we're sitting with Duncan and Pierre in the cafeteria, eating jacket potatoes with too much tuna and not enough cheese. Duncan got his with beans, and Axel has dared Pierre to try them, but he won't.

'Baked beans!' Duncan says, like he can't believe they've never had them. 'They're just … beans … in tomato sauce. You have them with jacket potatoes, or with toast … No?'

Axel shakes his head, visibly upset.

'*Non*,' he says. 'These beans, I do not understand.'

Axel has got many, many things going for him, but I have to say, not liking beans is a bit of a strike against him. Who doesn't like beans?!

'Tay!' a voice comes. I look up. It's Tommy, with his partner whose name I can't remember. He's very shy seeming, and sort of hangs back, but as Tommy slips into the seat next to me, he goes to Axel's other side and says hello in French.

'Good afternoon!' I say, suddenly thinking: *How the heck do I flirt?* I've forgotten! What kind of a teenager says *good afternoon* to somebody who isn't a prime minister? If Lucy and Star came and sat with me at lunch, I don't think we'd even say hello, or ask about one another's mornings. One of us would just launch into a story, without being asked, and that's just normal for us. Ooooooh, speaking of Lucy and Star, I must send that text about how their BBQ was. I still haven't done it! I will!

'Had double PE, so a wicked morning!' Tommy says, already shovelling food into his mouth. I glance down. He's got *two* jacket potatoes, one with beans and one with chilli con carne and cheese. 'Mr Peter's is such a legend. We had to do the beep test, you know, where you have to run to the line before the beep goes off? And the beep gets faster and faster?'

'Yeah,' I say. 'We did that at the end of summer term last year. Penelope Richards and Desiree Sanders both threw up.'

'Same today! But it was me! I did it though, I beat everyone. I've never sweated so much in my life!'

'You threw up?!' I say, because surely that's not what he's saying.

'Yeah!' Tommy says, throwing down his knife so he can use a fist to pump on his chest.

'Champion!'

'I don't know if I'm impressed or disgusted,' I say, and that's the honest truth.

'Oh,' Tommy says, pausing to give me that lopsided smile of his. 'You're impressed.

You're *so* impressed.'

'Thank goodness you're here to let me know,' I say, acting like I'm sooooo unmoved by his confidence, when actually my heart feels like it could beat out of my chest. Playing it cool takes a lot of work!

'Taylor Blake,' Tommy says, lowering his voice and leaning into me. It makes me do a sharp inhale of breath in shock – like, it takes a second for my brain to catch up to itself, but honestly, for a split second then he was coming so close I thought his lips might touch mine! Imagine if that happened, right in the middle of the cafeteria at lunch!! 'I'm always here to keep you on track.'

I'm so relieved to *not* have been kissed right here in the lunch hall (I mean, it's not ideal, is it?!) and what Tommy has said is so funny that I burst out into genuine laughter.

'You're an idiot!' I say, shaking my head, but giggly and cute, being a bit loud and hamming it up. It occurs to me that I should bat my eyelashes – that this is a thing people do, right? I mean, Lucy does it from under her fringe, and it always means getting out of trouble at school or getting extra cream on her decaf iced latte. So. Away I go, twittering at Tommy's little silly sayings and blinking more than I otherwise would in order to appear pretty and … whatever it is batted eyelashes achieve. A nice breeze?

Oh shoot. I've drifted off into my world and now Tommy is talking to a pal on the other table, and Axel seems enthralled by Pierre. I look around me. Duncan is a few seats down, a look of concern on his face.

'Are you OK?' he whispers behind Tommy's back as he leans forward to fist-bump yet another friend. The boy knows everybody! 'Have you got something in your eye?'

'No!' I whisper back, still behind Tommy's back. 'Duncan! Urgh!'

'What?!' Duncan hisses, but then Tommy is done with his legions of fans and sits back down properly, meaning order is restored before I have to spell out the concept of flirting to Duncan Higginbottom.

'So,' I say, scrabbling for something juicy to talk about. I see Madame Jones walking very fast from the selection of jelly and dry cake on sale today, towards the door, where Monsieur Toussaint is waiting for her. Monsieur Brown quickly follows, with his head down, like he doesn't want to be seen.

... I know what I should talk about!

'So, you'll never guess who Duncan and I walked in on having ... *relations*,' I say, in my best 'I have such gossip!' voice.

'Go on,' Tommy says. Then he lowers his voice. 'Wait – was it those two?' he says, using his thumb to point at Axel and Pierre.

'What?' I say. 'No, why would it have been Axel and Pierre?' Before he can answer I say, 'It was Madame Jones and Monsieur Brown!'

'No!' he says, acting grossed out.

'Seriously!' I squeal, and I'm probably being a liiiiiittle bit OTT because Lucy looks over from her table and pulls a weird face as if to say, *Have you lost the plot?!* It's not very supportive, really, and if she weren't so busy with all those face masks and BBQs, maybe I could let her in on Operation: Seduce Axel by Making Him Realise He Needs to Get a Move on Before Another Boy Snaffles Me Up!

(I'm still workshopping that, obviously.)

'Excuse us,' Axel says, standing up with his tray of food he has barely even touched. 'We are going for …' He waves a hand, and I nod.

'A walk?' I offer. 'OK.' Dammit. He's supposed to be *here* to bear witness to this flirting! At least he's got a taste of it, anyway. I add, 'See you at afternoon registration?'

'*Oui*,' Axel says, and then it's just me, Duncan and Tommy left, as his partner scurries after the boys too.

Duncan has barely spoken, and I'm suddenly really aware that he's watching me and Tommy like we're a tennis match: I talk, his gaze turns to me, Tommy talks, his gaze goes to Tommy. I kind of want to involve him in the chat, but I don't know what to say.

'Hey,' Duncan says, as Tommy fist bumps another Year 10 in hockey gear. 'You reading anything good right now?'

'Urm, yeah …' I say. I kind of don't want to admit to reading romance to him, though. I feel like Duncan probably reads philosophy, or something really highbrow and clever.

(Ooooooh! That would be a good column actually! *Why Do We Think Romance Is Less Intellectual than Other Genres? Any Reading Is Good!*)

'I'm reading *The Fault in Our Stars*,' he offers. 'Have you read it? It's so good!'

'Oh!' I say, and I don't know why I'm surprised. *Of course* Duncan reads John Green! 'I love that book! I've read it, like, six times!'

'Seriously?' Duncan asks. 'Don't tell me what happens. I'm just at the bit where they've met Van Houten in Amsterdam … I just don't understand how a book about dying teenagers can be so funny? It literally makes me laugh out loud!'

'Same,' I smile.

'Well, I'll let you know what I think tomorrow because I've got about a hundred pages left. I should finish it tonight …'

'You're fast,' I comment.

'Yeah, I could spend all day every day reading, to be fair,' he says. 'I love it!'

'Reading?' Tommy says. I didn't realise he was listening, but his friend has moved on to another table now. 'Like, for fun? Don't you have a life?'

'Hey!' I say, swatting his arm. 'I have a life, *and* I read a novel a week! Sometimes two!'

Tommy arches an eyebrow. 'Yeah, well,' he says. 'You're different.'

I pull a face. 'That doesn't sound good …' I say.

'No!' Tommy insists. 'It is! I actually wondered if you … well. If you fancied, like, going out one day? To the cinema?'

'Oh!' I say, taken aback. I have two thoughts at the exact same time: WHY ISN'T AXEL HERE TO SEE THIS! And also, well, at least I can tell Axel about this, which is almost as good.

'Yeah,' I say. 'OK.'

'Cool,' Tommy says, with a nod.

'Cool,' I echo, and then there's a pause that lasts a thousand years.

'Cool,' Duncan says, under his breath, taking the mick – but before I can shoot him a dirty look the bell goes, and Tommy dashes off.

'I'll text you, yeah?' he asks, halfway to the door, and I say, 'Yeah, OK,' still trying to work out how to sound both effortless and interested. *How to Be Parisian When You're Not from Paris* doesn't have a chapter on that.

I'm still mulling that over as I watch him go.

And then it hits me.

I've just agreed to a date. A date! With a boy!!

'I've never been on a date before,' I say, mostly to myself, but as Duncan happens to be there he replies, 'No, me neither.'

Then he says, 'Actually, Taylor, I was going to ask if you wanted to go to the cinema with *me* …'

I look at him. I sense a solution to my problem here – the problem being, of course, that everyone wants to go to the cinema except the one boy I actually really *want* to go on a date with. Axel.

'Why don't we all go?' I suggest brightly, thinking all I have to do is get a group of us together, and then engineer sitting next to Axel. 'It could be a fun group thing, couldn't it?'

'Oh,' Duncan says, standing up. 'A group thing. Yeah. I didn't think of that.'

My brain starts working in overtime now. The cinema in town is normally fully booked because it's really small, but if we can get in it would be PERFECT because they have all these battered old sofas and that means Axel and I could snuggle up on one together. Tommy is a hero and he doesn't even know it!

As Duncan and I leave lunch, we walk past Madame Jones and Monsieur Toussaint by the theatre block, having an argument of some sort. The French teacher is jabbing his finger in her face.

'*Non!*' he says, in this strong, angry, *passionate* voice. '*Non, non, non!*'

He stands quite close to her, and we both freeze to watch the scene unfold. I can't tell if we should say something, because a) they're teachers and it's none of our business, and b) it looks like he's going to cry, like Madame Jones has upset him?

'Should we do something?' I whisper, and Duncan whispers back, 'Probably?'

But then Monsieur Brown appears, striding across the quad and coming up very close to Monsieur Toussaint, like he's squaring up to him! For a fight! In geography we once watched a video about peacocks, how they rile up all their feathers to attract a mate, and that's what this reminds me of: Monsieur Brown has ruffled all his feathers, and with all his tail on show he's shouting, in a very unconvincing accent, 'That's ENOUGH! *S'IL VOUS PLAÎT!*'

Madame Jones looks *mortified* when she clocks that we've seen, making us immediately unfreeze and make a break for it to the other side of the theatre studio, half laughing and half holding our breath to make sure we don't get in trouble. And who do we run into but Ms K!

'Whoa!' she says, holding up her hands in surrender.

'Sorry, miss!' Duncan and I say in unison. I look at him right as he looks at me, because it's a shock we've spoken in perfect harmony. He pulls a face.

'Jinx,' I say, right as he does.

'Jinx again!' we say, and then everyone laughs because it's no good, apparently we're just going to keep saying the same thing at the same time for ever and ever.

'Peas in a pod,' Ms K says, smiling. I shrug, like, *What can you do, huh?*

'Well,' she presses, 'whilst I'm *literally* running into you—'

'I think we ran into you, miss,' Duncan offers, and she nods.

'I think you did too, Duncan,' she says. 'But let me take the opportunity regardless to say: Taylor, that work you sent me is excellent! Thank you for that!'

I feel myself blush, and don't really know what to say.

'The columns need an edit, but once we've chatted about that I'll get them in this week's *Register*, and then the next in a few issues' time, if that's OK with you?'

Before I can say YES, OF COURSE IT IS!! she presses: 'And your competition submission is excellent. Really … thoughtful. So all in, my favourite email of the day!'

She trots off with a flourish, and Duncan looks at me with a big, wide, open friendly face – and, it has to be said, an impressed face, too.

'Whoa,' he says. 'Congratulations!'

He opens his arms and I let out a little squeal and fling myself at him in excitement. Two columns to be published! That came from MY BRAIN!! Duncan catches my weight and then spins me around so that my feet are off the floor.

'Argh!' I say, getting dizzy, but it's funny, and I'm laughing, and Duncan is laughing too. We quickly stop, though, when some horrid Year 10s pass by.

'Get a room!' one says as he passes.

His friend joins in: 'Yeah, dude! You're drooling!'

They look at Duncan as they say it, and he goes bright red and looks at the floor. But I refuse to let them ruin our moment!

'Screw you!' I say to their backs, and hold on to Duncan's arm in a show of solidarity. He gives me a weak smile, but I can tell it has embarrassed him.

What I can't figure out, though, is why somebody suggesting Duncan and I are romantic makes me feel embarrassed, too.

He's just my friend! Ewwww!

15

Members Only

Me: *I need my friends!*

Lucy: *I'm here. What's wrong?*

Me: *I need kissing advice*

Lucy: *Of course you do ... you're obsessed*

Me: *THIS IS NOT NEWS!*

Star: *Sorry, was just finishing fencing practice. What's wrong Taylor?*

Me: *Can we do Starbucks tomorrow? PLEASE! I need to make Axel realise I'm the girl of his dreams! It's T-minus one day until the party!*

Star: *What does T-minus even mean anyway? What does the 'T' stand for?*

Me: *I think you're getting distracted ...*

Star: *Sorry. Starbucks. To talk about the party. OK!*

Lucy: *Me and Amelie are soooo excited for it. It will be fun!*

Me: *If I get kissed it will! See you tomorrow morning to plan!*

Me: *I know you're busy with your Frenchies, but I need ya*

Lucy: *It's OK, they know the way to school*

Me: *It's just, in times of need, who ya gonna call?*

Me: *NOT GHOSTBUSTERS!*

ME: *MEMBERS ONLY!!!*

Star: ☺

Me: *Drinks on me!*

Me: *Well, Mum!! xxxxxx*

I'm desperate to sound out this whole Operation: Make Axel Realise I'm the Woman of His Dreams (still workshopping). So here we are with our usual order: strawberry cream Frappuccino for Star, a decaf iced latte for Lucy and a mango and passionfruit Frappuccino for me. I nearly went rogue and plumped for a black Americano, but then I remembered

Axel isn't here so I don't have to impress anyone and I can drink what I like.

'I don't know what it stands for, actually,' I tell Star, who once again has brought up what 'T-minus' means. 'Maybe it's …'

'Take-off!' squeals Lucy, suddenly, pleased as punch she knows.

'Ahhh.' I nod. 'Yeah. Astronauts say it, don't they? God. It's so strange – so few people *are* astronauts but we *all* say loads of stuff they do. They've had more of an impact on the English language than Shakespeare!'

'Do *not* say that man's name in my presence,' says Star with a shudder. She adores English class – we all do – but *Macbeth* was not her vibe. 'I'm still scarred from last year's—'

'SOLILOQUY!' Lucy and I both shout at the same time, making the barista behind the counter turn and frown. I pull a face that I hope she knows means *sorry!*

'Soliloquy!' mimics Star, cringing. 'Mrs Hawthorn and her *Macbeth* soliloquies. I don't think I will ever recover.'

'She did say that word *a lot*,' I acknowledge.

'Yeah, but always with the hair flick!' says Star, full of outrage. 'All of it: that play, that hair flick, all of it!'

'I don't think we do any more Shake— Sorry, *that man's* stuff, if it's any consolation,' Lucy offers, rubbing Star's arm.

'It isn't,' Star whispers, hamming it up. 'I'm scarred for life.'

Lucy and I look at her, all full of pretend and over the top sympathy. I mean, it *is* fair enough, really: Mrs Hawthorn's English class last year felt like it went on for a century. Everyone tells you Shakespeare is boring, but I'd promised Mum I'd give him a chance and then … Mrs Hawthorn managed to make it worse than any of us feared. Mum got me *Macbeth: The Emoji Version*, which was quite entertaining, but when I tried to tell Mrs Hawthorn about it she told me she's a Bard purist and such lowering of intellectual standards are why she's ready to retire from the teaching profession and work for her brother-in-law's wine company.

'Wait,' Star says, changing the subject. 'I don't say anything else that astronauts say.' She looks between Lucy and me. 'Do I?'

'Houston, we have a problem,' I say.

'One small step for man, one giant leap for mankind …' Lucy says, putting on a funny voice.

'OK, I don't drop either of those into casual conversation,' Star says, slurping her Frappuccino. 'But fine. Point taken. Kind of.'

'Write it on the balance sheet!' I joke. 'In the transcript of this conversation, make sure it is noted that Star Bishop gave in and said we were right!'

Lucy pretends to type the information into her phone.

'Star … Bishop …' she mutters, wriggling her thumbs

and sticking out her tongue in faux concentration. 'Said ... we ... were ... *right* ...'

'All right, all right,' laughs Star. 'You pair of losers. Come on. We don't have long – what was so desperate to talk about, Taylor, that I had to get up forty-five minutes earlier this morning *thankyouverymuch*?'

'Yes, right. OK. On to business. Well,' I say, lacing my hands together in front of me like I'm about to pitch them for half a million pounds' worth of investment in my toilet brush company. 'The party is tomorrow, like we've said, and so this is it, I think. I think it will be my big first kiss. Things are going so well with Axel, and we're getting closer, and I just ... I feel it in my bones! It *has* to happen. It has to!'

I pull a funny face, an excited one, and expect the girls to do the same – except they don't. I swear Lucy and Star exchange A Look. You know when you know somebody has been talking about you? That they Have Thoughts and Opinions that they haven't told you yet? It's one those Looks.

'What?' I say.

'No, no,' Star smiles. 'Nothing. We know this means a lot to you.'

'Yeah,' I say. 'It does! And I haven't told you this bit yet, but I've been flirting with Tommy Tsao a bit, not to make Axel *jealous* exactly, but, you know ...'

Star frowns. 'That's not very nice for Tommy. If you're flirting with him and you don't mean it?'

'Yeah,' says Lucy. 'I'm Team Taylor, no matter what, but we actually thought you might really fancy him. You were laughing loads at his jokes at lunch yesterday, and he's always coming over to talk to you. He's a Year 10, he goes to our school … he *obviously* fancies you …'

Lucy has been impressed by Tommy ever since that day after the Co-op when she saw him smile at me and got all amazed.

'Urm,' I say, feeling defensive. On some level I know flirting with Tommy to get Axel's attention isn't the *kindest* thing I could possibly do, but it's not like I'm snogging him and asking him to take me to end-of-year prom whilst secretly trying to get with Axel. It's a grey area. 'I mean, I never said I fancied him back – if he even does fancy me, which we don't know that he does. I said from the start I like Axel. And I think Axel likes me too! We have these cute little chats, and the other day he even came into my room. He's kissed my cheek, too! I think he's building up to it. He always wants me to walk around holding his arm, by the way – have you seen that?'

'Yeah,' says Star. 'But what about Pierre?'

'No,' I say, wondering where she's got that from. 'I don't fancy Pierre! Oh. Also! I suppose yesterday Tommy did invite me to the cinema, but then it became a big group thing, if you want to come too.'

'Maybe,' says Lucy slowly.

'Yeah,' says Star. 'Maybe.'

I look at them both.

'And as for tomorrow,' I say, assuming that any moment now they're going to get excited and enthusiastic for me, that they're just slow on the uptake this morning because it's early. 'I thought I could straighten my hair but do sort of beachy, loose curls at the end? I think you can do that with ghds, I've seen a YouTube video on it. And I was thinking eyes not lips, because if I'm going to be kissed I can't be all gloopy and lip-glossy, you know? So maybe just tinted lip balm and a bit of mascara. All the French girls do minimal make-up, don't they? I really like it. *How to Be Parisian When You're Not from Paris* says—'

'Oh!' Star says. 'Here she goes!'

'What?' I say. 'Quoting the Bible?'

She shakes her head, and she's smiling, but … something doesn't feel right.

I stop talking. I look at Star. She looks down at the table. I look at Lucy. She pushes her empty cup away from her and chews on her bottom lip. My heart grows heavy in my chest, like a weight has been slowly tied to it and it's now sinking into my stomach.

'If there's something you two need to tell me,' I say, 'you can say it.' And then, even though I don't mean it, I add: 'I won't be offended or anything.'

Lucy sighs and pushes her fringe to one side. 'Don't get cross or anything,' she starts. 'It's just …'

Her sentence loses its wind.

Star supplies: 'It's just, since the beginning of term, it's been … a lot, all this talk of kissing and boys. It's been. You know.'

I shake my head. I do *not* know.

'A bit boring,' Lucy comments, just like that. A BIT BORING! I feel like she's just reached across the table and slapped me.

Whoa.

I'm BORING?!

I think I might be sick. What she's saying makes me feel light-headed.

'You've not even asked how we're getting on this week,' Star says. 'We've been having loads of fun with Amelie and Sophie, and they don't care about boys at all.'

I can't believe what I'm hearing.

'They've probably snogged loads of boys, that's why,' I say, and my voice is wobbling in a way I can't control. 'God. I can't believe this! You have no idea what it's like to be me, do you? All … *un-kissed*, with nobody to talk to about it!'

'We'll always listen to you, you know that!' says Star, in her kind and sensible way.

'Yeah!' agrees Lucy, but her features are neutral, not quite matching up to the strained tone of her voice. 'The Three Musketeers, Tay and two queers!'

I feel all strange, all embarrassed and ashamed. And because I feel that way, I don't want to hear them be kind now, or try and take back what they've just said. They obviously mean it! So. I want to be mad! Mad at myself, mad at them, mad at everyone! Have I really been that awful? Am I a horrible, ugly shell of a person with nothing to offer the world? Worthless? Are they trying to find ways to friend-dump me, like Horrid Anna did to her best friend in Year 8 and now they're school enemies? I hate that I'm questioning myself so much; it doesn't feel nice. At the end of the day my 'friends' should be supporting me and the things that are really important and special to me, and they're not! AND THAT DOESN'T FEEL NICE EITHER! It's all just a big mess.

'You've just told me I'm *boring*,' I say, and I hate how my voice wobbles. I try to take a breath. 'I need to go,' I mumble, and I can't think of an excuse why, and they don't ask. I just need to get out of there, because tears are burning my eyes and I don't want to cry in front of my friends. Well. 'Friends'. Do they even like me? It doesn't feel like they do. I'm the girl who never gets kissed, who poos in the woods, who's boring

211

and boy-obsessed, who nobody wants to be friends with. I'm a failure!

I'm vaguely aware that the walk to school is blurry, that I can't see properly, but I'm not actually crying. In fact, the mantra in my head is *don't cry yet, don't cry yet, don't cry yet*. I don't know when I *can* cry, only that I need a safe place to go. I can't believe this. I can't believe I'm going to throw a party where I hate everyone who is coming and they hate me and so might not even show up at all, which would be worse than a house full of people who don't like me. Imagine throwing a party and then the house is empty! WHAT WOULD AXEL SAY THEN!

This is awful. Horrible and awful and … and … and I'll go to Ms K's room. It will be safe there …

'Miss?' I say, knocking lightly on the door.

Ms K looks up from where she's sitting at her desk, fiddling with her computer. She seems stressed. I say that because she exhales really loudly before she spots me, and then it's like she remembers she's supposed to be approachable and I see her rearrange the features on her face with some effort.

'Taylor!' she says brightly. 'Come and save me from myself before I throw this computer out of the window, and all the Year 11 lesson plans with it!'

I creep inside, and I must look how I feel because then she says, 'What's going on?'

I try to avoid her eye contact, because the way she asks *what's going on* is really gentle, like she knows just by looking at me I'm not all right. But I don't know what to say – how to explain that I'm awful and my friends don't like me any more. I don't want Ms K to know that about me. She thinks I'm all right. I don't want her to suddenly pity me or something like that.

'Do you just want to sit for a moment?' she says. 'You can talk when you're ready?'

I nod, and slip into a front desk where I put my head on my hands and stare out of the first-floor window at the clouds.

Why me? I wish somebody had warned me that I'm so awful, so I could do something about it before even more people found out. I can't believe Lucy and Star have been talking about me! I feel so ganged up on!

I sigh deeply and keep watching the clouds. They float and float and float.

Eventually, I sit up properly, and Ms K stops what she's doing because she can tell I'm ready to talk. And I tell her everything. It's such a relief, actually. Once I start talking, I just can't stop! I tell her I still haven't kissed anyone, and I'm sure Axel likes me, and that Lucy and Star say I'm boring and that I'm just so hungry for *life*, you know? Hungry to live and have big loves and big kisses and big adventures, and if talking about that makes me boring to be around maybe I just won't ever have any friends, because I can't pretend this hunger isn't there! I can't!

'You don't have to pretend,' Ms K says. 'I see that hunger, Taylor, and I hope that you nurture it and it grows even wilder. You deserve all of those things. You deserve a life as big as you can imagine.'

'Thanks, miss,' I say.

'And you deserve to be kissed. Whenever the time is right, it will happen. And if you think you're the last person in the world to be kissed, just remember I didn't get my first kiss until I was seventeen.'

'Really?' I say, eyes wide. I can't imagine that. Ms K is pretty, for a teacher, and a few of the boys in class say she's fit.

'Really,' she says. 'And I'll tell you something else,' she adds. 'It was worth the wait.'

I give her some semblance of a smile.

'OK,' I say. 'Message received.'

She gives me a silly thumbs up and says, 'If it's not Axel, Taylor, I'm sure there are plenty of Crickleton boys who'd be up to the job, you know. You'll be fine. Kid, you'll move mountains!'

'You sound like Duncan,' I say. Ms K gives me a puzzled look. 'The Dr Seuss books, yeah? It's his favourite. In fact, huh!' I suddenly realise something. 'I called my competition poem "Moving Mountains" right after he told me about that book. I didn't realise!'

Ms K smiles, all soft around the eyes, a bit like Mum does when she's being sappy.

'Makes sense,' she says, almost to herself.

'What does?' I ask.

She shakes her head, like she's trying to get rid of a thought. 'He's a good boy, is Duncan,' she says. 'That's all I mean. It makes sense he'd tell you about that book.'

'Yeah,' I say, thinking, *Well actually, maybe I do have one friend left.*

'So you're feeling better?' she asks.

I nod.

'I think so,' I say. 'Yes.'

'Good,' Ms K says. 'Because I've got lower sixth waiting to come in for form time and you're holding everybody up.'

I laugh.

'Cheers, miss,' I say. 'You really know how to make a girl feel welcome!'

She winks at me. 'Get to registration,' she says. 'And don't you dare tell your form teacher you're late because of me!'

At lunch, I meet back up with Axel, who has been busy with the other Frenchies and their teacher all morning.

'Taylor!' he says in his glorious accent, kissing both of my cheeks. He's grinning! It's like he really is pleased to see me! Gosh, at least somebody is! 'I have had an idea. Can we escape the school food for lunch and go to the cafe?'

'Just you and me?' I say.

'Yes,' he grins. 'I cannot do this school food any more. I will buy us real food! Edible food, *non*?! No beans!'

I laugh.

'We'll be in trouble if we get caught,' I say, but to be honest eating lunch in the same school hall as the girls makes me feel queasy, so it's worth the risk to me.

'YOLO,' Axel says, holding up his hands like, *Am I right?!*

'YOLO,' I agree, and we slip out of the front gates when nobody is looking, arm in arm, off to a lunch date for two.

Crazy, isn't it? How the worst morning ever can give way to the best lunch ever? Everything can turn, just like that. One minute your friends have dumped you and you're crying your heart out, and the next you're being whisked off by a French boy who is so handsome it's entirely possible to get lost in his dimples!!

16

*P*ARTY DAY!!

Although. I'm ignoring Star and Lucy, because I'm afraid they are ignoring me. The only person who has messaged lately is Tommy, who says he can't wait for tonight. Since yesterday I've gone from upset to really angry that they think I'm boring and boy-obsessed. I was there for Lucy when she did nothing but talk about her budding crush on Star back when all that was happening! And Star went on and on about her parents' divorce, long after it happened, but I knew the best thing was to let her talk about it. We all get stuck on certain things, and a bit boring about them! That's what friendship is, listening to your pals talk about how they feel! You can't 'use up' talking-about-feelings time! It should be endless!!!

!!!!!!!!!!!!!!!!!

(THAT is how frustrated and angry and cross I feel!!)

So.

Yeah, I'm mad, but … I also hope that they still come to the party. And that they say sorry. And if they do, I'll forgive them, but only if they say they didn't mean it.

If they say sorry, I'll say sorry. That's what I've decided.

I really hate fighting. Knowing things aren't OK with us all is like walking around under a black cloud that threatens to rain at any moment. Like, you can get on with your life, but you're aware you could get soaked, aka could cry about it all, at any moment.

Anyhoo …

Axel has been with Pierre all day, so I'm feeling a bit insecure about getting that kiss tonight at the party, too. But I will say, me and Axel had *such* a nice lunch yesterday, and didn't even get caught being off premises! We ate pasta at the cafe with the wrought iron chairs, sat outside in the sun, and Axel told me about his family back home and how he wants to work in animation one day for somewhere like Pixar. We talked about books and films and TV – everything! I even asked him where Seoul is, because I forgot to google it. It's South Korea! So he's teaching me loads, too. I really felt like I had his undivided attention, and it was sooooo easy to chat with him. I almost forgot he's a boy I have a crush on! We were just friends, like Duncan and I are – Axel reminds me of him, how he asks questions and listens to the answers and then tells you what he thinks. And being friendly and chatty with him even made me forget about Star and Lucy for a bit.

It's Duncan, though, not Axel, who has come to the shops with me, on account of the fact that I haven't heard from the girls and Axel is, like I say, with Pierre. It's nice that he's helping, especially when everyone else has abandoned me.

'Chilli flavour?' he says, as I pick up some crisps to add to the basket.

'No?' I ask, suddenly doubting myself. 'I love chilli flavour crisps!'

'Divisive,' he comments, with a wag of his finger. 'If somebody gets a handful of those and thinks they're salt and vinegar, they're going to be in for a nasty surprise.'

'Sooooo … what?' I say. 'Plain crisps only? Or should I make little signs for them, to put by the bowls?'

Duncan clicks his fingers and goes into a 'finger point'. 'You,' he says, 'Are so solutions-focussed. You should put that on your CV under special skills. *Always know the best thing to do.*'

'I don't think that's a special skill,' I say drily. 'I think it's just having a brain that works?'

'Oft!' Duncan says, clutching his heart. 'She shoots, she scores. Man down!'

He falls to his knees, right there in the supermarket, reaching up to me with wide eyes like he's a man on his dying breath. I look at him. I wait. He continues to huff and puff, until he falls to the ground and lies there flat. An old woman comes around the corner and looks down, alarmed.

'You can just step over him,' I say. 'Don't worry.'

The woman gingerly skirts around Duncan's prone body, edging sideways until she's past him and can get to the piccalilli.

'You could catch something, lying down there,' she says to Duncan, who opens one eye as she leaves, looks at me, and then bursts into peals of laughter.

I'm laughing too.

'You're such an idiot,' I say, holding out a hand to pull him up.

'Nice to know you'd have my back if I collapsed!' Duncan cries. 'Telling little old ladies to climb over me!'

'You were in her way.'

'POSSIBLY DEAD, TAYLOR! I'm sorry if that was an inconvenience to somebody's shopping experience!'

'You're an inconvenience to *my* shopping experience!' I giggle. 'Come on. Let's pay.'

We bag up the party stuff and make for the walk home. It's late afternoon and the sun is low in the sky. The roads seem quiet, and the birds are chirping from their branches in a way that makes me feel like they're trying to say, 'It's nice out, isn't it! Enjoy it! Winter will be here soon enough!'

'Look at the colour of the sky,' I say, noticing that it is purply blue, like a lavender haze. 'Isn't that pretty?'

'You're the only person I know who makes a note of what colour the sky is,' Duncan says, but he looks, and nods, like he thinks it's pretty too. 'Or no, sorry. Not a note just for yourself. You say stuff out loud to make everyone else aware of nice things, too.'

'And that's a bad thing?' I ask.

'It's a *great* thing,' he replies. 'It's why I like being around you. You don't just exist, you know? You actually *live*.'

I let the compliment hang in the air. 'That's ... actually the nicest thing anyone has said to me,' I say, once I've decided I'm really touched. 'Thanks, dude.'

'You're welcome. Dude.'

He gives me a look.

'And by the way,' he says. 'You've inspired me to write a column, you know. I'd love to show it to you. I mean, I still think I'm a behind-the-scenes man, but it would be nice to get my ideas out there as well. Like you say, it's a special feeling, writing something that makes you feel understood, and other people understand themselves too.'

'Yeah!' I say. 'Send it to me! I think about asking people to read my rough drafts all the time. I get too scared. But now I think about it – nobody has ever asked me to read *their* rough drafts, either.'

'Ms K says workshopping rough ideas not only helps the person whose idea it is, but it also helps the person helping. If that makes sense? That was a lot of saying *help* in a sentence.'

I laugh. Duncan is cool, and I'm glad we've become friends. We've been talking so much that we're nearly home already!

'It makes sense,' I say. 'Like how I once helped Lucy study for the mid-year maths test, and it ended up meaning I got top marks because it accidentally polished my skills, too.'

'Exactly!' he says. 'Yes!'

'If you keep writing, you really will have to start that magazine for us, you know, so there's somewhere to put it all ... What did you call it? *The Instruction Manual*?'

'You remember!' he says. 'Was that the first time we talked, when I said that?'

'Yeah,' I say. 'I think it was. Weird that now here you are, food shopping with me for the party!'

'Life moves in mysterious ways ...' Duncan jokes. 'Is this your house?'

I'm already walking down the drive towards the front door.

'No,' I say over my shoulder. 'I just thought it looked like a good place to grab a few lemonades out of the fridge.'

Duncan loiters on the pavement, unsure if he should follow me. I put my bag down and get out my key. Waving it at him, I say, 'Seriously? Of course it's my house, you fool!'

Duncan rolls his eyes good-naturedly. 'With you I'm never quite sure ...' he says, and I shoot back, 'Now *that* I will take as a compliment.'

We bustle through to the kitchen and Duncan helps me unpack everything, sticking stuff that needs to stay cold in the fridge and making piles of things on the side that will need putting in bowls or on plates once I'm dressed. If I put the food out too early, I'm worried the soft stuff will have gone hard and the hard stuff gone soft by the time everyone gets here. Mum says that's what happened at my sixth birthday party, and there's been a family paranoia about repeating the mistake ever since. Nobody wants soggy crisps or dry cake.

'Right,' Duncan says. 'I'll go home and get ready, then – unless you need me for anything else?'

I shake my head. 'Nope. Thanks for everything you've done, you've been a lifesaver!'

'No worries,' Duncan tells me. He holds a hand up for a high five, and I'm just about to smack my palm to his when he says, 'Smell ya later, alligator!' It makes me pause mid-air.

'That's ... not how that goes?' I say, holding my hand aloft. 'Smell ya later, OR see you later, alligator?'

'Does it matter?' he says, still coming in for the high five.

'Kind of?' I say, trying to pull my palm back, but he grabs it with reflexes faster than mine.

'Hey!' I say, giggling, and I stumble forward – or he pulls me, or I pull him … I'm not really sure. Anyway, we end up standing really close to each other, and Duncan kind of laughs, but a shocked laugh, not a ha, ha laugh, and I stop breathing, and there's *a moment* that for a beat feels … nice? I think? And then I hear my mum shout, 'Hello!! I'm home!' and I yank my hand back, and then end up breathing like I've just sprinted a hundred metres in PE, and Duncan is looking at me like I've given him an electric shock.

What.

The.

Heck.

Was.

That!!!!!!

'Oh, hi! You must be Duncan!' Mum says, coming through to the kitchen. 'I'm Erica.'

We both turn to look at her, just people being totally normal where nothing strange or noteworthy has maybe-possibly just occurred.

Nope.

All good!

Nothing to see here!

Duncan clears his throat. 'Can I call you that?' he says. 'Or shall I call you Mrs Blake?'

Mum snorts a laugh. 'Well, I'm not married, so it's *Ms Blake*, and this isn't 1956, so yes, just Erica is fine.'

Duncan looks at me.

'A lot of things suddenly make sense with you,' he says, and Mum says, 'Duncan! Cheeky! I like you already!'

I make a noise that's as close to a laugh as I can manage, and then Mum is looking through what we've bought and asking for her debit card back and musing about moving furniture for the dance space we discussed. Duncan is happily chatting along with her, and I can tell Mum likes him. He's being really quite normal. I don't think what I thought just happened actually did happen. I was imagining it.

'You OK, bug?' Mum asks, running a hand down my back. In that moment, I make a choice to just carry on with the day and be as normal as Duncan is being.

'Yes,' I say. 'I'm good! Excited! I think you're right about the sofa – it's best on the back wall, yes.'

Duncan says he'll get one end if *Erica* (it's like they're best pals already! Jeez!) gets the other, and so I make everyone a drink, even though it doesn't seem very feminist to have a boy doing all the heavy lifting whilst I mix orange cordials like a turn-of-the-century wife. If they even had cordial then? Hmmmm. I wonder when cordial was invented?

'Perfect!' Mum announces, when I go through with the drinks.

We gulp them down and admire the room and Duncan looks at the time on his phone and says he has to get going if he's going to shower before the party.

'Gosh,' Mum says. 'Yes, absolutely, Duncan. I probably won't be here when you come back because I've promised to be out – I'm going to Starbucks for a monthly workshopping group. I'm an author, you see. A few of us local writers get together to share ideas and critique each other's work.'

'You're a writer?' Duncan says, glancing at me like, *Ah, like mother like daughter!* 'That's very cool!'

'Thank you, Duncan!' Mum says, and I know what's coming before she even speaks. 'I'm on TikTok, actually, if you want to give me a follow ...'

'OK, that's enough self-promotion, Mum!' I say, trying to sound jokey and not petulant or rude. Mum looks at me, registering the fact that she's dangerously close to cramping my style.

'Oh, yes, of course,' she says. 'It's been so nice to meet you! And thanks so much for the help – you've been a star.' She looks at me. 'Show Duncan out, darling, and I'll get a tablecloth and find some plates and bowls for the food? And then I've got some content to film – no rest for the wicked!'

'Thanks, Mum,' I say, rolling my eyes at her dropping her social media habits *again*, and then I hold out an arm towards the front door as a way to say to Duncan, *after you!*

'She's cool,' Duncan says, when we're on the doorstep. I get a sudden flashback to the other week, with Morgan and her boyfriend chewing off each other's faces outside her house. I instinctively look up to her bedroom window, in case she's watching me like I watched her. She isn't. Well. Either that or she's quicker than me at ducking out of sight.

'Taylor!'

I look to the road. It's Axel, walking hand in hand with Pierre.

'Oh, hey!' I shout, with a wave. The boys break apart and Duncan heads up the drive and says in an impressive and fluent-sounding French accent to Pierre, *'Timing parfait! Comment ça va? Avez-vous passé une bonne matinée?'*

I think he's asking how Pierre is, and I think Pierre says a long and complicated version of *yeah, good, thanks, mate.* Axel and I watch them turn to leave, and Duncan turns back to shout, 'Bye! *À plus tard!'*

'*À plus tard!*' I shout back, not sounding nearly as good as he does.

Grandma and Grandad pull up in their car before Axel and I even get back inside, all dressed up for what they call a

'Northern Soul' night. In my head I'm concocting a text to Members Only about what's just not-happened-but-kind-of with Duncan, before mentally deleting it because obviously we're not talking, and so the Members Only group chat is as silent as a Year 7 who has forgotten to do their homework. I'm going to have to process this alone.

'What it is? "Northern Soul"?' Axel asks Grandad. 'I do not know this music.'

Grandad ushers him in to the living room, and noticing how it's all been arranged for the party says, 'Ohhhh, now you're talking! Your first party, Taylor! Isn't this exciting! Isn't it nice, love?'

Grandma nods. 'It is. How lovely! How nice!' She's holding a book, and hands it over to me. 'I thought this was a bit of you,' she says, and I look at it. 'I found it in the charity shop today.' It's a book called *Bloodlender*. I turn it over and scan the blurb: It's about mysterious things happening in an old French manor. 'Oh!' I say. 'Thank you! It is!' She gives me a wink. 'Only in exchange for a preview copy of *your* new book, Erica,' Grandma says to Mum. She explains to Axel: 'I'm always her first reader, you know.'

Grandad pulls Axel down beside him on the sofa and gets out his phone to google videos of Northern Soul dancing. 'This is Northern Soul, Axel,' he says. 'Sound of my youth, this! Came from the British mod scene. It was a very northern thing, or the Midlands. See how everyone has on those button-down Ben Sherman shirts? And the jeans! I'd sit in a bath of cold water in my jeans to get them to shrink!'

'Put some tunes on, Erica love,' Grandma says, loitering around the sound system and clapping her hands. 'The dance floor is all ready for us, after all!'

Mum laughs and shakes her head, looking at me in a way that says, *What are they like, huh?* She finds a playlist on her phone and the music blasts out through our fancy connected speakers.

'Like this!' Grandad tells Axel, and he starts spinning around, Grandma moving to the beat too. This is a regular occurrence, to be fair. I've grown up knowing all about how they used to go to 'all-nighters' when they were barely older than I am now! Although they insist the world was a safer place then, and that if I sneaked out to go dancing in clubs there'd be trouble. Talk about double standards! Not that I want to go out all night dancing, but that is beside the point. It's no good having one rule for them but another for me, is it?

Axel joins them on our makeshift living room dance floor, trying to do what Grandma and Grandad do. He does a good job! Then he grabs my hand and spins me around, and I squeal with delight. He's really strong! And a really good dancer!

But then I have a funny feeling. As Axel reaches for my hand again, I think: *Wait. Axel was HOLDING HANDS WITH PIERRE?!* Is that what they do in France, then? I've not seen any other of the Frenchies holding hands. I did see men kissing each other on the cheek on holiday in Italy. And I suppose sometimes I hold Star or Lucy's hand. If girls can hold hands, why can't boys?

Axel spins me around again, and even Mum joins in for a bop. We spin and turn and let the rhythm carry us for one song, and then another, and I think how nice it is that Axel is so evolved. He likes my grandparents and gets on with Mum and holds hands with his friends because he cares.

And in less than a few hours, we will finally have kissed …

Oh my gosh!!!!

17

*A*nd we are a GO! It's party central up in here! Woo-hoo!

'Remember the rules,' Mum says, putting on her coat to leave. She seems nervous, now it's all happening. She keeps looking around anxiously, like four hundred teenagers and a beer factory are going to slip out from behind the curtains and have so much fun her house gets burned down. 'No alcohol or smoking,' she repeats. 'And—'

'… Nobody upstairs.' I help her with her coat and pat her back reassuringly. 'I've got it, Mum. I promise I won't let you down. This is too big of a deal to ruin.'

And then I'm suddenly overcome with a huge need to hug her tight, so I fling myself around her. 'Thank you, thank you, thank you, thank you, thank you!' I say, over and over again. It really is awesome that this is happening, that she trusts me and would even *consider* all of this. Not many mums would, and I do know that.

We stand like that for a beat, squeezing each other, and I know Mum won't let go first because she never does. When I pull away she's giving me that crinkly-eyed smile she does, like she could cry, and she says softly, 'You're growing up.' It's not a question, or even an exclamation. It's more of an observation, like she's remembering this moment and taking a picture of it in her mind. 'Auntie Kate says I have to let you spread your wings. I'm doing my best.'

I don't know what to say to that.

'Bye, bug-a-boo,' she adds, and I let her get away with it. It's actually all right to be called bug-a-boo sometimes.

THAT is how appreciative I am.

In the living room, Axel has picked the music – he's put on some smooth French rap. I think it's the same French rap he played for Grandma the other day, and I remember how much he made her laugh when he was trying to teach her the words. The food is out in bowls dotted everywhere, like a real, adult party. Mum is right: I *am* growing up! I suppose I just wish that in this moment things were OK with the girls. It went without saying that, when I first started planning this, we'd all get ready together. So it felt sad, putting on my make-up without them. I half expected them to just turn up, bags full of ghds and face glitter. But they didn't. I still haven't text them. They should text me! And if they decide not to come tonight, I'm just going to have to make a choice to enjoy it without them, even if that's hard.

I do wish they'd been here when I was trying to decide between a bold lip or a bold eye, though. I've done lipstick *and* eyeliner and can't help feeling that it might be a bit much. Mum said I looked beautiful, but she's biased. I look in the mirror by the front door and decide to scrub off some of the lipstick with my finger. It smudges to the edges of my lips, but that's better than it was. More 'un-done'. Very *How to Be Parisian When You're Not from Paris*:

Make-Up

Less is more. Go on dates bare-faced and wear red lipstick to the market. A sweep of mascara or a dash of tinted lip balm is more effective than inches of foundation and blusher. Skin is made to be seen – let it breathe. Before you leave the house, smudge something. 'Polished' is for wood floors, not faces.

I'm happier with it now. I feel *très chic!*

I prop the front door open with a doorstop so people can let themselves in without me having to act like some sort of doorman all night, and check the downstairs loo, where I've

233

even been allowed to light the fancy candle – Mum's best one! It's something she does if she has her friends over for book club, which is really wine-and-gossiping club. It's a good touch. Sophisticated.

I just want to remember this forever. Drink it all down because tonight is the night I will have my first ever kiss, starting the rest of my life where I'm not just boring Taylor Blake from Crickleton who has never gone anywhere or done anything, but rather Taylor Blake who throws chic parties and kisses boys and also knows actual real French people.

'Ready?' Axel asks from the doorway to the living room, his smile as wide as the moon. I grin back at him. 'Because, *moi*? I am excited!' He does a bum wiggle and I clap appreciatively.

'Let's party!' I cry, and he laughs his perfect laugh.

There is NOTHING worse than the ten minutes between when a party starts and when people actually arrive. Axel and I sit and wait on the sofa, him on his phone, me staring madly at the door, willing somebody to get here.

And then they do.

And they're all really nice to me!

'Hey, Taylor!' Kundai Bolou says with a fist bump, when he's never even spoken to me before.

'Tay-Tay!' Horrid Anna calls me, giving me an air kiss (lol).

'How do,' asks Tommy, arriving with his French exchange partner. 'Tonight's the night, then, is it!' he asks, also giving me a fist bump (what is it with boys and fist bumps?!). I freeze for a minute, thinking he's referencing me having my first kiss, but in hindsight I don't think he does. I think it was just something to say. 'What the hell is this music?' he adds, and the pair of them make their way through to the rest of the house.

When Duncan and Pierre arrive, Pierre gives me a quick hello and goes off to find Axel. Duncan holds out a thin rectangle shape wrapped in neat brown paper.

'Hey!' he says, and I didn't realise I'd been doing really short, shallow nervous breaths until I see him. He feels like a safety blanket, like I can breathe deep and actually relax and enjoy myself, because I know he'll look after me and help if I need it.

'Hey!' I say, and I open my arms for a hug. 'What's this?' I ask as he pulls away and gives me the present.

'For you,' he says, quite shyly. 'To say ...' His voice trails off. He suddenly reminds me of the old Duncan who didn't speak. It's a really bizarre feeling.

'To say what?' I ask, keeping my voice soft. I try to catch his eye, to let him know he can feel as safe with me as I do with him. That's what friends are for, isn't it?

He shrugs. 'Just open it,' he commands, almost as if he regrets giving it me and might take it back at any minute. And we can't have that! I love a present! I just wish I understood what it is *for*.

Because it's a brown paper wrapping, it doesn't give anything away. I rip the paper off eagerly, a few more people slipping by us to go inside, and a book with a purple cover is revealed. It has a cartoon drawing on the front, like a kids' book. I don't get it. Duncan and I talk about books quite a bit, but not books like this. It's says *Dr Seuss* on the cover, and I look up at Duncan questioningly. Our eyes lock and he's smiling wildly, madly, waiting for me to understand. I start to shake my head a bit, my way of asking for a clue, but when I look at it again I see it, *Oh, the Places You'll Go!* And that's when I realise. I look back at Duncan, smiling myself now, and then back at the cover once again. It's the book he spoke about, when he told me I was bound to succeed at what I want in life. It's 'our' book, I think, our own little in-joke. *And will you succeed? 98 and ¾ per cent guaranteed!*

'Oh, Duncan!' I say. 'Thank you! I can't wait to read it.'

It's so nice he's thought of me. Cute! It's so cute!

'Let me know what you think of it,' he says, stepping into the house. 'When you get a chance to flick through it.'

'I will,' I say. 'I'll just keep it safe ...' I look around for somewhere close by to put it. The only place really is under the stairs, with the shoes. 'Here,' I say, putting it between two pairs of wellies. 'Thanks again,' I smile, and Duncan nods.

'Now then,' he says, rubbing his hands together. 'Where are these chilli crisps I've been hearing so much about?'

I feel like I'm seeing the world through fogged-up glasses, or watching a TV show where the sound and the screen aren't properly synced up. I guess I'm kind of … floating through the evening? Like it's a dream. Not quite real.

But, like, it's all in a really good way. And Lucy and Star arrive! I see them loiter at the open front door, Amelie and Sophie behind them, and am torn between bounding over to welcome them or letting *them* find *me*. Axel comes over right as I'm trying to decide.

'Taylor, this is so much fun!' he says, grabbing my hand and twirling me around like he did earlier. I squeal with surprise, and when he pulls me in for a hug I think, *This is all exactly right.* All of it!

By the time I turn back, having decided that yes, I *will* welcome my friends into my house, they've already disappeared from view, and I see them five minutes later in the kitchen, pouring themselves a drink and passing bottles and cups between them and their Frenchies, the perfect, cosy little foursome. They haven't even come to say thanks for having them! How rude!

Well.

I'm deffo not going to approach them first now.

And now I don't know where Axel has gone. He was here just a minute ago. I look around and take in a few people sat on the stairs chatting, others on the sofas and chairs picking at the snacks. Two Frenchies have started dancing by the sound system, which feels promising. It's not a party without some dancing!

'I like your make-up,' Tommy Tsao says, appearing at my side. 'You don't normally wear it, do you?'

He is *so* tall. And no matter what I think about Tommy – his fist-bumping, for starters – he *is* always ready with a compliment for me. It's just normally followed by something less complimentary, like he can't be nice for too long, lol.

(Or not lol, really. I shouldn't encourage it!)

'Urm, I suppose not. Not a lot, anyway,' I say, and I'm aware of the smell of him. He's wearing a musky scent, and he's put gel in his hair as well, so it's all slicked back from his face.

'You look nice,' I tell him, gesturing to his open shirt over a T-shirt and his gold chain. 'I'm so used to seeing you in hockey stuff, or school uniform.'

'Yeah.' He nods, and he looks at me sideways on, and I see it, and the air feels all peculiar between us. I'm so used to Axel and Duncan, how relaxed and 'myself' I am with them, that now with Tommy I feel a bit half-hearted about it. Like yeah, he's a Year 10, but it shouldn't be this awkward … should it? Anyway, maybe me flirting with him has served its purpose, as cut-throat as that makes me sound. I'm pretty sure Axel will go in for the kill tonight!

'Make your move, man!'

One of Tommy's friends – a guy I don't actually know the name of, but I've seen at the park with him, and in the school corridor – has put both of his hands on Tommy's shoulders from behind, and is pretending to give him a massage, like he's a boxer about to go into the ring.

'Gareth,' Tommy says to him, and he sounds really annoyed. 'Go away, please!'

Gareth lets go of him and holds up his hands, then winks at me and walks off.

'Sorry about him,' Tommy says. 'Some people just need to grow up, I guess?'

'Right,' I say, and I'm looking around for Axel, but I still can't see him! It's so annoying!

Well, I suppose I should get flirtier with Tommy for when Axel re-emerges from the loo or wherever he is.

'Shall we get a drink?' I say. 'You don't have one.'

It's all very stilted, and I have to give myself a mental pep talk on laughing at Tommy's jokes more, except he's not really making any. In fact, it's like he's nervous. Tommy Tsao, nervous! Who knew that was even possible!

Tommy says, 'Yeah, lead the way,' and so I walk ahead, and Tommy is behind me where he … puts his hands on my waist! I'm so shocked I do a little yelp, and he leans in and says, 'Sorry! Is this OK?'

'Of course!' I say, and then I feel emboldened to take his hand instead – just for a minute. Long enough to be flirty. OMG!!

We sort out our drinks and I end up hoisting myself up on the kitchen counter, and it makes me just a tiny bit taller than him. Tommy leans his hips against the counter at the side of me, and gives me that smile again.

'You seem to be enjoying the exchange,' he asks. 'Seems like you really get on with your partner.'

I nod, trying to remember to smile, look interested, push the hair off of my neck … it's a lot.

'He's great,' I say. 'We really get on.'

'No way would my parents let me have a girl as my partner,' he says, and I notice it again: nothing he says is ever really a question.

'My mum gets it,' I say, and Tommy pulls a face like he doesn't believe me. 'As much as a mum can get it,' I add disloyally.

Tommy moves closer to me, so his arm is pressed against my leg.

'Cool,' he says.

And then I realise that none of this is about conversation at all. He doesn't really want to talk. There's so many people around and the music is pretty loud, but in a split second everything freezes and goes quiet, because Tommy Tsao is looking at me, then looking away, then looking at me again until I find myself leaning towards him, because this is it! A kiss! My first kiss! I can feel it!!!!!

The only thought in my head on loop is, *ohmygosh, ohmygosh, ohmygosh.* Tommy is looking at my mouth, and he moves forward too, reaching across me and craning so that there's ten inches between us, and then nine, eight, seven …

Boom. Those last six inches get closed in the blink of an eye, and my lips are nearly on Tommy Tsao's lips, and I can't believe I'm doing it, I'm about to kiss a boy. A Year 10 boy! It's really, *finally* happening!

Tommy makes a noise of pleasure – then a sort of gurgling sound. I know I'm supposed to keep my eyes closed so I do, but then I feel a warm gloopy liquid on my chin instead of his lips on mine, and then hear Tommy saying, 'Urgh, oh god, I'm so sorry.'

I can't figure out what happened. I open my eyes, and Tommy is no longer millimetres from me, but has turned to the kitchen sink, where a long stream of purple-coloured vomit is pouring from his mouth. I touch my chin. I look at my hand. That same purple-coloured vomit IS ON MY FACE.

Tommy Tsao threw up on me!

I start to gag – in humiliation or disgust I don't know – and stupidly put my hand to my mouth to try and stop myself ... and accidentally PUSH TOMMY'S SICK FROM MY CHIN *INTO* MY MOUTH!

And knowing I've got Tommy Tsao's sick in my mouth makes me gag even more, his vomit dribbling from the corners of my lips all down my top, and Tommy is next to me spewing his guts out as everyone else evacuates the kitchen shouting, 'Vom! Vom!' in various tones of hysteria.

I'm dry retching now, trying to get a handle on my digestive system. Eventually I stop. Tommy has stopped too: he's breathing heavily, panting, reaching his head under the cold tap to drink directly from it.

I look at his vomit on my top.

Whoa.

Literally, a kiss from me was enough to make a boy throw up.

Superb.

Great!

I grab a tea towel and wipe my face, trying to shut out the whispers from the lounge about Tommy Tsao being sick. Do people realise it's because of me?

I need to get out of here before they do.

I escape out of there, up the stairs – surely Mum's rule

about nobody upstairs doesn't extend to me! – and into the only room with a door that locks. The bathroom.

I slide the lock into the catch and sink to the floor.

It's only when I know I'm truly alone that the horrificness of what has just happened properly hits me: I made a boy throw up! We were about to kiss and I made him vomit!

And then I cry.

Big, horrible, ugly sobs.

The tears just keep. On. Coming.

18

*M*y working theory, after about fifteen minutes of crying my heart out, is that if I stay in here long enough Mum will come home and ask everyone to leave. Obviously that's if everyone isn't already getting their stuff together to go, because Caca Girl has become Vom Girl, making everyone she comes into contact with chuck up all over themselves. Best get out now! You could be next!!!

Oh god.

I will never live this down! Never, never, never! And all I wanted was for tonight to be this fun, magical, beautiful night, and yeah, with kisses.

But the thing is, I didn't even plan on kissing Tommy! It was supposed to be Axel! I wanted to kiss Axel! But Tommy was right there, and being so shy, and I don't know what came over me to think it might be a good idea. I stopped thinking, actually. I wasn't thinking, and I just went with what my lips told me.

That's the last time that will happen, mark my words.

I think I was just so desperate to be kissed that I lost myself for a second, not even caring who the kiss was with!

I wash my face with cold water and Mum's best cleanser, because if this doesn't call for it I don't know what will. I'd bleach my face if I could (but I know that would burn, and peel my skin off). (Although that sounds appealing right about now …)

I made Tommy Tsao throw up on me!

Every time I replay it in my mind, I start crying all over again.

'Taylor?'

A voice comes from the other side of the door.

'Taylor? It's us.'

I look hard at the door, like if I stare enough I will be able to see through it. But I don't need a see-through door to know who it is. I peel myself back up off the floor and slide the lock. They let themselves in, and close it again behind them.

'Come here,' Star says, enveloping me in a hug. Lucy wraps her arms around me from the other side.

'We love you,' she says into my back, and I've never been so pleased to see my friends in my life.

'I've been thinking I should jump out of this window and run forever,' I say, still the filling in their hug sandwich. 'I could run until I hit another country and then assume another identity and leave all this behind.'

'Nooooo,' coos Lucy, and I need a tissue to blow my snotty nose, so wriggle free and sit on the side of the bath. Lucy sits on the toilet – lid down, obviously – and Star leans against the sink.

'It's not that bad …' Star insists, and I give her a look. 'Is it?' she asks. 'What exactly happened?'

I don't think I can even say it. It's too embarrassing.

'Did Tommy Tsao really … throw up in your mouth?' Lucy asks gently. It's like she personally feels let down by him, champion of the Year 10 as she's been.

'Kind of!' I nod, wiping my nose with my hand. 'We were about to kiss, and—'

'You kissed Tommy?!'

'Yeah,' I say, and then I think about it. 'Well, no. I'm not sure!'

Star shakes her head. 'How can you not be sure?'

'It's all a blur!' I wail. 'I was sitting on the worktop, and he leaned in, and I thought it was going to happen and then I felt something on my chin, and then he turned away and was being sick in the sink and I realised when I opened my eyes that the thing on my chin was also his sick!'

'Nooooooo!' the girls say, in unison.

'Yes!' I exclaim. 'All this time, and this planning, and I finally get my first kiss and it makes the guy vomit all over me!'

Lucy shakes her head, certain. 'No,' she says. 'That wasn't your first kiss. That absolutely doesn't count.'

Star adds: 'And you didn't *make* Tommy be sick, Taylor. I promise! You're not, like, gross or whatever. He's fancied you forever! His friend Gareth was even telling us how you two were in the kitchen, finally getting together.'

'And then we saw you run up here …' says Lucy.

'And it took us a moment to figure out why,' concludes Star.

'I'm a laughing stock,' I say. 'Nothing I want ever works out. The kiss, you guys …'

'Water under the bridge,' declares Lucy. 'Honestly. Let's just go back to being friends, and everything being normal.'

'Really?' I snivel. I've never known Lucy to step down, to 'settle' an argument by suggesting the argument doesn't matter in the first place. Something doesn't feel right.

'Well,' says Star gingerly. 'You *have* been a bit distant, a bit off-radar. But now doesn't seem like the time to talk about it …'

'No,' I insist. Now isn't the time for Star's diplomacy. If things need to be said, let's say them! 'It is. If I don't have you two, what have I got?'

Star and Lucy look at each other, but I can't tell what they're thinking.

'Honesty game?' asks Lucy. 'Let's just … get it all out there?'

That is the Lucy I know.

'If it means sorting out whatever has been happening and then going back to normal, then yes!' I say. 'Honesty game!' I think about it for a second, and then add: 'You two have upset me, too, you know.'

'What?!' shrieks Lucy, outraged. 'Us?! You're the one high on first-kiss fever, disappearing and not joining in!'

'Yeah,' says Star gently. In typical Star fashion she adds, 'I'm sure we've all got our different interpretations of what happened, though. Maybe we can let Taylor speak first, and then we can?'

'God,' says Lucy. 'You really annoy me when you point out I'm not being very mature.' She furrows her brow, but dramatically, so it's obvious she's only half-joking. Lucy is such a force of nature, but she always listens to Star. Star has a very calming and reasonable effect on her.

'It's exhausting being the rational one all the time, if that's any consolation,' Star offers, with a similar expression playing across her lips. Even I cock an eyebrow at that comment. Star always thinks she's the voice of reason, and she normally is – but it's no fun if she points it out.

'Taylor?' she presses. 'Do you want to tell us *how* we've upset you?'

I shrug. It's hard being put on the spot, and I don't like confrontation. I'm not as confident as Lucy when it comes to all that stuff. But I suppose the worst has already happened tonight. What have I got to lose?

'It's just,' I say, scrambling to find the words. 'I wish you'd both really understand what it's like to be a kiss virgin, and be supportive with not *just* your *words*. Like, you *say* you get it and want me to have my fist kiss, but also … I don't know … you've not checked in a lot this week and it's felt like you've been talking about me behind my back or something, like deciding I've been a bad friend and so being a bit … catty, I suppose, whenever I've brought the kissing thing up.'

Lucy sighs. Star says, in Lucy's direction, 'Well, she's not wrong, is she? We have been annoyed, and we have been talking about her …'

'It just felt a bit boring! Not you wanting your first kiss being boring, but more just always hearing about it,' Lucy says, throwing her hands up in the air. 'You want your kiss, and we totally get that, but life still goes on and there are lots of other things, good things, to experience! And Amelie and Sophie are brilliant fun – you've missed a lot by not hanging out. Axel could have come too!'

'Axel wanted to hang out with Pierre …' I say. 'And it's the job of the host to do what they want, isn't it?! It's not my fault I got a boy! I do regret not coming to the BBQ though, and not asking about how your weeks have been. I should have checked in more, taken an interest in your French exchange experience. I've been a bit jealous, to be honest. Has it been amazing?'

Star shrugs, her eyes alight with the truth. 'It's been good, yeah …' she says. 'We just wanted to share that with you!'

'OK,' I say with a nod. 'So, like … what now?'

'What now is that we apologise to each other, have a big massive hug, and promise to all do better!' Star kneels down and puts her arm around my neck, and Lucy crouches down to make Star the filling to our friendship hug sandwich this time.

'I'm sorry,' we all say in unison.

'Best Friends Forever?' Lucy asks, her voice muffled by Star's hair.

'Best Friends Forever!' Star and I echo, before we untangle ourselves and resume our previous positions.

'And we won't talk about you any more,' Lucy offers.

'We were just annoyed.' Star shrugs gently.

'Be annoyed to my face next time,' I say, and Lucy says: 'Ditto!'

We sit, and I remember why I'm in here. I'm glad it's all sorted with the girls but URGH! Tommy Tsao!! Axel will never want to kiss me now he knows this has happened. I've blown it! I will never be kissed!

Lucy must be able to read my thoughts, because quietly she says, 'You'll have that lovely first kiss, you know. Don't worry about that. There's loads of time for romance ...'

I sigh dramatically. 'Isn't that just the problem?!' I howl. 'Time is trucking on! I'm the only girl in the year who isn't *living*! Who doesn't have adventures and big love affairs! I just make boys throw up! Axel will never want me once he hears about this ...'

There's another tap on the door.

'Go away!' says Lucy. 'Nobody is allowed upstairs!'

A voice from the other side says: 'It's Duncan!'

Lucy and Star look at me. I give a little nod. Duncan. I can see Duncan. He won't judge me.

Lucy gets up off the toilet seat and unlocks the door, pulling it open. I look up to see Duncan's smiling, kind face, but don't look at him for long. Because just beyond him is the guest room, and the door is ajar enough for me to see that Axel is sitting on the edge of his bed, next to Pierre, who he is kissing.

Duncan turns to see what I see, Lucy and Star doing the same, and we all gawp, jaws slack, until Duncan quietly spins on his heel to pull the guest room door closed and slips into the bathroom.

'What the hell?' I mutter. 'Axel and Pierre?! Did you know that?' I ask Duncan.

'Kind of.' He shrugs. 'I had a feeling.'

'Ohmygod,' I say, climbing into the empty bath and lying back to stare at the lights in the ceiling. 'Ohmygod,' I repeat. 'I made one boy throw up, and I made another boy gay!'

'That's not—' Lucy starts, but I snap at her: 'I know that's not how it works! Just let me be dramatic, would you!'

Everyone falls silent, and Duncan comes and sits at the edge of the bath. He reaches over and holds my hand.

'Don't let logic get in the way of a good story, eh?' he says, and I look at him and I can't help it. I laugh. I laugh, and it's like it breaks a spell for everyone else, because they all laugh too. Urgh! This is all so messed up!

'Not to alarm you,' Lucy says. 'But I feel like since you've been up here, the music has got a bit louder and things are rowdier down there? Do you want me to go and check?'

I turn an ear and get what she means. The last thing I want is the house trashed on top of all this.

'Do you mind?' I ask. 'I just need five more minutes to get myself together …'

'I'll go too,' says Star. 'Come on,' she tells Lucy. 'Let's go and get these kids under control, before Erica gets back …'

When they've gone, Duncan empties the glass Mum keeps our toothbrushes in, rinses it out and fills it with cold water. He holds it out to me. I take it gratefully, realising that I am, indeed, really thirsty.

'Shall we just sit for a bit?' Duncan asks. 'If the girls have got downstairs under control?'

I nod.

I stay in the bath and Duncan sits with his back against it, so I can just about see him in profile. He must be picking at a thread or something on the bathmat, because his gaze is down, his breathing even. He's nice. I'm starting to calm down now, and it helps that he isn't asking anything from me or after any gossip or even trying to make it all OK. He's just there. With me.

He looks so lovely, all polite and kind.

Maybe I got it wrong. Maybe nice boys aren't wet, or too quiet, they're just nice, and look after you, and don't ever make you feel crazy.

Duncan has never made me feel anything less than perfect, just as I am. 'OK,' I say, when I can hear the music has been turned down and it feels like I won't *die* if I have to re-enter the party. It will suck – but I'll survive. Just. 'I think I can manage going back downstairs now,' I declare.

'As you choose,' Duncan says, standing up and holding out a hand to help me climb out of the bath. He looks me up and down, and for a moment I get the feeling he's going to tell me something sweet, like maybe that I'm beautiful, but then he scrunches up his nose and says: 'Not to pry, but – I think you've got sick on your top?'

I look down. I'm covered. I go and grab a fresh T-shirt whilst Duncan waits at the top of the stairs. When I pass by Axel's room, the door is open again and he and Pierre are nowhere to be seen. Back down we go.

19

I am agog. The house looks virtually tidier than when the party started – there are two big bags of recycling by the back door, empty plates and bowls are in the dishwasher, and everyone is milling about finishing their drinks like we do this all the time, like we're all so used to an unsupervised adult-free party and know exactly how to behave.

The thing is, it's scarily close to us all actually knowing how to behave?

It's like being in a parallel universe, one where teenagers can … actually be trusted! And right on cue, Mum comes home.

Credit to her, she doesn't make a big scene. She slips through the front door, says a quiet hello to the few faces she recognises, and finds me in the kitchen.

'I'm impressed,' she says, going to get a drink from the fridge.

I shrug, like it's nothing. 'I enjoy surpassing expectation,' I grin, and Mum, Duncan and I go outside to the back patio, where we sit. Lucy and Star join us.

'Girls!' Mum says, raising her drink in salute. 'How's it been!'

'Good,' they chorus, looking at me with a smile.

'A boy threw up on me,' I say.

'Apparently,' Lucy offers caustically, 'it was nerves.' She looks at my mum. 'He really fancies Taylor, Erica,' she clarifies, and Mum nods, like, *Well, of course*. God bless her.

'Axel kissed Duncan's exchange partner, Pierre,' I continue.

'A not altogether surprising turn of events,' Mum says. 'Good for them!'

Gosh, did everyone see Axel and Pierre happening except me?!

'Horrid Anna taught everyone how to twerk properly,' Duncan says. 'So I am now able to add that to my university applications.'

'Excellent,' laughs Mum. 'Kid, you'll move mountains!'

Duncan looks at her, wide-eyed. 'You know Dr Seuss?' he says, and Mum exclaims: 'Of course!'

'Duncan's been telling me about that book,' I say. 'In fact, he got me a copy.'

'Oh, Duncan, that's very kind of you,' Mum says, right as Star leans into me and squeals, 'Duncan got you a *present*?!' I shrug, like it's no big deal, but then as the house gets quieter because everyone is taking the hint that it's time to leave, he stands on the back patio, all the sky getting dark around him, the garden lights making his eyes twinkle, and he smiles, and I smile back, and I start to find the edges of a thought.

Wait.

Duncan?

Do I ... fancy DUNCAN? DUNCAN HIGGIN-BOTTOM?!

THE BOY WHO NEVER SPEAKS?!

THE BOY WHO IS JUST A FRIEND?!

Except these past few weeks have taught me that not only does Duncan speak, he's funny, and kind, and charming, and just ... nice. His company is comforting. And what did Grandad say, that friendship wins the race? Maybe Duncan has been in the lead all along and I didn't even know it.

'Taylor!' Gareth hangs out on the back step, waving. 'Great party! You're a legend, man!'

Somebody else echoes, 'Yeah, you're a legend! Thanks!'

And as I get up to say goodbye to everyone properly, four more people say that: that I'm a legend.

Taylor Blake is a legend! Imagine that! It makes me feel all warm and proud inside.

'Well,' says Duncan. 'It's probably time for me to go.'

Lucy and Star interrupt to say Star's dad is here so they've got to go too, and they blow kisses across the room and say they'll text in the morning. Axel and Pierre are whispering sweet nothings to each other at the top of the drive – clearly they've been here for a while, finally some quality alone time away from the party madness – and Mum is still out back, giving us all our space. So there, at the front door, it's just me and Duncan, and I'm just so happy and so grateful for him.

'Thanks for coming,' I say. 'And for my present. That was really thoughtful.'

'No worries.' He shrugs. 'Enjoy.'

'Yeah,' I say, and I'm aware our voices are both getting quieter. 'I will.'

I'm so happy he's here, in fact, that I reach out a hand to his and squeeze, before pulling him in for a hug.

'Oh!' he says, holding me tightly. I can *feel* him blushing, and maybe I'm blushing too, but I don't care. As we stay like that I say, 'Duncan?' and he says, 'Yeah?'

'You know when I said about the cinema? About us all going?'

His arms loosen around me, and I take the hint that the hug is over.

'Yeah?' he says, looking at the ground.

'Shall just you and me go, maybe? After the exchange people go home?'

He looks up in surprise.

'Great!' he says. 'Yeah, that'd be wicked. I'd like that.'

'Me too.' I nod, and then Pierre yells, '*On y va, Duncan?*' and so he starts the walk up the drive, backwards, smiling at me, and I smile at him.

'Wait,' he says, halfway up. 'But what about Tommy? Aren't you and him …?'

'I'd prefer to go with you,' I say. And I mean it.

Inside, Mum is explaining to Axel that they can leave the furniture where it is, and they'll just sort it out in the morning.

'I'm too tired now,' she says, with a yawn. 'It has been such a long day – teaching at the university, then writing, and then out workshopping at Starbucks … *Demain*,' she insists with a wave of her hand. *Tomorrow*. 'Thank you for all of your help, though.'

'Thank you for the party!' Axel says, and his smile is undeniable. His whole face is lit up by something … and I suspect I know what it is.

'Night, Taylor,' Mum says, kissing my cheek. 'Turn off all the lights before you go up?'

'Will do,' I say. 'Love you.'

She ruffles my hair. 'Love you too, sausage.'

261

She kisses Axel goodnight too, and then it's just him and me left in the living room, standing at opposite ends.

'Did you have a good night?' I say shyly. I might have realised a few things about Duncan Higginbottom, but I sure do feel embarrassed about never noticing how gaga Axel is about Pierre. Honestly, I thought we'd run off into the kissing sunset together! How was I so blind?!

Axel's smile gets even wider, like that's possible.

'*Oui*,' he says. 'I had … how do you say? A magical time …'

I nod, digesting his enthusiasm. 'So, you and Pierre …?' I ask.

'Yes!' he grins. 'I am very happy! I did not know if he wanted to be only my friend, or if we could be together in a way that is romantic. We have been friends for a short time only. And now we have kissed!'

I nod. 'Did you always know you liked him?' I say. I can't help myself.

Axel nods. 'From the first time we meet, yes,' he says, in his imperfectly perfect English. I try to look happy for him.

'That's so nice,' I offer, but even I can tell that I don't sound genuine. Axel frowns.

'And you?' he asks. 'I have been so busy with Pierre I have not seen you! Was the party fun for you?'

'You didn't hear?'

Axel shakes his head.

262

'Tommy threw up on me,' I say, and when Axel narrows his eyes I realise he doesn't know what 'threw up' means. I make a gagging sound, and fling my hand in front of my mouth in a gesture I'm pretty sure is obvious.

'No!' he shrieks, horrified. 'Tommy did that on ... on *you*? But why?'

He wanders over to the sofa and sits down, resting his forearms on his thighs so he's leaning forward, eager for the details. I don't really know where to begin, so I think about how to explain as I plop myself down on the opposite end of the sofa, pulling my legs in under me.

'We nearly kissed,' I say, and Axel raises his eyebrows.

'Taylor,' he says. 'No! Not Tommy! Not for you!'

I sigh, and give a shrug.

'Can I tell you something really embarrassing?' I say, and Axel tips his head to the side, the picture of sympathy, and replies: 'Taylor, we are friends, *non*? Nothing is embarrassing when we are friends.'

Don't be so sure of that, I think. But at the same time, I trust Axel. I feel like tonight, I've realised Tommy isn't the boy for me, even if he is a Year 10, and I've cleared the air with Star and Lucy, and I've even agreed to a date with Duncan. I've been my best, most mature self! *Sacre bleu!* I really am a legend!

But this legend has just one truth left they need to reveal ...

'Don't laugh,' I say, 'but ...' I gulp down some air, trying to find my bravery. 'I thought that … you know … *you and me*?' I gesture with a finger between us, and Axel furrows his brow. Then I see his realisation, and his eyebrows shoot up towards his hairline in surprise.

'Oh!' he says, and he mimics what I've just done, wagging his finger between us to check he's catching my drift. I bury my face in my hands.

'I know!' I say. 'I got it so wrong! I just like your company so much, and you're so cool, and I thought … well! I don't know what I thought!'

Axel scoots over to where I'm sitting and pulls my hands away from my face.

'Taylor,' he says, forcing me to look at him. 'How do you say: no big deal? I do like you! I like you so much!'

He looks into my eyes, all handsome and French, and he sort of nods, willing me to believe him.

'I love being your partner! You are so cool also!' he says. 'I think we are fantastic friends!'

I nod. 'I can't believe I thought you fancied me,' I say.

Axel puts his finger under my chin, exactly like he did that day at school and I melted at his touch.

'Taylor, if I liked girls, you would be the girl I liked, OK?'

'Really?' I ask.

'Really,' he says, with a smile. 'But …'

'OH GOD!' I say. 'I knew there would be a but!'

Axel rolls his eyes. 'You are so dramatic,' he laughs. 'I love it!'

I pull a face. What on earth is he going to say next?

'Duncan,' he states. 'I think you and Duncan …'

My jaw drops in shock.

'What?' I ask. 'How did you …?'

Axel shrugs. 'The way you look at him,' he says. 'It is the way I look at Pierre, I think.'

I put my hand over my mouth. How is Axel so perceptive?! Even more perceptive than me, about my own feelings?!

'I didn't know I liked him,' I admit. 'Until tonight.'

'So I think you did have a good party, then. In the end.'

I nod.

'I think I did, yeah,' I agree. 'In the end.'

20

Members Only

Star: *How's it going, Taylor? What's it like with you and Axel now
that you know he's with Pierre?*

Lucy: *WHICH WE ARE VERY SORRY ABOUT!*

Star: *Well, I was sorry until DUNCAN HIGGINBOTTOM suddenly
entered stage left!*

Lucy: *Who'd have thought?!*

      Me: *Not me! Not anyone!*

      Me: *But yeah, it's nice with Axel.
         It's like, now that I can chill about
         the snogging (or lack thereof!)
         I can see what amazing friends
         we make.*

Me: *We're even at Grandma and Grandad's right now, because Grandad said over FaceTime that his dahlias have had a surprising second late bloom and he's going to straighten out the leaves between two matchsticks so they're even prettier. Axel loves Grandad's garden so wanted to see all the flower action and Grandad couldn't wait to show him!*

Lucy: *I understood about ten per cent of that text*

Me: *Axel charms mothers, grandmothers, boys, girls AND my grandad! I'm so happy I met him!*

Me: *thanks for asking how I am.*

Me: *HOW ARE YOU TWO?! We need to do our fanfic ASAP, as soon as they've gone! I miss it!*

Star: *We do! Let's make a date!* ☺

Star: *I'm so tired from fencing*

Lucy: *A bit bored of being a host now, tbh. It was really fun for a bit but I miss just watching TV in my room by myself! lol*

'Lovely boy,' Grandma says as we observe them through the living room window. 'I think you've made a friend for life there.'

'Yeah,' I say, smiling. After the initial shock of his romance with Pierre I've calmed down. *Of course* they're in love. Of course they are! I was so blinded by first-kiss fever that I sort of overlooked the obvious: the hand-holding, the secret whispers, the sketches, the constant desire to be near him ... Axel and I have had a good laugh about how blind I've been! And the girls have been so nice to check up on me too.

'And the party went well?' Grandma asks, refilling her tea from the pot.

'It was soooo good,' I tell her. 'Everyone kept calling me a legend! And ... I asked a boy out, too. On a date.'

I don't know what comes over me, revealing such a private thing to her. It's just, since it happened I keep wanting to talk about him, and I think about him all the time too. It's like a plot twist in my own life: Duncan Higginbottom! I keep reading the book he gave me, and it's not a silly kids' book like I thought. It's this really nice story about losing your way and finding your way and knowing that ups and downs are a part of life. It makes me feel really understood, like Duncan gets me. I keep replaying all our conversations and everything we've talked about, mining it for clues that he likes me too. But he does, doesn't he? He must! Being all blush-y, and helping with the party, and being nice to Mum and buying me the book in the first place.

'And who is this boy who has caught your eye?' Grandma

asks. 'The one Grandad saw you talking to on the bus? Tommy?'

'Actually,' I say, 'no. It's my friend Duncan. I thought he was this quiet boy at the front of the class who never spoke, but then he's been doing the French exchange too, and it turns out he likes writing and works on the *Register*, and we just have loads in common. I didn't even know I wanted to ask him to the cinema until I did, if that makes sense. I thought we were just friends!'

Grandma chuckles. 'Oh, I know that feeling,' she says. 'Your grandad and me,' it was exactly the same! I was quite the belle of the ball back in the day, you know. What is it they say? Wait, don't tell me!' She closes her eyes and calls up a memory. Then her eyes fling open and she declares: 'I was the whole vibe! Isn't that what they say?'

'Oh my goodness,' I giggle. 'Grandma!'

'It's true! I was the whole vibe! I had my pick of boys. And your grandad, he was my friend – he was the only one who asked me what I thought about things and listened to the answer. We'd talk for hours, we would. Hours! And then I realised it was that friend I wanted to tell everything to: funny things, silly things, all of that. And then boom: I fell for him. My friend became my boyfriend.'

'Axel says friendship is the most important thing in the world,' I say, and Grandma nods.

'Wise boy!' she notes.

'I can't believe you've been married for almost fifty years,' I say.

She shrugs and gives a big sigh. 'It's easier when you like each other as friends,' she smiles. And then she adds, with a naughty twinkle in her eye: 'He's still an idiot who drives me potty sometimes, though. I mean, most of the time, if we're honest. But he's *my* idiot.'

'Awww, that's nice,' I say. 'I hope I have my own idiot one day, too.'

21

Members Only

Star: *Guys, the frenchies are all at their final day briefing tomorrow morning! Let's hang!*

Lucy: *What you thinking*

Star: *That we take @Taylor to Starbucks and talk about The Boy Who Never Speaks*

Lucy: *We want to know everything, Tay!*

Me: *YES PLEASE!*

When I get there, my mango and passionfruit cooler is already waiting for me, and they sit in one side of the booth, hand in hand, grinning up at me. I can't tell if I'm in trouble, or if they think that they are.

'Hello ...' I say uncertainly, slipping into a chair opposite. 'This is all very ...' I don't know how to finish the sentence. Star widens her grin even more.

'We're being good friends,' she says.

'And we would also like every single last morsel of gossip re: asking Duncan out,' Lucy chimes in. I pull a face, a face that means *can you even believe I did that?!* The girls break into a squeal of glee, like no, they can't! The woman behind the counter issues a stern *shhhhh* like this is a library, not a coffee shop, but we take the hint.

'Duncan Higginbottom?!' Star stage whispers. 'I can't believe it!'

'I know.' I shrug. 'Neither can I, to be honest.'

'Have you seen him since? Like, is it weird, or normal ...?'

I shake my head. 'I haven't seen him, no. It was only on Friday night! Give me a minute!'

'And when are you going out?' Lucy presses.

'We didn't get that far.' I shrug. 'This is like the Spanish Inquisition! You're making me sweat!' I exclaim, wiping my palms on the thighs of my jeans.

'Well, we could *not* care ...' Star threatens jokingly, and I roll my eyes.

'Nooooo!' I say. 'This is much better. I love it really.'

Lucy shakes her head good-naturedly, fringe whipping her face. 'I knew you did,' she says. 'God ... Duncan

Higginbottom! Who knew! I had Axel on my bingo card, Tommy Tsao on my bingo card … but not Duncan.'

'Ohmygosh,' Star says, her eyes going wide. It's spooky, but somehow I know what she's going to say before she even says it. 'Tommy Tsao just walked in. Taylor, *do not* turn around.'

I freeze. Tommy slipped out of the party after the Vomiting Incident, and I haven't heard from him since. I was so convinced it was my fault on Friday, but today, after the space of a weekend, I can see that it was probably no one's fault. It was just a thing that happened? Like, an uncontrollable event.

I look at the girls, not even wanting to move my body an inch. I am totally frozen. Tommy can't see my mouth, if he's even seen me at all, but I barely move it as I say, 'What's he doing?'

Star's eyes flicker beyond my shoulder. 'Buying a drink,' she says, also not moving her lips. We're all talking to each other like plastic Barbie dolls.

'Should I say something?' I ask. 'What should I say?'

'I don't know …' Lucy replies, with a shrug. 'Maybe just say hello?'

'Ask if he's feeling better?' Star suggests.

I remain as still as possible. 'Maybe he hasn't seen me,' I say. 'I need more time to workshop what to say …!'

And right as I speak, my eyes flicker up to the mirror behind Star's and Lucy's heads, where Tommy is perfectly visible and at the exact moment I see him, he sees me. I try to smile, but it comes out as more of a grimace-type thing. Tommy pulls an equally weird face. Oh god. He looks so sad! I felt mortified about being thrown up on, but it never occurred to me he must feel mortified to be the one doing it!

Before I can decide what to do, he turns and makes for the door.

'Gah!' I say, finally able to move again. 'He just looked so sad! I should go and say something.'

The girls just look at me, obviously not knowing the best way to advise me.

'Right?' I clarify, but before the answer I push back my chair and go out on to the street, looking left and right to see which way he's gone.

'Tommy!' I call, when I see him. He turns around. I can't tell if he's happy or sad I've come after him.

'Hey,' I say, doing a funny jog towards him, which is really no quicker than a walk, but it gives the impression I'm eager to see him.

'Hey,' he says, with a nod. 'You all right?'

'Yeah,' I say. 'You?'

'Yeah,' he replies, and we stand. Tommy gives a nervous smile, and I feel awful that I ever tried to flirt with him to make somebody else jealous. He's a nice enough boy, but he's not the boy for me. I think I just got a bit carried away that he's a Year 10. But I should never have used him to make another boy like me. That wasn't right.

'Sorry about your party,' Tommy says, right as I open my mouth and say, 'I'm so sorry for last Friday.'

We both stop speaking, in case the other wants to finish.

This is so awkward!

'I wanted to text, but …' he says. He doesn't finish the sentence.

'It's OK,' I reassure him. 'I didn't text either …'

He nods, like fair play, yeah, I have a point.

Eventually, he says: 'Everyone is talking about what a legend you are. You know. Because it was such a good party.'

'Not for everyone …' I reply, a cautious joke.

'I know …' Tommy says, not giving me a laugh. He's right. It's too soon for jokes. 'I really am sorry for the being sick thing.'

'Sorry if I made you sick,' I say, and Tommy shakes his head. There really is no way for us to laugh this off. Tommy is the most unsmiling I have ever seen him.

'I was just nervous,' he tells me. 'I really wanted to make a good impression on you. Every time I see you I always say a stupid thing or act like an idiot, and I don't know why. Well. I do. It's because I like you.'

I smile at him. Gosh. He's being really quite heartfelt and kind. It's disorientating!

'You probably don't even want to be my friend now, but … I wondered if you still wanted to go to the cinema with me? If I haven't put you off? I can promise you there will be absolutely no vomit. Zero.'

I smile.

'You haven't put me off,' I say. 'But …'

'I knew there'd be a but,' he says sadly.

'There's actually somebody else I'm going to the cinema with,' I tell him. I figure I had better be honest and tell him the truth. I've been unkind enough. 'He's just my friend right now, but I think it might become more? So I don't want to lead you on or anything. You know. If you want it to be romantic or whatever.'

I actually can't believe I've just said all that! That I have been so grown-up and mature as to be honest, even though my preference would be to cover my eyes and pretend none of this is happening!

Tommy holds out a hand, smiles and says: 'Friends?'

I take it.

'Friends,' I say, and that is that.

22

I can't believe the exchange is coming to an end. I've spent years excited to finally host a French person in my house, to finally be in Year 9, old enough to do it, and in the blink of an eye it's finished! Well, basically, anyway. We're doing a 'goodbye ball' in the hall tonight, which is less of a ball and more a lacklustre excuse for a party with Monsieur Brown as the DJ and a bit of food which even I can see isn't as good as the food I had at my party. Not to be big-headed or anything. It's just … fact.

'This isn't as good as your party,' Axel tells me with grin, as if he can read my mind. It makes me feel *very* proud. Nothing has really worked out like I thought it would, but it's all worked out for the best. Pierre snuggles into Axel's shoulder beside him, holding on to his arm.

'Hard agree,' says Lucy with a meaningful grin.

'You're all very kind,' I say, right as the music changes to something slow and floaty.

'Oooooh!' says Star. 'Slow dance time!' She holds out a hand to Lucy and says, 'My love, please may I have this dance?'

Lucy giggles and says, 'Oh, all right then!' I love to see how she softens with Star. It's sort of how I feel with Duncan, I think, that this one particular person is a safe place to be your most relaxed self.

Axel and Pierre slink off to the middle of the hall too, and I stand there, suddenly self-conscious, watching all these couples with their hands on each other's waists: including Tommy, who has commandeered a French girl, her head is resting on his chest as they sway. If I felt any guilt about turning him down this morning, it evaporates. I think Tommy is going to be just fine.

'Fancy a shuffle?'

I turn around. It's Duncan.

'Oh, hello,' I say. 'Fancy seeing you here!'

'With the power of speech and everything,' Duncan grins, and he holds out a hand. I do the same, and he takes my fingertips and walks me to the edge of the dance floor.

'I don't know what I'm doing,' he says, as we stand opposite each other.

I laugh. 'And I do?' I ask.

We both look around, to see how everyone else is doing it.

'OK,' Duncan suggests. 'How about you put this hand here …' He gently takes my hand and puts it on his shoulder. 'And put this other hand here on my hip …' I look up at him: there's not much space between us. I feel a lump form in my throat.

Duncan mirrors the way I'm holding on to him, opposite hand on my shoulder, the other on my waist. And then we sort of … move from side to side? It's all very awkward. Very, very awkward.

But then, Duncan shifts his hand a bit to pull me closer, his grip firm on the bottom of my back, and it makes the six inches between us become four, and I'm close enough to smell him. I could burst into flames. My blood is pumping harder and faster through my veins than it ever has before. When we talk, it is in a hushed whisper. I don't know if that's because we're so close it doesn't need to be any louder, or because we're afraid to break the spell that has fallen over us.

'It's been good, the exchange, hasn't it?' Duncan says, pulling away slightly so I can see his face better as he speaks. It means his face is *very* close to mine, and my tummy lurches like a car with the brakes suddenly slammed on. We could kiss, if we wanted to. And I don't have words to describe how much I want Duncan to kiss me. It's a bodily *ache*.

'Really good,' I whisper, and I think, *I hope my breath doesn't smell. I wish I'd had a Tic Tac.*

Duncan dares to shuffle more theatrically, whipping me around in a spin. It makes the room whir, like a fairground ride. I giggle nervously.

'I saw that in a film,' he says, colour in his cheeks. 'I've always wanted to try it.'

'Maybe a little warning next time,' I say, and his face falls. 'Hey,' I say. 'I'm kidding. I like dancing with you.'

'I like dancing with you too,' he says, and it's here. The moment. We're going to kiss! We're going to kiss! We're going to kiss!

I think of *How to Be Parisian When You're Not from Paris*. They say be available, but aloof. I wish I knew what that meant! What is 'aloof'?!

… And then the music changes, Monsieur, or should I say DJ Brown clumsily switching from a smooth, slow song into a fast, janky beat.

Whatever spell we had has been broken.

'Oh,' says Duncan, in surprise. 'Vibe shift,' he laughs, and it makes me laugh too.

'Dance-off?' I say, because we can hardly have our big romantic moment now. I *really* want to kiss Duncan, but not so much that I want it to be soundtracked by a Meghan Trainor remix.

'Are you sure you want to challenge this?' Duncan asks, before busting out an almost-perfect robot dance.

'How do you do that!' I squeal. 'Teach me! Teach me!'

After that, all the songs are dance-y ones, so we bop and spin and robot and Lucy shows us dance moves called 'feed the chickens' and 'wash the windows', and before long we're inventing ridiculous dance moves and giving them even more ridiculous names.

'Play the trumpet!' cries Axel, and we all pretend to play the trumpet.

'Disco fever!' Duncan shouts, pointing across his torso from floor to ceiling.

'Do the vomit!' Tommy yells, and we hold our stomachs and pretend to be sick to the beat of the music.

When I pause for a break, searching out a drink, Axel comes with me. We're both hot and sweaty messes, and it turns out tonight *is* fun, just in a different way. It's like because we all know this is the end, we're all truly letting go, all being as silly as we like because it's the end of days.

'What a trip!' Axel says. 'Fantastic!'

I smile. 'Good,' I say. 'I am happy if you're happy.'

Our gaze drifts out over to the dancers, where Pierre and Duncan are doing a dance move that looks like casting a fishing line and 'catching' Star and Lucy.

'So, you and Duncan ...' Axel says. 'I was right?'

I shrug.

'I was right.' He nods. *'Il n'est rien de réel que le rêve et l'amour ...'*

'What does that mean?' I ask.

'I think, *Nothing is true, except dreams and love.*'

I nod. 'You're very French sometimes,' I grin. 'Do you know that?'

'And you, Taylor Blake, are sometimes very, very English.'

'I'm OK with that,' I say, with a wink. Because do you know what? I am. It's not so bad here in Crickleton.

Ms K appears at the hall doorway then, waving something in the air. She's looking right at me – I go over.

'I hoped you'd still be here,' she says, with a big smile. 'Because I wanted to be the one to give you this.'

She hands over the paper she's holding. It's this week's *Register.* And on the back, taking up almost the whole page, is my very first published opinion column: 'You Don't Have to Go into STEM!'

'Oh my gosh!' I say, staring at it like if I blink, the words could disappear. 'Miss, thank you! Oh, thank you so much!'

23

'*H*ello! It's just us! Your favourite grandma and grandad!'

Grandma and Grandad let themselves into the house, like they always do, telling the same joke that they always do. *Of course* they're my favourite grandma and grandad – they're my *only* grandma and grandad! They come through to the kitchen, where Axel, Mum and I are having our last breakfast together.

'Bonjour, *tout le monde*!' Grandad announces, casting his arms out wide like he might burst into song. And yup! He's wearing his beret. And a massive grin. Axel opens his arms, openly impressed, and stands up to give Grandad a hug.

'Share the love!' Grandma says, once they've embraced. She gives Axel a squeeze too. 'You're like one of the family now,' she tells him as they hug. Axel towers over her; it's funny to see. 'It's been lovely having you here, *mon petit choufleur.*'

'Grandma, you know that means *my little cauliflower*, don't you?' I laugh. 'Where did you even hear that?!'

'She's got a pocket book of French phrases in her handbag,' Grandad says. 'We found it in the pound shop.'

Grandma raises her eyebrows and nods proudly. '*C'est vrai*,' she says smugly, and Mum says: 'All those years I wanted you to come visit me in Paris and you said you would as soon as you spoke the language, and now fifteen years later you've finally started to learn!'

'Best book a trip in, then.' Grandad nods, giving Axel a wink. 'We'll be coming to visit in no time!' he says, and Axel says: 'You can be my guest!' He seems to remember something then. 'Oh!' he says, patting Grandad's beret with a light touch. He digs into the front pouch of his backpack and pulls out … his own beret!

'You see!' Grandad cries, as Axel sticks it on his head at a jaunty angle. 'Look at you! Even more handsome!' We all laugh, and Axel looks thrilled with himself to have been the cause.

'I have become more French in England,' Axel says, and we all laugh, because we know what he means.

Grandma and Grandad start pouring themselves coffee before deciding that actually, they'd prefer to put the kettle on *for a cuppa*, when Mum asks: 'Have you seen this?'

She points at a copy of the *Register* by the orange juice. Grandma pulls up a seat and theatrically pulls on her glasses.

'*Crickleton High Lost Property will be laid out on the bollards at the front gates ...*' she reads, confused.

'Other side,' I laugh. She turns it over.

'You Don't Have to Go into STEM!', by Taylor Blake!' she reads. She's smiling so wide I'm worried her lips will fall off her face! 'This is fantastic, Taylor! Look at this, David!' she says, handing it to Grandad, who has sat down beside her and is picking at half a *pain au chocolat* like he couldn't possibly take the whole thing ... except he will, in about thirty seconds. He loves his food. He'll probably take a whole other one after that. No judgement!

'Well, well, well,' he mutters under his breath, skim reading it and smiling. I think he's welling up.

'Oh gosh, Grandad, don't *cry*,' I say, and he looks at me all happy and impressed and says, 'How can I not? This is marvellous, Taylor! You're so clever! We said you'd get that feminist manifesto in there soon enough! And I'd have never thought of it this way – you make an excellent point.'

'And to think you said there'd be no room for opinion pieces in the *Register*,' Mum says. 'I knew you'd get a byline again. I just didn't think it would be this soon when you've been so busy!'

'Well, you're all very kind,' I say, genuinely touched. 'But!'

287

I add, clapping my hands. 'Let's not forget what today is really about: saying goodbye to Axel!'

We all look at him, coffee cup halfway to his mouth, and his eyes go wide at the sudden attention.

'*Au revoir?*' he says, looking side to side, before taking a big dramatic slurp. It makes me giggle. He's really loosened up this week, really got in on the family humour. Grandma is right: he *does* feel like one of us!

'We've got you a little something,' Grandma announces, pulling a family-sized bar of Dairy Milk and a Crickleton keychain out of her handbag. 'To remember us by,' she says, sliding them across the table.

'*Merci …*' says Axel, his voice soft, turning over the keychain in his hand. He seems genuinely touched. 'I think I should have bought something also … but … *je suis désolé*, I didn't!' We all laugh again. It's part jolly, part sad. We've all really taken to him this week. He's kind of like what I'd imagine a very close cousin to be – family but also a great friend.

'I've prepared a little speech,' Mum says, and already her voice is wobbling. I know I gave her a hard time about being cool and not embarrassing me with her Francophile ways, but I know it's meant a lot to her, being able to use her French again. She's been happy and sing-songy. I mean, Mum is always in a pretty good mood, but even with the party – we *really* caught her on a good day. A good week!

She coughs to clear her throat, and then reads some French off a piece of paper from her pocket. The only words I can really catch of her speech is *un plaisir*. Presumably that means 'a pleasure', but whatever she's said, Grandma and Grandad are as clueless as me, but Axel looks like he's going to cry. He stands up again and gives Mum a big hug, pulling off his beret and sticking it on her head. He says something to her in French, and Mum bops his nose, like she used to do to me when I was little.

'Go on,' Mum says, wiping her eyes. 'You little cauliflowers. You'll be late if you don't go now! Are you sure I can't drive you?'

'No, Mum,' I say. 'We walked it here, we'll do a pilgrimage walk back.'

And off we go, tears in everyone's eyes.

I'm glad it's sunny, that Axel gets to remember Crickleton in this hazy low light.

'It was a good week,' he says, as we plod along.

'I agree,' I say.

'We both found love,' he comments, and I smile.

'And friendship,' I suggest, and he grins.

'And friendship,' he agrees. 'I am a boy,' he continues. 'And you are a girl. It was a …' He wafts his hand about, trying to think of the word. 'How do you say? A misunderstanding?'

I can't help but laugh. 'Yes,' I say. 'A misunderstanding. I am a girl, you are a boy, and I am very happy there was a mistake.'

'Me too. I think when you come to France next year, you come as my guest, OK?'

'I'd like that,' I tell him, because it really is what I've always wanted: to know somebody who isn't from here – no matter how OK this town might have actually turned out to be.

'My English friend,' he says, as the school gates come into view. 'I have wanted an English friend for a long time, Taylor Blake.'

'Come here,' I say. 'Let me hug you.'

Axel lets the tears flow.

The Frenchies all throw their stuff at the bottom of the coach, in the storage bit, and busy themselves hugging people and saying goodbyes. The air is sorrowful, but content: I think I'd be missing home if I was away for a week, no matter how much fun I'd had, so I get it. They're OK with going home.

Pierre arrives with Duncan, and throws his arms around Axel. I think they're both going home with more than they arrived with. Duncan looks at me shyly, and I grin.

The girls arrive, both with tears in *their* eyes, too (there's lots of crying today!!) because they've had so much fun hosting Amelie and Sophie. I feel a twinge of regret that I didn't get to know their partners very well. Hopefully I can spend more time with them when the Frenchies host us next year. Although god, that seems such a long way away. Tommy carries his partner's bag and seems like he can't wait to throw him on the coach, but looks sadder when he hugs the girl he was dancing with last night. The boy moves on fast – but good for him.

And then there's Madame Jones, standing by the bus with Monsieur Toussaint, one leg kicked back behind her as she leans against it, curling the end of her hair around a finger and giggling like … well, I want to say giggling like a schoolgirl, but I don't know anyone who giggles like that, and I *am* a schoolgirl!

Monsieur Jones loiters near us, watching them furiously. I look from him, back to them, back to him.

'I'd go and mark your territory if I were you, sir,' I say, and I half expect him to shoot back a, *'En Français, s'il vous plaît!'* But he doesn't. He narrows his eyes at me, weighing up what I've said, and a hush descends across my little group, me and Star and Lucy and Duncan and Tommy all falling quiet, unsure of what is happening but knowing it is something big.

Monsieur Brown takes a massive breath and launches

into action, marching towards the coach and shouting in a voice that's really deep and manly, 'Carrie!'

Madame Jones looks over and her knees sort of buckle, like she's swooning, and Monsieur Brown grabs her hand and pulls her close like he's going to snog her face off, and all the students gasp as we clock what's happening: two teachers! Snogging!

… But it actually doesn't get that far. Madame Jones (Carrie, lol) giggles and Monsieur Brown stops millimetres from her face. She says something, and he decides to kiss her cheek instead, very chastely. It's quite sweet, actually, if you forget for a second that they're teachers.

'Way-heyyyyyy!' shouts Tommy, and we all burst into a spontaneous round of applause, even the Frenchies – except for Monsieur Toussaint, who climbs on to the bus and sits at the front, refusing to look out of the window. Monsieur Brown does a double fist pump, and we all cheer again before the Frenchies board the coach and we fall quiet, silently waving them off.

'Starbucks?' Lucy asks when they turn out of the school drive, out of sight.

I shake my head.

'No,' I say, because this feeling that I have to go home and capture this moment is so strong I think I might *run* back. 'There's something I need to go and do …'

* * *

I feel really emotional after this week. Axel is right: we both got our loves (or crushes, at least), and we made great friends. But I also feel like I've learned things about myself, too. I know that sounds really dramatic and grand, but it's true!

I skipped going to Starbucks with the girls because I can feel words brewing in my fingertips. I'm glad Mum is out teaching at the university when I get home, and I can use the key under the flowerpot to let myself in to a quiet house, where I can curl up on the sofa with my laptop. I make myself a cordial and grab a KitKat, and look out of the window to the garden for a bit. It makes me think of Axel, how much he loved Grandma and Grandad's garden. Finally I get settled, and I let the words pour out:

I've spent the week with a stranger in my house. A stranger who ate at my kitchen table and followed me to school. But, by the end of the week, they weren't a stranger any more. They were a friend!

I had huge expectations for the French exchange. I thought it was going to be my first step into a wider world – a world where I knew people from other countries! What I didn't expect is that it would make me appreciate where I am from even more. It's not about who I can be as much as who I already am.

I appreciate the way my mother welcomed this stranger into my home. I appreciate how my grandparents wore berets and learned French rap. And I even appreciate the look on my exchange partner's face when he tried fish and chips for the first time, or British coffee. He hated both! But it was hilarious!

I appreciate the effort the teachers made. I appreciate seeing my town with new eyes, from the museums to the woods. They're not mind-blowing, but they're home! And I especially appreciate how having strangers here found me friends from within my own classrooms: everyone who did the exchange ended up becoming friends, in one way or another, and that is priceless.

They say you should be yourself because everyone else is already taken. Well, after this week, I finally understand that! I always wished I had been born somewhere else, somewhere more exotic or cool. But after this week, I get it! We're all just people who have hopes, and dreams, and crushes, no matter where we are from. And we all need each other!

I'd sign up for the exchange again in a heartbeat. Because, truthfully, it put an extra beat into my heart, and definitely a skip in my step.

I finish writing. I'm crying – tears are streaming down my face! And it's because of that that I know this article isn't an article at all, and it isn't for anybody else. This is for me, like a diary entry. Something to keep, so I remember this forever.

24

'I want to look like myself,' I say, remembering the last time Star did my make-up, that day in the girls' toilets. 'Not too much eyeliner, not too much lipstick … just natural-looking.'

'The sort of natural that takes two hours and the three of us to get right?' Lucy quips, and I roll my eyes.

'Shut up, you!' I say, but I'm just messing. I'm so happy that they're here, helping me get ready for MY FIRST EVER DATE!! I'm pleased that everything is back to normal. I've tried to be a better friend, asking them more about themselves and how they found the exchange, but they're also giving me room to just freak the heck out about (did I mention this?) MY FIRST EVER DATE!!! I couldn't do it without them.

'I think you should do lip balm instead of lip gloss,' make-up artiste Star says, blending something over my eyelid. 'Because when you kiss, you don't want it to be gloopy and gross.'

I feel like I could be sick, but in a good way. An excited way.

'Oh wait,' she adds, thinking. 'Was it *you* who gave *me* that piece of advice?'

I did, but that's not what I want to talk about.

'Do you really think we will kiss?' I ask, eyes still closed.

'At this point … yes,' says Star. 'Don't you think, Lucy?'

'I think, let's just enjoy it all for what it is. There was so much pressure for kissing at the party and look what happened. Tonight doesn't have to be *all* your firsts: first date, first kiss …'

'Now who is being mature!' observes Star. 'Urgh! I see why you hate it when I get that way now. I feel all shallow in comparison!'

'Yin and yang, babe,' Lucy giggles, 'Yin and yang.'

'OK, eyes open,' Star commands, and I look at her as she narrows her eyes, appraising me. 'Good,' she says, and Lucy gives me a thumbs up.

'I'll start on your hair,' Lucy says. 'So we don't end up rushing.'

She plugs in the ghds and puts them on the metal of the radiator whilst they warm up. As we wait, she brushes through my hair and then pins bits up, out of the way, so she can get to the layers underneath.

'What are you two up to tonight?' I say, remembering to talk about something other than Duncan.

'That's cute,' Lucy laughs, going in on the first bit of my hair.

'What?' I say.

'Trying to be all easy-breezy and asking us about what we're up to, when all you want to do is talk about Duncan!'

'I'm trying my best!' I squeal. 'Of course he's all I want to talk about! At least right now!'

'It's OK,' Star says, giving me a tiny bit of mascara. 'Your efforts have been noted, and appreciated.'

'Thank you,' I say. 'I'd like it timestamped in the transcript of this conversation, please.'

She pretends to write in the invisible notebook in the palm of her hand.

'Done and done,' she smiles, stepping back to give me the once-over. 'Now,' she muses. 'I think we've nailed it, don't you?'

'Shift out of the way of the mirror and I'll tell you!' I giggle, and she acts offended, clutching her imaginary pearls, but she giggles too, and steps aside so I can see myself. She's right – I look good! Not too much make-up, just sort of fresh-faced and dewy. I'd make the authors of *How to Be Parisian When You're Not from Paris* proud, I think.

'And you're comfortable in your outfit?' Lucy asks again, for the millionth time.

'Yes!' I say. 'I know it's not the fanciest, but I'm honestly just so exhausted from trying to dress like the Frenchies that it's a relief to dress as myself tonight. I think jeans and a T-shirt is a good vibe. Me, with nice hair.'

'You with nice hair, perfect,' declares Star, and Lucy smooths down the last part of my hair, adding in a flick to the bits around my face, and together we look at my reflection once more.

'I feel really emotional,' Lucy says. 'Is that weird?'

'Yes,' says Star, with a light giggle. 'But I feel it too, so we're both weird.'

They stand either side of me and wrap an arm around me each, and I say, 'I love you guys. Thanks for this.'

'Just make sure you tell us *everything* when you get home,' Star says. 'OK?'

'Unless we go and sit two rows behind them and spy ...' says Lucy, and for a split second I can't tell if she's joking. 'Oh my gosh!' she laughs. 'Taylor! Calm down. Look at your face! We're not going to spy.'

Before I can say anything, the doorbell rings. I swallow, hard.

'Hello! Duncan! Nice to see you again!' I hear Mum say downstairs. I check myself one last time and say, 'I'd better go. She'll be pouring him tea and talking about the numbers her last TikTok video got if I don't.'

'Go,' Star says with an excited squeal. 'We'll come down when he's gone. Poor boy doesn't need an audience.'

'So of course, I was getting my past perfect and past continuous tenses mixed up,' Mum is saying to Duncan, who is politely sitting on the sofa. Instead of social media, she's talking to him about her other love: French. Like mother, like daughter! 'Because my French is so rusty! I'm thinking of taking a refresher course, but I suppose what I need is a conversation partner, somebody to just chat and practise with that way. Maybe Axel will FaceTime with me! Or his parents. Now there's an idea …'

'Taylor!' Duncan exclaims, when he sees me. The words seem to dash out of his mouth involuntarily, because he shuts his mouth quickly once he's spoken, like he's trying to stop any further words from escaping.

'Hi,' I say, and I know it's 'just' Duncan, my friend, a guy who I've spent loads of time talking to recently, a boy who is the easiest boy in the world to hang out and chat with. But. He's never been the Duncan who picks me up at my house wearing a shirt. He's really made the effort! He's got gel in his hair, too, and a small bunch of flowers in his lap.

'These are for you,' he says, as he spots me seeing them. 'Just to say … you know … urm …'

'That's really sweet, Duncan,' Mum says, I think sensing he needs rescuing. 'How about I take those and put them in water? I'll stop chattering on now – you don't want to be late! I'm going to set up my phone and lights and make some content for my TikTok account. Wish me luck!'

I shoot Mum A Look and tell Duncan I'll just get my coat.

'Have a good evening, Erica,' Duncan says, getting up to follow me. 'I promise I'll have her home by nine p.m.!'

Mum sticks her head around the door of the kitchen. 'She's not your responsibility,' she says. 'Taylor, make sure you have *yourself* home by nine, OK? You know I trust you!'

'Thanks, Mum!' I say, before telling Duncan: 'Can you tell she's a single mother doing it on her own? No woman needs a man?'

Duncan holds up his hands 'I see it, I like it, I respect it,' he says. 'Now. Shall we?'

'We shall,' I say, stepping out into the early night.

We meander up the drive and make a left to the top of the hill in a bit of an awkward silence. We're going to walk to the small independent cinema in town. I'm happy to be here, but I feel like I don't know how to find my way to the usual

302

back-and-forth conversations we have. What am I supposed to say? *Good day? How's it going? What have you been up to today?* It all feels so … things you'd say to an elderly auntie you haven't seen since you were seven.

'Can I hold your hand?' Duncan says, breaking the quiet between us. A bolt of happiness shoots through me, bursting into a million fireworks. What a straightforward way to ask the question. And in such a straightforward way would I like to answer!

'Yes,' I say, holding it out, and he takes it and he's warm and firm and lovely, and then suddenly the silence doesn't seem as big, it seems comfortable. I sneak a peek at him, all sandy hair and soft features. I can't believe this boy was under my nose this whole time! Like an actor in the wings of the stage, waiting for his cue.

'I read the book you gave me,' I say, and I don't even overthink saying it. I have the thought, and then I say it out loud.

'Yeah? And what's the verdict?' Duncan asks.

'It's really good,' I say. 'I suppose I thought it was a kids' book, but—'

'But it's not really, is it?' Duncan smiles. 'But there's something about it being written in rhyme …'

'Yes!' I agree. 'That's what I was going to say! It makes something really scary, this idea of having setbacks sometimes easier to understand? Because it's done in a fun way. It's got me thinking about how we tell stories. Like, not every big sad story needs a big sad delivery?'

'I think there's a word for that, for when comedy and sadness are side by side.' He clicks the fingers on his free hand. 'Damn. I can't remember.'

'Minus ten points for you, then,' I say, and Duncan rolls his eyes.

'So the uncertain and awkward part of this date is over?' he asks.

I laugh.

'It *was* uncertain and awkward for a minute there, wasn't it?' I say.

Duncan shrugs. 'You've come through though,' he says. 'You're dragging me into the micky-taking and sarcastic part of the date quite happily!'

'I'm glad you said quite happily,' I tell him. 'Otherwise I'd have told you to get back into the awkward bit!'

Duncan laughs. 'No, no! Here we are! I've dreamed about being here with you!'

He says it as a joke, but as soon as he's said it it's like we both know he means it.

'Not in a creepy way,' he says, pulling a funny *oooops!* face. 'Just. I've always thought you were really cool. And now you're being cool in my presence. On purpose.'

'Duncan,' I say, deciding that it's OK to continue to rib him. 'This whole *nobody-knows-who-I-am, I'm-just-the-quiet-boy-at-the-front-of-the-class* routine is over now. There's no hiding. You're a copy editor extraordinaire, Ms K's second-favourite writer ...'

'No idea who her first-favourite writer is ...' he says. I point at myself, and he nods with a smile. 'Obviously,' he concludes.

'My point being,' I say, 'I'm happy to be here with you, too. You, Ceek!'

'Ceek!' he exclaims. 'I forgot about that! Cool geeks unite!'

'Cool geeks unite!' I echo.

We round the corner and there's the cinema, a sign for the comedy we're going to see lit up outside.

'It's supposed to be really good,' Duncan says, nodding at the poster.

'Yeah, the reviews are really good, I think,' I say.

Inside, we queue for our tickets. Still holding hands!! And when Horrid Anna from the year above comes in with her parents, she sees us and I pretend I haven't seen her, but I know she's clocked that Duncan and I are here on a date. And if she knows, it means everyone at school will know soon enough. She's such a gossip!

'I've got this,' Duncan says, when we get to the front of

the queue. Before I can protest, he says, 'Popcorn, too? With a Smarties topper?'

I don't know what to say. I don't know what the feminist politics are of having a boy pay for your ticket and snacks. It doesn't *feel* very feminist, and I'm sure Mum wouldn't approve.

But before I can say anything Duncan has handed over his card and we're already walking towards the theatre.

'I'll pay next time,' I say, and Duncan wiggles his eyebrows.

'Already talking about a next time!' he says. 'I'll take it!'

We get settled in our seats, and I don't mean to compare boys to each other, but I do have a thought. I think, Duncan and I like to talk about the same things. Tommy always seemed bored by what I'm interested in. Why did I ever think I could make myself fancy him?! This is so much better.

I'm having so much fun!

The movie is brilliant, and we hold hands nearly the whole time, breaking occasionally to wipe the sweat off our palms. We find all the same bits funny, even the bits other people don't laugh at, and when we come out we regale each other with impressions of our favourite parts of the film.

'No!' Duncan laughs, as we flop down on the bench outside the cinema. 'When he says to that guy, *Don't do that, we've only been married two days!* And then drops the watermelon! That was hilarious!'

'Yeah,' I laugh, putting on a voice to mimic the actor. 'Oh! Watch your fruit, sir!'

People trickle out beside us as others line up for the next showing.

'We should probably shut up now,' I say. 'We don't want to spoil it for everyone else.' I nod towards the line, and Duncan takes the hint.

'I would say that I should get you home, but as your mother rightly pointed out, you are your own responsibility so … you should be getting yourself home? As I just happen to walk beside you?'

I look at the clock face of the big clock tower in the marketplace. It's quarter to nine.

'I just need to go to the toilet,' I say, standing up. 'Those large Cokes are no joke.'

'Same,' Duncan says. 'Meet back here in two?'

I do a soldier's salute. 'Yes, sir! Thank you, sir!' I even do a funny march towards the toilets, not even caring that everyone is watching me be ridiculous.

I don't really need to pee. It actually just occurred to me that if we are going to kiss, I should probably have a Tic Tac and put on more lip balm, but if I did it in front of Duncan I thought it might come across as *expecting* a kiss to happen, when it's all supposed to be very natural and unplanned and surprising, *à la* what Lucy said, not to mention *How to Be Parisian When You're Not from Paris*!

The Moment

All a Parisian woman needs to know is this: you
cannot force the moment. The moment will find
you when the time is right …
And then all you must do is enjoy it!

The mascara Star put on my lashes has leaked under my eyes – I really did cry with laughter at the movie – so I tidy myself up, freshening my breath and moistening my lips. I look at my reflection. Despite myself, I think, *This is it! The last time you'll look at yourself as a kiss virgin!!*

'All good?' asks Duncan outside, and I nod. 'In that case,' he says, 'may I hold your hand again?'

I grin. 'You may,' I say, and even though it's cold now my heart beating like a big old brass band keeps me warm, and we pass the walk back to my house talking about the movie some more.

'And not forgetting,' Duncan says, once we reach the top of my drive. 'You did say next time you'll pay, which means there has to be a next time …'

His voice has gone softer, and we're facing each other.

I half wonder if Mum is twitching the curtains from her writing studio. Not that I care. Why would I, when I've had so much fun, and the only thing that could make tonight any better is to KISS? Plus, I do know that Mum would never spy. If she thought it was going to happen, she'd give us our privacy. She gets it.

Duncan still has my fingers laced through his, so if I pulled at his hand he'd have to step closer. Should I do that? Is that too forward? I look at him shyly, the chat between us now having petered out into quiet, the sky darkened. He's looking down at his shoes, and I'm looking down at my shoes, and our foreheads are tipped towards each other.

I take a breath. I try to enjoy the moment instead of skipping to the *really* good part. I take a breath and look up, right as Duncan does, ready to close my eyes and lean into the only thing left to do ... when Duncan says, 'Right then! I'll let you get inside! Thanks for a lovely time! Bye!'

And then he's gone. He practically *runs* to the top of the road, not even turning back. It's like he's made his great escape!

What the heck!

I was busy over here thinking about finally kissing and he can't get away fast enough?!

I AM SO TERRIBLE AT THIS! I'm awful at this! I thought things were going so well and I was wrong, wrong, wrong!

I walk to the front door totally stunned. I can't believe that just happened. But then as I go in and Mum yells from the writing studio, 'Taylor? Is that you?' I know for a fact I'm about to burst into tears. I can't even shout out hello, I just kick my shoes off and bolt upstairs and climb into bed fully clothed, pull the duvet up over my head, and I cry, and I cry, and I cry.

25

I don't text Duncan, because I don't know what to say. And I ignore pleas for gossip in Members Only, for the same reason. I must have literally cried myself to sleep because I wake up in the same clothes I wore out last night, minus my jeans, which I vaguely remember taking off at 2 a.m., too hot and uncomfortable.

But then, at a quarter to nine, Duncan texts me. It says, *Thanks for a great time last night!* And has a smiley face at the end. Am I hallucinating? Did we experience the same ending to the date? Thank god it's a Saturday and I can stay at home, in my room, hidden away from the world! I get up for a wee and see the toothbrush glass Duncan gave me some water in, the night of the party. I open my curtains pull out a book from off my bedside table (reading *always* cheers me up!) and *Oh, the Places You'll Go!* falls to the floor. I kick it under the bed. Duncan is everywhere! I'd like ten minutes of thinking without his face popping into my head!!

'Urgh!' I huff and puff, and Mum yells upstairs, 'Bug? Are you up?'

I'll bet it's killed her to be so patient. She gave me my space last night, which was very awesome of her. I know she loitered at my bedroom door for ages, and she knocked and asked if she could do anything, but when I said no she didn't push it. But today is a new day, and Erica Blake won't let me get away with hiding, as much as I want to.

'I've put in the last of the frozen croissants!' she yells. 'And made fresh juice!'

I mean, yeah, I'm sad. But I'm not going to skip on freshly baked croissants. I'll go down for one and show my face, and then get on with my moping.

'Morning, beautiful,' she says, as I pad into the kitchen in yesterday's T-shirt and my underwear.

'Morning,' I mumble, wiping sleep from my eyes.

Mum pretends she's totally not interested in me sitting down, in me pouring my juice, in me putting some butter and jam on my plate ready for the pastries. She idly looks out of the window, makes her coffee, and I know what she's doing. I tell her so. I say, 'Mum. You're so obvious.'

'What?' she says, like butter wouldn't melt.

'You're waiting for me to speak first,' I say. 'So I don't feel claustrophobic. There's a whole chapter on it in *Raising Empowered Teens*.'

'You've been reading my library books?' Mum says, amusement playing across her face.

'If there are going to be books written about us, I'd like to know what they say.' I shrug.

She pulls out the croissants and plates them up, slipping into the chair opposite me. We help ourselves, and for a minute I forget all about being sad, because everything is just so delicious. And then she looks at me over the rim of her coffee cup, and even though I know she's trying to be discreet she isn't. *Raising Empowered Teens* would fail her for this look. This is *not* being 'hands off'.

'Do you want to talk about it?' she asks eventually.

I knew it! I knew she'd crack! Not that I blame her. I'd be curious too.

'Not really,' I say, but she catches my eye and smirks, because being surly and moody doesn't suit me and we both know it. 'Well,' I say, deciding that OK, I'll tell her, but I'll be strong and act like it's not a big deal.

But then I try to finish that sentence, and I burst into tears.

'Oh, darling!' she says, coming to sit beside me. She puts her arm around me as I let the tears flow – I'm surprised I have any left, to be honest, after last night. They are big, horrible sobs, the sort of tears that well up faster than you can swallow them down and so make everything twenty times more dramatic than you want them to be.

'Oh, love …' Mum says, stroking my back, and I end up crawling into her lap like I did when I was four and had scraped my knee. I curl up on her, clinging to her neck, and she rubs my back under my T-shirt.

'Darling,' she says. 'Did he … hurt you? Did he pressure you, or …?'

'What?' I say, pulling away. 'No! Oh gosh, no!'

She's *met* Duncan, right? He wouldn't hurt a fly!

'You can tell me if he did. You won't be in trouble …'

I shake my head and try taking some big breaths. More sobs come, but I'm breathing deeper. I can't look right at Mum – I'm too embarrassed – so I stare at the ceiling, willing the tears to stop coming. Mum pushes my juice towards me and I take several sips, the cool liquid running down my burning throat. It helps.

I'm OK.

I'm feeling better.

'I feel really embarrassed,' I say sadly.

'Dates can be embarrassing,' she tells me. 'Did I ever tell you about when I went on a date when I was nineteen, and my period came early and I leaked all over my WHITE trousers?'

314

'No!' I say. 'That's awful!'

Mum nods. 'Yup,' she says. 'And that's not the worst bit. The worst bit is that we were in a pub garden, and a woman came over to tell me – you know, girls look after each other like that, don't they? And as soon as my date realised what had happened, he acted like he didn't know me! Just wandered off and never came back!'

'Seriously?!' I ask her, snivelling back some snot so disgustingly that Mum grimaces and hands me a tissue.

'Seriously,' she says, as I blow my nose. 'Your Auntie Kate has some toe-curlingly bad stories, too, but I'll let her fill you in. It wouldn't be fair for me to gossip about her.'

'Will you gossip about me?' I ask.

'Never,' Mum tells me, drawing an 'x' over her chest and adding: 'Cross my heart.'

I sigh.

'There was no kiss,' I say finally.

There.

I've told her.

Mum doesn't say anything. It's like she's waiting for more information.

'And I thought there would be?' I clarify. 'We had a really nice time, and we held hands, and then when he walked me home I thought it would finally happen and he sort of … ran off.'

'Ran off … literally? Or lost his confidence?' Mum asks. Huh. I hadn't thought of it like that. Lost his confidence? The notion never occurred to me.

'I don't know,' I say. 'He sent a text this morning to say he had a nice time.'

'Polite boy.' Mum nods.

'Well, not really. Not if he doesn't like me that way. If he doesn't like me that way he shouldn't say he had a nice time, he should say thanks, but let's just be friends.'

'I see what you mean,' Mum says. 'I take your point …'

I sigh again. This is all such a mess.

'But …' she presses. 'Well, I've only met him twice, but he seems very emotionally mature, Taylor. I don't think he'd say he had a nice time if he didn't.'

I don't know what to say to that. Why didn't he kiss me then? Why did he launch himself back up the road like he couldn't get away from me fast enough?

'Look,' Mum says, tucking my hair behind my ears. 'I can't read minds, so I don't know for sure what is in Duncan's heart. But I do know this: You are an infinitely kissable, beautiful girl, and Duncan looks at you like you're the stars, the sun, the earth and the moon all rolled into one. He might just be nervous, or even trying to make sure the moment is absolutely perfect, because he wants to impress you, or maybe he likes you so much that he believes you're worth perfect.'

'Do you think I'm silly for getting upset over a boy?' I say.

'Silly? Taylor, no! Why would I ever think you're silly!'

'You don't get upset over boys. You don't even date! You don't need anyone!'

Mum pulls a face, and I can't tell what it means.

'Well,' she says eventually, 'maybe I never met anyone who makes me feel how Duncan makes you feel. You know, it's not about *needing* someone, a boyfriend or a kiss or whatever … it's about *wanting* it. And there is nothing wrong with wanting someone! Wanting to share experiences with somebody – especially something as lovely as a first kiss … wanting a friend and comfort and romance … that's totally normal, bug-a-boo. And getting upset over a boy isn't silly or weak. I hope you know that. In fact, I don't think I tell you often enough how proud I am of you, how much I admire you. I admire your hunger for romance, your zest for life … this … *fearlessness* that you have. You love hard, and trust easily, and you know that being excitable is better than playing it cool. Honestly, you're the best of all teenage girls on the cusp of it all, ready to dive in with a wide-open heart, and that's what makes you so utterly special, darling. Don't ever change – hold on to that hunger and that zest, because lord knows as you grow up, life will try and knock it out of you. Resist. Keep that heart open – *especially* when it comes to wanting to kiss a boy you really like!'

She bends down to give my forehead a kiss.

'Knowing you, you probably suspect it's not very feminist to get upset over a boy, but I promise you: It's just as feminist to want friendship and romance with a boy as it is to *not* want these things if you choose not to. Feminism is all about equality and freedom of choice. Men don't sit around wondering if they're allowed to have crushes! So you shouldn't either. Go after what you want, even if the only reason is because you just *want it*!'

I feel better now, like the heaviness in my chest has been pricked with a pin, so it can leak out of me.

'Did you text him back?' Mum asks.

'No.' I shake my head. 'Not yet.'

'Do you know when you'll see him again?'

'At school, I suppose,' I say. 'And we have the prize-giving ceremony for the writing competition on Monday, too.'

Mum nods. 'Well,' she says, wrapping her arms even more tightly around me. It's like she doesn't want to let me go. 'Whether you text back or not, don't be too hard on him. Be the nice girl you naturally are, and try to keep that heart wide open, OK? Even when it feels hard. We have to have wide-open hearts to make it all worthwhile.'

'OK,' I say, and she kisses the top of my head.

'Now get off me,' she says, 'because I've lost all feeling in my legs.'

I laugh, and climb off, but from where I sit next to her I

still stretch my legs out so they're in her lap and she can hold my feet.

'By the way,' I say, remembering who paid last night. 'Who should pay for a date? Because last night Duncan paid. Was that wrong?'

I brace myself to hear I should have been more assertive and paid my share, but she just laughs.

'Oh, bug-a-boo, it really doesn't matter,' she says. 'Just let him pay, if he offers. Clearly Duncan knows that chivalry isn't dead yet.'

I decide to shower and brush my teeth so that I'm a bit fresher, and make my bed and open a window so that yes, I can continue wallowing, but I can also do it with a bit of fresh air and without smelling like BO. I keep picking up my phone and looking at Duncan's text, still not sure what to make of everything. I feel loads better after everything Mum said, though. He's a good, kind, nice person to know, and I can't force somebody to snog me. I can't punish him by giving him the silent treatment.

I do need a little bit more time to nurse my ego, though.

At around 4 p.m., I get an email. It's from Duncan. My immediate thought is: *Oh, so NOW you're eager?! I didn't reply to your text, so now you're doing another method of communication?!* It's not a kind reaction. I know that!

Despite myself, I open it. The subject line intrigues me. It says, *I couldn't help myself!*

In the body of the email, there's just a link over the words *Click here*, like it could almost be spam. I might regret doing this when my whole computer gets a virus! But I'm too curious not to …

A website comes up: www.theinstructionmanual.co.uk – and in case I didn't get it, the same words are in big capital letters at the top of the screen, too: THE INSTRUCTION MANUAL. The rest is mostly blank, like it's a template for what the *Instruction Manual* could be. It's got bold, blocky colours and headings at the top for *culture*, *opinion*, *sports* and *about*. I click on the headings, which all lead to blank pages. Except *About* …

In this section, there's my photo, and underneath is Duncan's. My photo is of half my face, taken from the side, and I'm laughing, tipping my head back. I think it was taken last week. I had no idea Duncan had snapped it. Next to it, it says: *Head Writer.* Then: *Taylor Blake is the best writer in all of Crickleton, and probably all of the world. She has eyes that light up and a laugh that makes you want to hear it forever. Everyone wants to know her, because she is really special.*

Next to Duncan's picture is says: *Editor. Taylor was there the first ever time he talked. Before that he was mute.*

320

This is so cute! Does it mean Duncan really does want to launch this as a project together? It would be very awesome if he does: It's one thing having somebody let you write for their publication, but having *our own* publication is *legendary*. People think I'm a legend because of a party? Well, what if I had my own online newspaper!

I obviously can't ignore this. Especially after everything Mum said, it's blatant that no matter what, Duncan and I have a special friendship, whether kissing is involved or not. I hit reply and type: *GAME ON! I'll send you ten ideas for articles by Monday x*

If Duncan *doesn't* want to kiss me, and only wants to be my friend, maybe it wouldn't really be that bad. Not when we can do something like this together. I could settle for this.

You know. When I'm done being humiliated.

26

Members Only

Lucy: *Good luck tonight!*

Star: *Thinking of you, writer extraordinaire!*

Star: *And definitely not wondering what it will be like to see Duncan!*

Lucy: *Nope! Definitely not!!*

'You lied.'

I put my phone away before Duncan can see me talking about him on the screen. His voice comes from behind. It's the first time I've seen him since Friday night. I kept thinking I'd bump into him at school, but bizarrely I didn't. I couldn't help but wonder if he was keeping his distance. But here we are, in the lobby of Lady Manners, where we've agreed to all meet up – him, me and Ms K – before the creative writing prize-giving ceremony.

'I have a habit of that,' I say, because it sounds witty. I actually have no idea what I'm supposed to have lied about, but he's smiling, so it can't be that serious.

'Ten ideas before the end of the weekend,' he said. 'You said you'd send ten ideas, but I haven't seen any ...'

I nod. 'I've got them,' I say. 'But it struck me that you emailed from your school address, when, if we're going to have our own website, you should be emailing me from Duncan at theinstructionmanual dot com ...'

He narrows his eyes. 'And so ...?' he says, crooking an eyebrow.

'And so I set those up. And if you log in to your new official email, I think you'll find my pitches, from *my* official email. And I sent eleven. Just to be extra.'

Before Duncan can reply, Ms K appears.

'You're both here!' she says. 'Excellent! How are you? How do you feel?'

Duncan shrugs. 'No expectations,' he says. 'It's all experience, isn't it?'

Ms K shakes her head like she can't believe what she's hearing. 'Duncan,' she says. 'Your maturity and level head continue to impress me. What other Year 9 boy would say such a thing. Isn't he wise, Taylor?'

My phone beeps again. It's a photo of Mum, Grandma and Grandad, holding up a piece of paper that says: *Good Luck, Taylor!* Underneath Mum has texted: *We're so proud of you. Text as soon as you've won!*

'A wise boy with a bad haircut,' I quip, reading the message and then slipping my phone on to silent mode. Duncan looks horrified and touches his head and says, 'Hey!' but I wink at him, to let him know I'm kidding.

Ms K laughs, and tells us we can go into the hall in a moment, but shall we go around and look at all the submissions out on display? They're all up on big boards, divided up by year group and category. On the Year 9 board it says BECOMING in big letters at the top, with a dozen or so entries pinned below.

'There you are,' Duncan points out, and it occurs to me it's the first time he's seen my entry. I reread it as he checks it out, reminding myself of what I said:

Moving Mountains

He sees me. It came as a surprise.
Kindred spirits, he and I.
I like my laughter more now.
To make him smile is to win gold.
And silver.

And bronze.

He believes in me, and it makes me strong.

He knows what I can do.

I didn't know that's what I was waiting for.

But all along it was you.

'Oh!' I say, before I can stop myself. Duncan looks at me, questions in his eyes.

'Bit much, isn't it?' I say, because I'm embarrassed. But … I've just learned something about myself. I've just learned that what I thought was a poem inspired by Axel during the French exchange actually isn't that at all. Now I've read the book Duncan gave me, I understand why I called my poem 'Moving Mountains'. It's because that's what we talked about when he told me about it, the day I said I wanted to write and be a journalist and travel the world. The day he listened, and didn't ignore me like Tommy or say something poetic like Axel. Duncan heard me talk about my dreams and told me I could do them: 'And will you succeed?' he'd quoted. 'Ninety-eight and three quarters per cent guaranteed!'

I think my poem is for Duncan! And that I've liked him as more than a friend for way longer than I realised!!!

'It's good,' Duncan says, bumping his shoulder against mine. 'I think you could win with that, you know.'

My throat is dry and I can't respond. Can Duncan tell it's

about him? I have no idea if he likes me or not, but I've told myself it doesn't matter because we make an excellent team, whatever we are romantically. But seeing my words up there for everyone to see … everyone is going to know I have a crush on him, aren't they?

'There's a symmetry between your entries,' Ms K says, pointing out Duncan's. 'Which is poetry in itself, isn't it?'

I follow her finger to see Duncan's poem. It's my first time seeing it. It's called 'Mountains and Other Things', and underneath, in smaller writing, says: *Inspired by Dr Seuss, for her.*

Now I really can't breathe. Is the 'her' me? I look at him, but he's looking at his favourite place: the floor. I drag my eyes back to his work, and force myself to keep reading even though I might DIE of a HEART ATTACK at any moment!!

Mountains and Other Things
Inspired by Dr Seuss, for her

Sometimes I feel invisible
Like half a person or less
But then you say my name
And suddenly I couldn't care less
About what other people think,

Or what other people do
The person who makes me smile
I've got to admit: it's you
You're funny but you're kind
And always speak your mind
You're driven and you're bold
With you they broke the mould!
And what I want to tell you,
Is that because you're so deeply you
Is that I feel braver about this life
I can move mountains too!

'Whoa,' I say, 'Duncan! That's so good!'

'Nooooo,' he says, still not looking at me. 'I don't know. It's not as good as yours.'

'They're both fantastic,' Ms K says. 'And like I say, they're a nice pair. Now come on, let's go and take our seats. The ceremony is about to begin.'

We fuss about getting seated, and my brain is working even more overtime than it normally does. I'm pretty sure Duncan *does* like me! Which means Mum could be right: everything is fine between us, and the right moment will come. I feel my shoulders drop and it's easier to keep my chin held high. I'm even smiling! I can't help it!

'I really did like your poem,' I tell Duncan as Ms K pops to the loo.

'Not too soppy?' he asks. I shake my head.

'The perfect amount of soppy,' I say, and then I pull a face, and Duncan laughs, and it all feels normal again. THANK GOODNESS!!

'And just for the sake of clarity,' Duncan says, 'do I really have a bad haircut?'

'I was yanking your chain, pal,' I laugh, and he does a dramatic sigh, like it's really been weighing on his mind.

'You didn't text me back,' he says plainly. 'I've been worried.'

Before I can stop myself, I say: '*You* ran away from *me*! I've been worried!'

'I'm an idiot,' he says, and I roll my eyes.

'Don't say that, Duncan,' Ms K says, slipping back into her seat beside me. 'A bit daft, yes, but not an *idiot*.'

'Thanks, miss,' Duncan laughs. 'I appreciate the pep talk.'

'She wouldn't be calling you daft if she knew what you'd done this weekend …' I say, trying to sound all mysterious.

'Dare I ask?' Ms K says.

I stifle a giggle.

'I'll tell you, miss, but you can't get upset. Because it might compete with the *Register*, you see.'

329

'Go on …' she challenges.

'He's set up an online newspaper!' I announce, unable to keep my big mouth shut! 'For us to run together! Called the *Instruction Manual*!'

Duncan pulls it up on his phone and shows her the site template.

'Wow,' Ms K says. 'This is great! But why do this instead of the *Register*? You've been writing amazing stuff for that, Taylor, and you're doing such good work there too, Duncan!'

'We're just playing,' Duncan says. 'Seeing what it might be like. There'd be no word count like there is for the school paper, and we could write what we wanted.'

Ms K nods. 'You could,' she says. 'Well. I'm impressed! Let me know how you get on with it! Will you be taking submissions from other students?'

Duncan looks at me. I shrug.

'We're still developing the idea,' I say.

'But we have official email addresses!' Duncan adds.

'Oh, well, if you've got official email addresses …' Ms K smiles, and Duncan rolls his eyes and says, 'We'll keep you posted, miss. We might even let you write for us. You know – if your pitch is strong enough.'

We all laugh, and only start to hush as the head of Lady Manners takes to the stage to welcome us. The lights dim slightly, so there's more of a spotlight on the stage, and Duncan's knee knocks against mine. I look at him, half of his face illuminated from the lights at the front. I grin. He grins too. I don't even care if I win. I'm just happy to be here, with him, talking about writing websites and mountains, laughing, having fun.

We sit through what feels like twenty million categories before they get to ours, but when we realise it's us, Duncan and I both sit up straighter, at the edge of our seats, paying attention to every last word. I don't know who grabs whose hand, but we're clutching each other's fingertips and I feel a thousand volts of energy pulsate through my body. The head says our names as part of the wider list of submissions, and says things about how the standard was so high, it was a really tough choice for the judges, blah, blah, blah.

'I wish he'd get on with it!' I whisper, and a girl in front of me turns round and smiles, like she wishes he would too. I have a premonition that Duncan is the winner. I feel it in my gut. I might be biased, but I really do think his poem is the best.

'And the winner is …' the head says, and I grip Duncan's hand even tighter. '… Candice Smithers!'

'What!' Duncan whispers, but it turns out Candice is the girl in front of us, so I make sure to give a little whoop, because I don't want her to think we're sore losers. She stands up and goes to collect her prize: a small medal and a book token for twenty pounds.

'I thought for sure you were the winner!' Duncan tells me as we clap once more, but I really don't mind. Like he said earlier, it's all experience, isn't it.

The clapping quietens, and it's then the best thing ever happens.

We've stopped holding hands, but Duncan reaches across to my lap and grabs it again. I grin at him. He grins at me. And we sit that way for the rest of the evening, hand in hand, losers in writing … but winners, I think, in something else.

'Well,' Ms K says, when it's all over. If she's noticed Duncan and me continuing to hold hands, even as we walk back to the entrance hall, she hasn't said anything. 'You've both got highly commended, which, if you ask me, is only right, and so the judges are not *total* fools. They know good work when they see it.'

'You're biased, miss, but thanks,' I say.

'Facts are facts.' She shrugs, and I think she's taking our loss harder than we are. 'And we can start thinking about the next competition. If you have time now you've got your own website! I was thinking, let's shoot for something national next. Why not, you know?'

'Sounds good,' Duncan says, and I know before he even says it that he's going to walk me home. I can just tell.

'Well done both of you, anyway,' Ms K says. 'I'd better let you get home. And me – I've got a hot date with a bowl of cereal and my Netflix account!' We all laugh, but I only realise a beat too late that she isn't kidding. 'See you tomorrow!'

'See you tomorrow, miss!' Duncan and I say, and I'm right: without asking, Duncan starts to walk with me.

27

We get the bus, sitting side by side and trundling through the Crickleton streets. And then Duncan gets off with me at my stop, and we head towards my house, and it's like an exact replay of Friday night. He stands opposite me, and we're still holding hands, and the air between us gets all still and serious.

'I've never kissed anyone before,' he suddenly says. 'I keep thinking I'm going to kiss you, but I feel a bit nervous, to be honest.'

As if to prove his point he lets out a big exhale with a giggle, which is most definitely an anxious thing.

'I've never kissed anyone either,' I say, touched by his honesty. Duncan's poem said I make him braver – well, when he's honest and truthful like this, he inspires me to be brave and do the same too.

'What?!' Duncan exclaims, creasing up his face like he doesn't believe me. 'Are you joking?'

I don't know if I'm offended by the incredulity in his voice.

'No …' I say.

'But …' Duncan counters. 'I thought you'd kissed loads of people!' He must register the look on my face because he adds: 'Not in a bad way. It's just, well, everyone fancies you.'

'Everyone fancies me?!' I repeat. 'Oh my god, they so do not. What are you even talking about?!' Duncan must be so nervous that he's just chatting rubbish now. I mean, it's cute if he thinks other people like me, but, like … they don't. Hence being a kiss virgin, just like him!

Duncan pulls a face, like he doesn't know what else to say, and it makes me laugh.

'Well,' he says. 'I do. I fancy you.'

I stop laughing. Duncan's voice has got low now, and somehow we're standing closer than we were before, like the magnetic pull is getting stronger and stronger.

'I fancy you too,' I say. 'You're funny, and kind, and say what you mean.'

Duncan nods.

'Well, what if I say I'd like to kiss you?' he asks.

Holy moly – *yes! Yes, yes, yes*, I think! Let's do it! Suddenly my whole body stands to attention. I can feel the light breeze of the night dancing across the skin of my arms, across the back of my neck. My heart thumps, pulsing blood around my body in massive swooshing movements, keeping me alive and alert and awake and *here*. Here, now, and ready. I have waited years for this, imagined it so many times. And yet I've been a fool, really, because even in my wildest dreams I couldn't have imagined anything more amazing than doing this now, with Duncan, a boy who it took me so long to understand is actually incredible. I really like him! And he really likes me! And I feel all nervous and scared but it's a good nervous and scared, like I've been queuing for a roller coaster for ages and now I'm on it, and we've gone up to the top slowly, slowly, slowly, and it's the big dramatic pause before the really big drop. *Whooooosh!* That's how my tummy feels: like it knows the big roller coaster drop is about to happen, and is equal parts eager and terrified.

My voice drops as low as his, so we're both basically whispering. I daren't speak any louder: in fact, I can't!

'I'd like that,' I tell him. I have never meant something more in my whole life.

And then it happens.

Duncan steps forward to close the last of the gap between us, and I swallow hard and dare to put my face closer to his. Duncan gives a shy smile, and it makes me smile, and we're both smiling as our lips touch, but then I surrender to what is happening and close my eyes to feel everything as deeply as humanly possible, and I'm not smiling any more.

It's everything I hoped it would be.

It's gentle, and sweet, and with a boy I really, really, like.

Duncan's mouth is soft and inviting. It's like he's excited to be kissing me, but taking his time, too, like he might want to remember this as well.

Electricity fizzes through me as I kiss him back, not wanting this moment to end.

I'm glad I waited.

I'm glad it's with him.

It's better than any French kiss or movie kiss, or anything I've read about in a book.

The kiss is perfect.

I wish it could go on forever.

Publishing Credits

It takes a village to get a book to publication, and so I'd like to say an incredibly big and special thank you to:

Literary Agent: Ella Kahn

Commissioning Editors: Carla Hutchinson and Alex Antscherl

Desk Editor: Jessica Bellman

Copy-Editor: Jess White

Proofreader: Jane Baldock

Authenticity reader: Eva Echo, with Write Up

Art Director: Laura Bird

Design Assistant: Grace Barnes

Illustrator: Lucia Picerno

Production: Nicholas Church

Marketing: Sophie Rosewell

Publicity: Grace Ball

UK Sales: Sally Wilks, Frances Sleigh and team

Export Sales: Sarah McLean, Hattie Castelberg and team

Audio Editor: Ashleigh James

Translation Rights Sales: Barney Duly, Jo Blaquiere, Lucy Gibbs, Yas Langley

WhatsApp support and ideas: Charlotte Jacklin, Sarah Powell, Lucy Sheridan

Beta reader: Imogen Thompson

. . . and a massive thank you to you, too, for reading. See you for the next one!

Coming soon

TAYLOR BLAKE
SEIZES THE DAY

Spring 2025

About the Author

Laura Jane Williams (she/her) is known as the queen of the meet-cute. She is the author of eight romance novels for adults, several non-fiction titles, and her work has been translated into languages around the world. When she's not telling stories, Laura likes movie marathons, parenting, and throwing weights around at the gym. *Taylor Blake Is a Legend* is her debut teen novel.